On the

Frank L. Packard

"'Was you thinkin' av lavin', Mr. Holman?'"

ON THE IRON AT
BIG CLOUD
BY
FRANK L. PACKARD

NEW YORK
THOMAS Y. CROWELL, COMPANY
PUBLISHERS

Copyright, 1911,
BY THOMAS Y. CROWELL COMPANY.
Published September, 1911.

TO
MY FATHER
Lucius Henry Packard

CONTENTS

PAGE

I. Rafferty's Rule
....
                               ....
1 II. The Little Super
....
                               ....

22   III. "If a Man Die"

43   IV.   Spitzer

66   V.   Shanley's Luck

92   VI.   The Builder

123 VII. The Guardian of the Devil's Slide

153 VIII. The Blood of Kings

182 IX.   Marley

210 X.   The Man who didn't Count

237 XI.   "Where's Haggerty?"

256 XII. McQueen's Hobby

274 XIII. The Rebate

292 XIV. Speckles

308 XV. Munford

323

ON THE IRON AT BIG CLOUD

I
RAFFERTY'S RULE

The General Manager of the Transcontinental System glared at the young man who stood facing him across the office desk. "Why, you wouldn't last three months!" he snapped.

"I'd like to try, uncle."

"Humph!"

"I'm qualified for the position," young Holman went on. "I've done my stint with the construction gangs and I've spent four years in the Eastern shops. You promised me that if I'd stick I'd have my chance."

"Well, if I did, I didn't promise to put you in the way of making a fool of yourself and a laughing-stock of me, did I? You may be qualified technically, I don't say you're not. In fact, I've been rather pleased with you; that's one reason why you're not going out there to tackle something you can't handle. If men like Rawson and Williams can't hold down the job, what do you expect to do?"

"No worse than they, at least," Holman answered, quietly. "Look here, uncle, that's just the point. There aren't any of the men want the position, so I'm not jumping anybody to take it. I'll not make any laughing-stock of you, either. I'm not going out as the Old Man's nephew; just plain Dick Holman. If I don't make good you can wash your hands of my railroad career."

"Young man," said the General Manager, severely, "don't make rash statements."

He pushed the papers on his desk irritably to one side. Then he frowned. Two years ago, when the road had dug, blasted, burrowed, and trestled its right of way through the mountains, they had built the repair shops for the maintenance of the rolling stock, and from the moment the first brass time-check had been issued the locomotive-foremanship of the Hill Division was no subject to be introduced with temerity anywhere within the precincts of the executive offices. One man after another had gone out there, and one after another they had resigned. "Hard lot to handle," Carleton, the division superintendent, had replied to the numerous requests for explanation that had been fired at him. And now Dick wanted to go. The general manager's fingers beat a tattoo on the desk and his frown deepened into a scowl. "You're a young fool," he grunted at last.

And Holman knew that he had gained his point. "That's very good of you, uncle," he cried. "I knew you'd see it my way. When may I start?"

"I guess you'll get there soon enough," his uncle answered grimly. He rose from his chair and accompanied Holman to the door. "Well, go if you want to, but remember this, young man, you're going on your own terms. When you resign from *that* position, you resign from the road, understand!"

"All right, uncle," Holman laughed in reply. "It's a bargain."

Three days later, as Number One pulled into Big Cloud, Holman swung himself to the platform. Up past the mail and baggage cars, the steam drumming at her safety, a big ten-wheeler was backing down to couple on for the run through the Rockies. There was the pride of proprietorship in his glance as his eyes swept the great mogul critically, for in his pocket was his official appointment as Locomotive Foreman of the Hill Division, vice Williams, resigned.

It was not until the last of the Pullmans had rolled smoothly past him that he turned to take stock in his surroundings. The first impression was not prepossessing. Before him, just across the yard filled with strings of freight cars, were the low, rambling, smoke-begrimed shops and running shed, while beyond these again the town straggled out monotonously.

To the westward, through the mountains, were the curves and grades that wrenched and racked and tore the equipment he would hereafter be accountable for. To the eastward—but "eastward" was only two hundred yards away, for there his eye caught the "Yard Limit" post, that likewise marked the end of the division.

If after this cursory survey there still lingered any illusions of the picturesque in Holman's mind, they were rudely dispelled by the interior of the barn-like structure at the side of the platform that did duty for station, division headquarters, general storeroom, and anything else that might seek the shelter of its protecting roof. The walls were adorned with such works of art as are afforded by the Sunday supplements, interspersed here and there with an occasional blue-print and time schedule. The furnishings bore unmistakable evidence of having seen service with the construction staff when the road was in the making. At the right of the door, as Holman entered, the despatcher was poring over the train sheet.

"Sure," said he in answer to Holman's inquiry, "that's the super over there."

Holman crossed the room and proffered his credentials.

"Glad you've come," was Carleton's greeting, as he rose and extended his hand. "We've been expecting you. Williams went East this morning on Number Two. Sit down. That's your desk there."

Holman glanced at the battered table toward which the other pointed, then back again to the four days' growth on the super's face.

Carleton grinned. "Fixings aren't up to what you boiled-shirt fellows down East are used to. Out here on the firing line most anything goes. I've been requisitioning office fixtures for months. Ain't seen any way-bill of them yet, Davis, have you?" he called across to the despatcher.

Davis got up with a laugh and joined the other two, "No," said he, shaking hands with Holman, "not yet."

"And not likely to, either," continued the super. "It's rough and ready out here, Holman. The staff quarters up there," he jerked his thumb toward the ceiling, "are all-fired crude, and the Chinese cook is a gilt-edge thief and most persuasive liar; but we've got the finest division of the best railroad in the world, and we're pushing stuff through the mountains on a schedule that makes Southern competition sick. We're young here yet. Some day, when the roadbed's shaken down to stay, we'll build the extras."

The enthusiasm and bluff heartiness of the super was contagious. Holman put out his hand impulsively. "We've heard a lot of you fellows down East," he said, "and I'm glad 'I've got a chance to chip in." His eyes swept around the room and came back to meet the super's smilingly. "Even if accommodations *are* below 'Tourist Class,'" he added.

So Holman came to the division and joined the staff. Spence, chief dispatcher, had shaken his head. "Twenty-eight and locomotive foreman of *this* division with the roughest, toughest bunch on the system's pay-roll to handle! Hanged if he isn't a decent sort, though, even if he will shave and wear collars. Imagine Williams with creased trousers! And say, his wardrobe—he's actually got a dress suit with him! Wouldn't that ground the wires! Who is he, Carleton? Got a pull with the Old Man?"

"Didn't inquire," returned Carleton bluntly. "Let him try out."

If the super waited before passing judgment on the latest addition to the staff of the Hill Division, the shop hands did likewise—but for another reason. They waited for Rafferty. Rafferty was boss. Who Rafferty's boss was, was his affair, and it did not concern them. What Rafferty said—went. It was two weeks before he delivered his verdict.

"A damned pink-faced dude!" he announced and terminated his remark with a stream of black-strap juice by way of an exclamation mark.

The fiat had gone forth!

Down in the pits, stripping the engines of their motion gear, the fitters passed resolutions of confidence in Rafferty's judgment, and among the lathes and planers the machinists did likewise. The concurrence of the forge gang was expressed by a vicious wielding of the big sledges that sent showers of sparks flying from the spluttering metal whenever Holman was sighted coming down the shop on a tour of inspection—a significant intimation to him to keep his distance. And that the sentiment of the shops might not be lacking in unanimity, the boilermakers, should Holman have the temerity to pause for an instant before a shell on which they were at work, would send up a din from their clattering hammers intolerable to any but the men themselves whose ears were plugged with cotton waste.

As for Holman, he might have been entirely unconscious of the hostility and ill-will of his subordinates for all the evidence he gave of being aware of it. He was busy mastering the routine and details of his new position. For a month he said nothing; then one morning over at headquarters he turned to Carleton, who was reading the train mail that had just come in.

"Why did Williams resign?" he asked quietly.

"Eh?" said Carleton, startled out of his calm by reason of the suddenness of the question.

"Why did Williams resign?" Holman repeated.

"Oh, I don't know. Tired of the life out here, I guess," Carleton evaded.

"Was it Rafferty?"

Carleton turned sharply to scrutinize the other's countenance. Holman was gazing out of the window.

"It was Rafferty," Carleton admitted after a moment.

Holman's gaze never shifted from the window. "Why wasn't Rafferty fired?" he asked in the same quiet tones, but this time there was just the faintest tinge of accusation in his voice.

Carleton's face flushed. An instant's hesitation, then he answered bluntly: "He weighed more, that's why!"

"Oh!" said Holman significantly. "Then why didn't you recommend Rafferty for the position long ago and save all the trouble?"

"I would have if he could do anything more than sign his name."

Holman turned angrily to face the super. "So," he cried, "when a fellow comes out here he has to play a lone hand, eh? A show-down with Rafferty, shop hands, and the whole division drawing cards against him. You, Carleton, I didn't put you down as a man with a pet."

Carleton got up and put his hand on Holman's shoulder. "Don't do it, either," he said quietly. "Don't run off your schedule that way, son. It has always been man to man, and I wasn't appealed to. So far it has been all Rafferty. It's easier to get a new foreman than a new shop crew, so I haven't interfered."

"I don't understand," said Holman blankly.

The super laughed shortly. "Rafferty has the men where he wants them. If he got on his ear he could tie us up so quick we wouldn't know what happened. A nice thing for me to admit, isn't it? But it's so. I suppose I should have nipped the whole business in the bud, but I kept on hoping that each new man would beat Rafferty at his own game. Has he got you going, too?"

Holman gathered up the repair reports from his desk and started for the door. "Game's young yet," he flung over his shoulder as he went out.

From the office Holman walked up the yard to the spur tracks at the end of the shops where three or four engines were waiting their turn for an empty pit. He glanced at their numbers, comparing them with the papers he held in his hand, then turned and walked back, pausing on the way to inspect an engine, bright and clean as fresh paint and gold leaf would make her, that had been hauled out of the shops that morning. He passed in through the upper doors to the fitting-shop. Already another engine had been shunted in to replace the one that had gone out. Her guard-plates, links, cross-heads, main and connecting rods were lying on the floor beside her, and the labor gang were jacking and blocking her up preparatory to running the wheels out from underneath her. There was a trace of heightened color in Holman's face as he turned to look for Rafferty.

The boss fitter was in his usual place. Down the shop, hands dug deep in his trousers pockets, legs spread wide apart, he swung slowly round and round on the little iron turntable that intersected the hand-car tracks where they branched out in all directions through the shops. As Holman approached he stopped the motion indolently by allowing the toe of his boot to trail along the floor around the table.

Holman's manner was quiet and his voice was soft, almost deferential, as he spoke: "I see you have 483 finished, Mr. Rafferty."

Rafferty looked down from his superior two inches and said: "Yis."

"And," continued Holman, "you've run in 840 in her place."

"Yis," said Rafferty again, this time even more indifferently than before.

"Well, now, really, Mr. Rafferty, I'd like to know why you did it? You know I told you yesterday to be particular to take 522 next." Holman's tones were more nearly those of apology than of expostulation.

For answer Rafferty gave a little shove with his foot and the turntable began to revolve slowly. During the circuit Rafferty coolly gave some directions to the men nearest him, and then as he once more came round facing Holman he stopped. "Fwhat was ut you was sayin', Mr. Holman?" he drawled.

"This is the biggest division on the system, isn't it?" Holman asked inconsequently.

"Eh?" demanded Rafferty.

"Longest division — most mileage — covers quite a stretch of country," Holman amplified.

"Oh!" returned the other with a grin. "Well, you'll be thinkin' so if you ever sthay long enough to git acquainted wid ut."

"Perhaps that's the reason I am beginning to feel cramped — I've only been here a month, you know," Holman smiled.

"Fwhat d'ye mean?"

"Why, curiously, it doesn't seem big enough or wide enough or long enough for even *two* men."

Holman purred his words in soft, mild accents, and Rafferty, understanding, sneered in quick retort: "Was you thinkin' av lavin', Mr. Holman?"

"No," said Holman, slowly, "I don't know that I was. I thought perhaps the matter might be adjusted, and I'd like to ask your advice. Now, if you were locomotive foreman and you found that the foreman of this shop, in a dirty, low, underhanded fashion was discrediting you with the men, and furthermore flatly disobeyed your orders, what would you do, Mr. Rafferty?"

By the time Holman had completed his arraignment, Rafferty was mad—fighting mad. "I'll tell you fwhat I'd do," he yelled, shaking a great horny fist under Holman's nose. "I'd plug him good an' hard, that's fwhat I'd do! See!"

"Rather drastic," Holman commented after a pause, during which Rafferty drew back and with hands on hips stood scowling belligerently. "But desperate cases sometimes require desperate remedies, and I don't know—but—that—" his fist shot out and caught Rafferty fairly on the point of the jaw—you're right!"

Rafferty, staggering back from the impact of the blow, set the table whirling. His feet went out from under him and he fell sprawling to the floor. As he picked himself up, Holman sprang toward him and swinging twice landed two vicious smashes on Rafferty's face. Then, except for a confused recollection of a rush of men, that was all Holman remembered until he opened his eyes to find himself in his bunk at headquarters with Carleton bending over him.

"You're a sight," Carleton commented grimly. "What was the muss about?"

Holman explained. "I took Rafferty's advice and plugged him, you see, and after that——"

"After that if it hadn't been for old Joe, the turner, running over here to tell us, they'd have killed you. Don't you know any better than to stack up against Rafferty like that, let alone the whole gang? Did you expect to do them all up?"

"No, not exactly. I expected there'd be something coming to me, but I had to do it. I'll admit, Carleton, I was in a blue funk, but I just *had* to. Moral effect, you know."

"Yes," said Carleton savagely, "the moral effect is great! It will be as much as your life is worth to put your head inside those shops again. You don't know the men you're dealing with out here."

"You're wrong, dead wrong, Carleton, I do. You said it was man to man, didn't you? Well, then, either I'm running the shops or Rafferty is. Rafferty has the men with him because he's a bully and they're afraid of him. It was mere force of habit made them pile on to me. You wait until they're cooled off a bit and see."

But Carleton shook his head. "You're a bloomin' fool," he summed up judicially, "but here, shake! You've got your grit with you, if you did leave your sense behind."

For the rest of the morning Holman nursed his injuries, but at one o'clock he was at his desk again. Five minutes afterward Rafferty came in. He was not a pretty sight with his cut lip and battered eye as he limped past both Spence and Holman. With a vindictive glare at the latter he marched straight across the room to where Carleton sat. He leaned both hands on the super's desk.

"Ut'll be just a show-down, Mr. Carleton, that's all there is to ut. Me or him, which?" he announced.

Carleton tilted his chair back, put his feet up on the desk and his thumbs in the armholes of his vest. "State your case, Rafferty," he said calmly.

"Case!" Rafferty spluttered. "Case is ut? I'm sick av bein' bossed bye kids out av school that was buildin' blocks whin I was buildin' enjines. I quit or he does!" Rafferty jerked his thumb in Holman's direction.

"Is that all you have to say, Rafferty?"

"That's about the size av ut."

"Very well, Rafferty, you can get your time," said Carleton quietly.

For a moment Rafferty stared as though he had not heard aright, then he swung round on his heel only to turn again and face the super with a short laugh. "All right, Mr. Carleton, you're the docthor. It's satisfied I am. Whin I go out, every bloomin' man in the shops 'ull go out wid me!"

Carleton's feet came off the desk like a shot, his chair came down to the floor with a bang, and the next instant he was standing in front of the boss fitter.

"See here, Rafferty," he blazed, "you know me — the men know me. While I've held the bank there's been fifty-two cards in the case and every mother's son of you has had a square deal. You know it, don't you? No man on this division ever came to me with just cause for complaint but had a chance to state his grievance on a clear track and no limit on his permit either. Now, I'm entitled to the same line of treatment I hand out, and I won't stand for threats!"

Rafferty shifted uneasily and to hide his confusion reached for his "chewing." "We've nothin' agin you, Mn Carleton, an' I'm givin' you fair warnin'," he mumbled as his teeth met in the plug.

"When you make trouble on this division you make trouble for me," said Carleton bluntly. "As for warning, I give you warning now that if you start any disturbance in those shops it will be the worse for you. Now go!"

They watched him through the windows as he crossed the tracks. Finally, as he disappeared inside the shops, Carleton turned with a grave face.

"I'm afraid it's going to be a bad business," he said.

"You don't mean to say," Holman burst out, "that the men are fools enough to quit just because one man with a grouch says so, do you?"

"I told you that you didn't know the class of men out here — they're partisan to the core — it's bred in them. I'm not blaming you, Holman — not for a minute! As I said this morning, I've seen it coming for a long while — long before Williams gave up the ghost. Now it's here, we'll face the music, what?"

"It's mighty good of you to say so, old man," said Holman, slowly, "but I've put you in a bad hole, and it's up to me to get you out of it. Inside of two weeks with the repair shops on strike our rolling stock won't be able to handle the traffic." He put on his hat and started for the door.

"Where are you going?" Carleton demanded.

"Rafferty's not going to have this all his own way. The men have no grievance, and I don't believe they'll follow him out if they're talked to right. I'm going over."

"Not if I know it, you're not," said Carleton grimly. "There may be a coroner's inquest before this affair is settled, perhaps more than one if things get nasty, but I'm hanged if I propose starting in that way this afternoon."

"That's all right," Holman replied doggedly. "Just the same, I'm—Eh? What's up, Carleton? What's wrong?"

Spence had bent suddenly over the key, and Carleton, with a startled exclamation, was staring at the words the dispatcher was hastily scribbling on the pad. Holman leaned over the super's shoulder and even as he saw Carleton reach to plug in the telephone connection with the roundhouse, he read the message: "Number Two wrecked Eagle Pass. Send wrecker and medical assistance at once." The next instant he was flying across the yard to the shops.

As he burst in through the door he was greeted with a snarl. The men were massed in a body around one of the locomotives in the fitting-shop, and Rafferty, from the cab, was talking in fierce, heated tones. At sight of the master mechanic he stopped short and with an oath leaped from his perch straight for Holman. The crowd divided, making a lane between the two men, then, with startling suddenness, breaking the ominous silence that had fallen, there came three short blasts from the shop whistle—the wrecker's signal. It halted Rafferty when but an arm's-length from the locomotive foreman. Then Holman spoke:

"You hear that, men? Number Two has gone to glory up in Eagle Pass. You, Rafferty, get the wrecking crew together, *quick!* The rest of you get back to work."

"You're a liar!" Rafferty yelled. "A measly, putty-faced, starch-shirted liar, d'ye hear? Ut's a plant! You can't work any sharp trick loike that on me!"

There was a low, menacing growl from the men and they edged in close. But Holman gave them no heed; he took a step nearer Rafferty, looking straight into the other's eyes.

"Rafferty," he said quietly, "you've a wife and kids, haven't you? And you're a railroad man, aren't you? Well, there's wives and kids and mates up there in that wreck. The other affair can wait until we get back. Now, will you go?"

And Rafferty went — at the head of the wreckers — out into the yard where the switching crew were working like beavers making up the relief train. Two passenger coaches to serve as ambulances, behind them a flat, then the wrecking crane, the tool car, and a caboose. As Rafferty was piling his men into the train, Holman raced across the tracks to the station. On the platform the doctors, hastily summoned, were crowded around Carleton. Holman stopped beside them. "We're all ready, Carleton," he announced; then to the others: "You fellows had better get aboard; we'll be off as soon as we get the track."

"Spence will have the line clear in a minute," said Carleton, as the doctors started for the coaches. "I'm sending a dispatcher up with you; he can tap in on the wires. How many men did you scrape up?"

"The regular crew."

"And Rafferty?"

"He's going along."

"I don't know how you did it, and there's no time for explanations now; but I think, Holman, you'd better leave Rafferty behind."

"And have the whole crew quit, too? It's no use, Carleton, he's got to go. That's all there is to it."

Carleton shook his head doubtfully. "I don't like the idea of you two getting up there together. There's no need of you going, and you'd better not go. You don't know the man; if you think he'll forget——"

"You're wrong, I do. I told you so before; anyway, it's too late now — we're off. Here's Spence with the orders."

Before Carleton could reply, Holman had grabbed the tissue and was running for the train. As he swung himself into the cab of the engine and handed Hurley, the driver, his orders, Rafferty climbed in from the other side.

At sight of Holman, Rafferty hesitated and half turned around in the gangway to go back to the caboose; but Holman reached out and caught his arm.

"Stay where you are, Rafferty," he said quietly. And during the nerve-racking thirty-mile run to Eagle Pass no other words passed between them. Sometimes in the mad slur of the locomotive as she hit the tangents their bodies touched; that was all.

Holman, by virtue of railroad etiquette, had climbed to the fireman's seat and once or twice he had glanced around at the great bulk of the man behind him, at the grim, set features, at the eyes that would not meet his, and wondered at his own temerity in inviting a physical encounter. And what good had it done? Was Carleton right after all? Perhaps. And yet behind the stubbornness, the self-will, the purely physical, there must be the other side of the man. If he could only reach — it only touch it. He *had* touched it. His appeal for the injured.

Hurley was eating up the miles as only a man at the throttle of a wrecker with clear rights could do it. A long scream from the whistle that echoed through the mountains above the pounding, deafening rush of the train brought Holman back to his immediate surroundings. Another minute and they had swung round the curve and thundered over the trestle that made the approach to the Pass.

Half a mile ahead of them up the track they saw the horror. Hurley latched in his throttle and began to check. As the brake-shoes bit into the tires, Holman slipped off his seat and faced Rafferty. There was a curious look in the other's eyes, and Holman understood. Understood that here Rafferty was his master—and knew it. So this was the meaning of it. This was how he had touched the other's better nature! Rafferty had cunningly seized the opportunity of placing him at an even greater disadvantage than before. For an instant he hesitated as he bit his lip, then he canceled the personal equation. "Go ahead, Rafferty," he said quietly, answering the unspoken challenge, "you're better up in this sort of thing than I am. You're in charge."

And Rafferty without a word swung himself from the cab.

To Holman the first five minutes was unnerving. It was his first bad wreck. Down East it had never been his province to go out with the crew—nor was it here, he reflected grimly, and at that moment was grateful for the veteran Rafferty. It was like some hideous nightmare to him. All along the line of burning wreckage lay the dead, their silence the more awful by contrast with the shrieks and cries of the wounded still imprisoned in the wreck. And then the feeling passed and he worked—worked like a madman.

Once a woman had caught his arm and, sobbing, dragged him toward the stateroom end of one of the Pullmans. Through the smoke and scorching heat of the flames he had fought his way in, then back with the child. The woman had thrown her arms hysterically around his neck.

It was all a mad, furious turmoil, and he gloried in it. The crunch of the ax through glass and woodwork, the wild rush into the heart of things to stagger back blinded and choked with his helpless burden. The fierce joy if life still lingered; the tender reverence if life were gone.

Up the track toward the engine there was a crash and a chorus of excited cries. He rushed in that direction. A half-dozen of the wrecking crew were grouped around the forward baggage-car. As Holman reached them, disheveled, clothes torn and scorched, face blackened with smoke and daubed with blood where glass and splinters had cut him, the men drew back aghast, staring white-faced.

"By God!" one cried. "It's *him!*"

"Of course it's me! Are you crazy? What's the matter with you?"

The man pointed to the blazing car. "Some one said you was in there, and he went in after you just before she crumpled up."

"Who?" Holman shouted.

"Rafferty."

Holman made a dash for the car. The men held him back. "Don't try it, sir; it's too late to do any good."

He shook them off, and with his arms crossed in front of his head to protect his face he half stumbled, half fell through the opening that had once been a door. The car was half over on its side. The trunks, dashed into a heap on top of each other when the car had left the track, were all that supported the burning roof timbers. Between the trunks and the edge of the car there was a little space with the floor at an angle of forty-five degrees, and along this, head down, Holman crawled blindly. The floor was already beginning to smolder, the metal-bound edges of the trunks blistered his hands as he touched them. His senses reeled, but on and on he crawled, and in his mind over and over again the one thought: "Rafferty! My God, Rafferty!"

Then his hands touched something soft, and slowly, painfully, inch by inch, he struggled back dragging Rafferty after him. Somehow he reached the door, then a confused jumble of noises and nothing more until he returned to consciousness, and to the knowledge that he was back in his room at Big Cloud with the almond-eyed factotum in attendance.

"Belly much better? Likee eat?" inquired that individual solicitously.

Holman grinned in spite of the pain. "No," he answered; then as he closed his eyes again he muttered: "Tell Carleton I was right."

And he was, for two days afterward Rafferty publicly abdicated. He gathered the men in the fitting-shop and mounted to the cab of an engine jacked halfway up to the ceiling as before, only on this occasion it was at noon hour and not in the company's time. His words were few and to the point, delivered with a force and eloquence that was all his own:

"I sed he was a damned pink-faced dude, so I did. Well, I take ut back, d'ye moind? An' fwhat's more, I'll flatten the face av any man fwhat sez I iver sed ut!"

II
THE LITTLE SUPER

Tommy Regan backed the big compound mogul down past the string of dark-green coaches that he had pulled for a hundred and fifty miles, took the table with a slight jolt, and came to a stop in the roundhouse. As he swung himself from the cab, Healy, the turner, came up to him.

"He's a great lad, that av yours," Healy began, with a shake of his head — "a great lad; but mind ye this, Tommy Regan, there'll be trouble for me an' you an' him an' the whole av us, if you don't watch him."

"What's the matter this time, John?"

"Matter," said Healy, ruefully; "there's matter enough. The little cuss come blame near running 429 into the pit a while back, so he did."

"Where is he now?" Regan asked, with a grin.

"Devil a bit I know. I chased him out, an' he started for over by the shops. An' about an hour ago your missus come down an' said the bhoy was nowheres to be found, an' that you was to look for him."

Regan pulled out his watch. "Six-thirty. Well," he said, "I'll go over and see if Grumpy knows anything about him. Next time the kid shows up around here, John, you give him the soft side of a tommy-bar, and send him home."

Healy scratched his head. "I will," he said; "I'll do ut. He's a foine lad."

Regan crossed the yard to the gates of the big shops. They were still unlocked, and he went through into the storekeeper's office. Grumpy was sorting the brass time-checks. He glanced up as Regan came in.

"I suppose you're lookin' fer yer kid again," he said sourly.

"That's what I am, Steve," Regan returned, diplomatically dispensing with the other's nickname.

"Well, he ain't here," Grumpy announced, returning to his checks. "I've just been through the shops, an' I'd seen him if he was."

The engineer's face clouded. "He must be somewhere about, Steve. John said he saw him come over here, and the wife was down to the roundhouse looking for him, so he didn't go home. Let's go through the shops and see if we can't find him."

"I don't get no overtime fer chasin' lost kids," growled Grumpy.

Nevertheless, he got up and walked through the door leading into the forge-shop, which Regan held open for him. The place was gloomy and deserted. Here and there a forge-fire, dying, still glowed dully. At the end of the room the men stopped, and Grumpy, noting Regan's growing anxiety, gave surly comfort.

"Wouldn't likely be here, anyhow," he said. "Fitting-shop fer him; but we'll try the machine-shop first on the way through."

The two men went forward, prying behind planers, drills, shapers, and lathes. The machines took grotesque shapes in the deepening twilight, and in the silence, so incongruous with the usual noisy clang and clash of his surroundings, Regan's nervousness increased.

He hurried forward to the fitting-shop. Engines on every hand were standing over their respective pits in all stages of demolition, some on wheels, some blocked high toward the rafters, some stripped to the bare boiler-shell. Regan climbed in and out of the cabs, while Grumpy peered into the pits.

"Aw! he ain't here," said Grumpy in disgust, wiping his hands on a piece of waste. "I told you he wasn't. He's home, mabbe, by now."

Regan shook his head. "Bunty! Ho, Bunt-*ee!*" he called. And again: "Bun-*tee!*"

There was no answer, and he turned to retrace his steps when Grumpy caught him by the shoulder. The big iron door of the engine before them swung slowly back on its hinges, and from the front end there emerged a diminutive pair of shoes, topped by little short socks that had once been white, but now hung in grimy folds over the tops of the boots. A pair of sturdy, but very dirty, bare legs came gradually into view as their owner propelled himself forward on his stomach. They dangled for a moment, seeking footing on the plate beneath; then a very small boy, aged four, in an erstwhile immaculate linen sailor suit, stood upright on the foot-plate. The yellow curls were tangled with engine grease and cemented with cinders and soot. Here and there in spots upon his face the skin still retained its natural color.

Bunty paused for a moment after his exertions to regain his breath, then, still gripping a hammer in his small fist, he straddled the draw-bar, and slid down the pilot to the floor.

Grumpy burst into a guffaw.

Bunty blinked at him reprovingly, and turned to his father.

"I's been fixin' the 'iger-'ed," he announced gravely.

Regan surveyed his son grimly. "Fixing what?" he demanded.

"The 'iger-'ed," Bunty repeated. Then reproachfully: "Don't *oo* know w'at a 'iger-'ed is?"

"Oh," said Regan, "the nigger-head, eh? Well, I guess there's another nigger-head will get some fixing when your mother sees you, son."

He picked the lad up in his arms, and Bunty nestled confidingly, with one arm around his father's neck. His tired little head sank down on the paternal shoulder, and before they had reached the gates Bunty was sound asleep.

In the days that followed, Bunty found it no easy matter to elude his mother's vigilance; but that was only the beginning of his troubles. The shop gates were always shut, and the latch was beyond his reach. Once he had found them open, and had marched boldly through, to find his way barred by the only man of whom he stood in awe. Grumpy had curtly ordered him away, and Bunty had taken to his heels and run until his small body was breathless.

The roundhouse was no better. Old John would have none of him, and Bunty marveled at the change. He was a railroad man, and the shops were his heritage. His soul protested vigorously at the outrage that was being heaped upon him.

It took him some time to solve the problem, but at last he found the way. Each afternoon Bunty would trudge sturdily along the track for a quarter of a mile to the upper end of the shops, where the big, wide engine doors were always open. Here four spur-tracks ran into the erecting-shop, and Bunty found no difficulty in gaining admittance. Once safe among the fitting-gang, the little Super, as the men called him, would strut around with important air, inspecting the work with critical eyes.

One lesson Bunty learned. Remembering his last interview with his mother, he took good care not to be locked in the shops again. So each night when the whistle blew he fell into line with the men, and, secure in their protection, would file with them past Grumpy as they handed in their time-checks. And Grumpy, unmindful of the spur-tracks, wondered how he got there, and scowled savagely.

When Bunty was six, his father was holding down the swivel-chair in the Master Mechanic's office of the Hill Division, and Bunty's allegiance to the shops wavered. Not from any sense of disloyalty; but with his father's promotion a new world opened to Bunty, and fascinated him. It was now the yard-shunter and headquarters that engaged his attention. The years, too, brought other changes to Bunty. The curls had disappeared, and his hair was cut now like his father's. Long stockings had replaced the socks, and he wore real trousers; short ones, it is true, but real trousers none the less, with pockets in them.

When school was over, he would fly up and down the yard on the stubby little engine, and Healy, doing the shunting then and forgetting past grievances, would let Bunty sit on the driver's seat. In time Bunty learned to pull the throttle, but the reversing-lever was too much for his small stature, and the intricacies of the "air" were still a little beyond him. But Healy swore he'd make a driver of him—and he did.

The evenings at the office Bunty loved fully as well. Headquarters were not much to boast about in those days. That was before competition forced a double-track system, and the train-dispatcher, with his tissue sheets, still held undisputed sway. They called them "offices" at Big Cloud out of courtesy—just the attic floor over the station, with one room to it. The floor space each man's desk occupied was his office.

Here Bunty would sit curled up in his father's chair and listen to the men as they talked. If it was anything about a locomotive, he understood; if it was traffic or bridges or road-bed or dispatching, he would pucker his brows perplexedly and ask innumerable questions. But most of all he held Spence, the chief dispatcher, in deep reverence.

Once, to his huge delight, Spence, holding his hand, had let him tap out an order. It is true that with the O. K. came back an inquiry as to the brand the dispatcher had been indulging in; but the sarcasm was lost on Bunty, for when Spence with a chuckle read off the reply, Bunty gravely asked if there was any answer. Spence shook his head and laughed. "No, son; I guess not," he said. "We've got to maintain our dignity, you know."

That winter, on top of the regular traffic, and that was not light, they began to push supplies from the East over the Hill Division, preparing to double track the road from the western side of the foothills as soon as spring opened up. And while the thermometer crept steadily to zero, the Hill Division sweltered.

Everybody and everything got it, the shops and the road-beds, the train crews and the rolling-stock. What little sleep Carleton, the super, got, he spent in formulating dream plans to handle the business. Those that seemed good to him when he awoke were promptly vetoed by the barons of the General Office in the far-off East.

Regan got no sleep. He raced from one end of the division to the other, and he did his best. Engine crews had to tinker anything less than a major injury for themselves: there was no room in the shops for them.

But the men on the keys got it most of all. As the days wore into months, Spence's face grew careworn and haggard; and the irritability from overwork of the men about him added to his discomfort. Human nature needs a safety-valve, and one night near the end of January when Regan and Carleton and Spence were gathered at the office, with Bunty in his accustomed place in his father's chair, the master mechanic cut loose.

"It's up to you, Spence," he cried savagely, bringing his fist down with a crash on the desk. "There ain't a pair of wheels on the division fit to pull a hand-car. Every engine's a cripple, and getting lamer every day. The engine ain't built, nor never will be, that'll stand the schedule you're putting them on through the hills, especially through the Gap. That's a three per cent, with the bed like an S. You can't make time there; you've got to crawl. You're pulling the stay-bolts out of my engines, that's what you're doing."

Carleton, being in no angelic mood, and glad to vent his feelings, growled assent.

Spence raised his head from the keys, a red tinge of resentment on his cheeks. He picked up his pipe, packing it slowly as he looked at Regan and the super. "I'm taking all they're sending," he said quietly. He reached over for the train-sheet and handed it to the super. "You and Regan here are growling about the schedule. It's your division, Carleton; but I'm not sure you know just what we're handling every twenty-four hours. It's push them through on top of each other somehow, or tell them down-East we can't handle them. Do you want to do that?"

"No," said Carleton, "I don't; and what's more, I won't."

Spence nodded. "I rather figured that was your idea. Well, we've about all we can do without nagging one another. I'm near in now, and so are you and Regan here, both of you. I've got to make time, Gap or no Gap. There's so much moving there isn't siding enough to cross them."

"You're right," said Carleton; "we can't afford to jump each other. We're all doing our best, and each of us knows it. How's Number One and Two to-night?"

Spence studied for a moment before he answered: "Number One is forty minutes off, and Number Two's an hour to the bad."

Carleton groaned. The Imperial Limited West and East, officially known on the train-sheets as One and Two, carried both the transcontinental mail and the de-luxe passengers. Of late the East had been making pertinent suggestions to the Division Superintendent that it would be as well if those trains ran off the Hill Division with a little more regard for their established schedule. So Carleton groaned. He got up and put on his hat and coat preparatory to going home. "Look here," he said from the doorway, "they'll stand for 'most anything if we don't misuse One and Two. They're getting mighty savage about that, and they'll drop hard before long. You fellows have got to take care of those trains, if nothing else on the division moves. That's orders. I'll shoulder all kicks coming on the rest of the traffic. Good-night."

When Bunty left the office that night and walked home with his father, he had learned that there was another side to railroading besides the building and repairing of engines, and the delivery of magic tissue sheets to train crews that told them when and where to stop, and how to thread their way through hills and plains on a single-track road, with heaps of other trains, some going one way, some another. He understood vaguely and in a hazy kind of way that somewhere, many, many miles away, were men who sat in judgment on the doings of his father and Spence and Carleton; that these men were to be obeyed, that their word was law, and that their names were President and Directors.

So Bunty, trotting beside his father, pondered these things. Being too weighty for him, he appealed: "Daddy, what's president and directors?"

Regan's temper being still ruffled, he answered shortly: "Fools, mostly."

Bunty nodded gravely, and his education as a railroad man was almost complete. The rest came quickly, and the Gap did it.

The Gap! There was not a man on the division, from track-walker to superintendent, who would not jump like a nervous colt if you said "Gap!" to them offhand and short-like. A peaceful stretch of track it looked, a little crooked, as Regan said, hugging the side of the mountain at the highest point of the division. The surroundings were undeniably grand. A sheer drop of eighteen-hundred feet to the cañon below, with the surrounding mountains rearing their snow-capped peaks skyward, completed a picture of which the road had electrotypes and which it used in their magazine-advertising. What the picture did not show was the two-mile drop, where the road-bed took a straight three per cent and sometimes better, to the lower levels. So when Carleton or Spence or Regan, reading their magazines, saw the picture, they shuddered, and, remembering past history and fearful of the future, turned the page hurriedly.

But to Bunty the Gap possessed the fascination of the unknown. He was wakened early the next morning by his father's voice talking excitedly over the special wire with headquarters about the Gap and a wreck. He sat bolt upright, and listened with all his might; then he crawled noiselessly out of bed, and began to dress hastily. He heard his father speaking to his mother, and presently the front door banged. Bunty was dressed by that time and he crept downstairs and opened the door softly.

It was just turning daylight as he started on a run for the yard. It was not far to the office, — a hundred yards or so, — and Bunty reached there in record time. Across the tracks by the roundhouse they were coupling on to the wrecker; and answering hasty summons, men, running from all directions, were quickly gathering.

Bunty hesitated a minute on the platform, then he entered the station and tiptoed softly up the stairs. The office door was open, and from the top stair Bunty could see into the room. The night lamp was still burning on the dispatcher's desk, and Spence was sitting there, working with frantic haste to clear the line. In the center of the room, the super, his father, and Flannagan, the wrecking boss, were standing.

"It's a freight smash," Carleton was saying to Flannagan—"east edge of the Gap. You'll have rights through, and no limit on your permit. Tell Emmons if he doesn't make it in better than ninety minutes he'll talk to me afterward. By the time you get there, Number Two will be crawling up the grade. She's pulling the Old Man's car, and that means get her through somehow if you have to drop the wreck over the cliff. You can back down to Riley's to let her pass. We'll do the patching up afterward. Understand?"

Flannagan nodded, and glanced impatiently at Spence.

The super opened and shut his watch. "Ready, Spence?" he asked shortly.

"Just a minute," Spence answered quietly.

Bunty waited to hear no more. He turned and ran down the stairs and across the tracks as fast as his legs would carry him. He scrambled breathlessly up the steps of the tool-car and edged his way in among the men grouped near the door. He was fairly inside before they noticed him.

"Hello," cried Allan, Bunty's bosom friend of the fitting-gang days, "here's the little Super! What you doin' here, kid?"

"I'm going up to the wreck," Bunty announced sturdily.

The men laughed.

"Well, I guess *not* much, you're not," said Allan, "What do you think your father would say?"

"Nothing," said Bunty, airily. "I just comed from the office," he added artfully, "and I'll tell you about the wreck if you like."

The men grouped around him in a circle.

"It's at the Gap," Bunty began, sparring for time as through the window he saw Flannagan coming from the office at a run. "And it's a freight train, and—and it's all smashed up, and——"

The train started with a jerk that nearly took the men off their feet. At the same time Flannagan's face appeared at the car door.

"All here, boys?" he called. Then he announced cheerfully: "The devil's to pay up the line!"

Meanwhile, Bunty, taking advantage of the interruption, had squirmed his way through the men to the far end of the car, and the train had bumped over the switches on to the main line before they remembered him. Then it was too late. They hauled him out from behind a rampart of tools, where he had intrenched himself, and Flannagan shook his fist, half-angrily, half-playfully, in Bunty's face.

"You little devil, what are you doing here, eh?" he demanded.

And Bunty answered as before: "I'm going up to the wreck."

"Humph!" said Flannagan, with a grin. "Well, I guess you are, and I guess you'll be sorry, too, when you get back and your dad gets hold of you."

But Bunty was safe now, and he only laughed.

Breakfastless, he shared the men's grub and listened wide-eyed as they talked of wrecks in times gone by; but most of all he listened to the story of how his father, when he was pulling Number One, had saved the Limited by sticking to his post almost in the face of certain death. Bunty's father was his hero, and his small soul glowed with happiness at the tale. He begged so hard for the story over again that Allan told it, and when he had finished, he slapped Bunty on the back. "And I guess you're a chip of the old block," he said.

And Bunty was very proud, squaring his shoulders, and planting his feet firmly to swing with the motion of the car.

The speed of the train slackened as they struck the grade leading up the eastern side of the Gap. Flannagan set the men busily at work overhauling the kit. He paused an instant before Bunty. "Look here, kid," he said, shaking a warning finger, "you keep out of the way, and don't get into trouble."

It would have taken more than words from Flannagan to have curbed Bunty's eagerness; so when the train came to a stop and the men tumbled out of the car with a rush, he followed. What he saw caused him to purse his lips and cry excitedly, "Gee!"

Right in front of him a big mogul had turned turtle. Ditched by a spread rail, she had pulled three box-cars with her, and piled them up, mostly in splinters, on the tender. They had taken fire, and were burning furiously. Behind these were eight or ten cars still on the road-bed, but badly demolished from bumping over the ties when they had left the rails. Still farther down the track in the rear were the rest of the string, apparently uninjured. The snow was knee-deep at the side of the track, but Bunty plowed manfully through it, climbing up the embankment to a place of vantage.

His eyes blazed with excitement as he watched the scene before him and listened to the hoarse shouts of the men, the crash of pick and ax, and, above it all, the sharp crackle of the fire as the flames, growing in volume, bit deeper and deeper into the wreck. Fiercely as the men fought, the fire, with its long start, kept them from making any headway against it. Already it had reached some of the cars standing on the track

From where Bunty stood he could see the track dipping away in a long grade to the valley below. They called that grade the Devil's Slide, and the wreck was on the edge of it, with the caboose and some half-dozen cars still resting on the incline. As he looked, far below him he saw a trail of smoke. It was Number Two climbing the grade. By this time the excitement of his surroundings had worn off a little, and the arrival of the Limited offered a new attraction.

He clambered down from his perch and began to pick his way past the wreck. Flannagan, begrimed and dirty, was talking to Emmons. "I don't like to do it," Bunty heard Flannagan say, "but we'll have to blow up that box-car if we can't stop the fire any other way, or we'll have a blaze down the whole line. The train crew says there's turpentine—two cars of it—next the flat there, and if that catches—Hi, there, kid," he broke off to yell, as he caught sight of Bunty, "you get back to the tool-car, and stay there!"

And Bunty ran—in the other direction. He knew Number Two would stop a little the other side of the wreck, and that there would be a great big ten-wheeler pulling her, all as bright as a new dollar and glistening in paint and gold-leaf. When he pulled up breathless and happy by the side of Number Two, Masters, the engineer, was giving Engine 901 an oil round, touching the journals critically with the back of his hand as he moved along.

At sight of Bunty, the engineer laid his oil-can on the slide-bars and grinned as he extended his hand. "How are you, Bunty?" he asked.

And Bunty, accepting the proffered hand, replied gravely: "I'm pretty well, Mr. Masters, thank you."

"Glad to hear it, Bunty. How did you get here?"

"I comed up with the wrecker-train. It's a' awful smash."

"Is it, now! Think they'll have the line cleared soon?"

"Oh, no," Bunty replied, eyeing the cab of the big engine wistfully. "Not for ever and ever so long."

Masters' eyes followed Bunty's glance. "Want to get up in the cab, Bunty?"

"Oh, please!" Bunty cried breathlessly.

"All right," said Masters, boosting the lad through the gangway. Then warningly: "Don't touch anything."

And Bunty promised.

It was only four hundred yards up to the wreck; but that was enough. Masters and his firemen left their train and went to get a view at close quarters. When it was all over, it was up to the wrecking boss and the engine crew of Number Two. Flannagan swore he blocked the trucks of the cars on the incline; but Flannagan lied, and he got clear. Masters and his mate had no chance to lie, for they broke rules, and they got their time.

Be that as it may, Bunty sat on the driver's seat of the Imperial Limited and watched the engineer and fireman start up the track. He lost sight of the men long before they reached the wreck. They were still in view, but he was very busy: he was playing "pretend."

Bunty's imagination was vivid enough to make the game a fascinating one whenever he indulged in it, and that was often. But now it was almost reality, and his fancy was little taxed to supply what was lacking. He was engineer of the Limited, and they had just stopped at a station. He leaned out of the cab window to get the "go-ahead" signal. Then his hand went through the motion of throwing over the reversing-lever and opening the throttle. And now he was off; faster and faster. He rocked his body to and fro to supply the motion of the cab. He sat very grim and determined, peering straight ahead. He was booming along now at full speed. They were coming to a crossing. "*Too-oo-o, toot, toot!*" cried Bunty at the top of his shrill treble, for the rules said you must whistle at every crossing, and Bunty knew the rules. Now they were coming to the next station, and he began to slow up. "*Ding-dong, ding —*"

Bang!

Bunty nearly fell from his seat with fright. Ahead of him, up the track, there was a column of smoke as a mass of wreckage rose in the air, and then a crash. Flannagan had blown up a car. Bunty stared, fascinated, not at the explosion, but at the rear end of the wreck on the grade. He rubbed his eyes in bewilderment, then he scrambled over the side of the seat. He paused half-way off, looking again through the front window to make sure. There was no doubt of it: the cars were beginning to roll down the track toward him. He waited for no more, but rushed to the gangway to jump off. Then he stopped as the story Allan had told about his father came back to him. Bunty's heart thumped wildly as he turned white-faced and determined. No truly engineer would leave his train; his father had not, and Bunty did not.

The reversing-lever was in the back notch where Masters had left it when he stopped the train. It was Bunty's task to reach and open the throttle. He climbed up on the seat and stood on tiptoe. Leaning over, he grasped the lever with both hands and pulled it open. What little science of engine-driving Bunty possessed, was lost in the terror that gripped him. The runaway cars were only a couple of hundred yards away now, and, gaining speed with every rail they traveled, spelt death and destruction to the Imperial Limited, if they ever reached her. The men at the top of the grade were yelling their lungs out and waving their arms in frantic warning.

The train started with a jolt that threw Bunty back on the seat. For an instant the big drivers raced like pin-wheels, then they bit into the rails, and aided by the grade, Number Two began to back slowly down the hill.

Bunty picked himself up, his little frame shaking with dry sobs. The freight-cars had gained on him in the last minute, and had nearly reached him. Again he leaned over for the throttle, and hanging grimly to it, pulled it open another notch, and then another, and then wide open. 901 took it like a frightened thoroughbred. Rearing herself from the track under her two hundred and ten pounds of steam, she jumped into the cars behind her for a starter with a shock that played havoc with the passengers' nerves. Then she settled down to travel. The Devil's Slide is two miles long, and some pretty fair running has been made on it in times of stress; but Bunty holds the record,—it's good yet,—and Bunty was only an amateur!

It was neck and neck for a while, and there was almost a pile-up on the nose of 901's pilot before she began to hold her own. Gradually she began to pull away, and by the time they were half-way down the hill the distance between her and the truant freight-cars was widening. The speed was terrific.

Pale and terror-stricken, Bunty now crouched on the driver's seat. Time and again the engineer's whistle in the cab over his head signaled, now entreatingly, now with frantic insistence. But Bunty gave it no heed; his only thought was for those cars in front of him that were always there. He cried to himself with little moans.

There was a sickening slur as they flew round a curve. 901 heeled to the tangent, one set of drivers fairly lifted from the track. When she found her wheel base again, Bunty, shaken from his hold, was clinging to the reversing-lever. He shut his eyes as he pulled himself back to his seat. When he looked again, he saw the freight-cars hit the curve above him, then slew as they jumped the track and, with a crash that reached him above the roar and rattle of the train, the booming whir of the great drivers beneath him, go pitching headlong down the embankment.

Bunty rose to his knees, and for the first time looked out of the side window, to find a new terror there as the rocks and trees and poles flashed dizzily by him. He turned and looked behind. A man was clinging to the hand-rail of the mail-car, and another, lying flat, was crawling over the coal heaped high on the tender. Bunty dashed the tears from his eyes; he was no "fraidy" kid. He stood up, and holding on to the frame of the window, staggered toward the throttle. As he reached for it, 901 lurched madly, and Bunty lost his balance and fell headlong upon the iron floor plate of the cab. Then it was all dark.

Number Two pulled into Big Cloud that night ten hours late, and it brought Bunty. His father and Carleton and Spence and the shop-hands were on the platform. From the private car, which carried the tail-lights, an elderly gentleman got off with Bunty in his arms. The men cheered, and while the master mechanic rushed forward to take his son, the super and Spence drew back respectfully.

"Mr. Regan," said the old gentleman, with tears in his eyes, "you ought to be pretty proud of this little lad."

Regan tried to speak, but the words choked somehow.

The old gentleman swung himself back upon the car. "Good-by, Bunty!" he called.

And Bunty, from the depths of the blanket they had wrapped around him, called back, "Good-by, sir!"

When Bunty was propped up in bed, his father told him how the express messenger had stopped the train and carried him back into the Pullmans.

Bunty listened gravely. "Yes," he said, nodding his head; "they was awful good to me, and the man that tooked me off the train told me stories, and then I told him some, too."

"What did you tell him?" Regan asked.

"Oh, 'bout trains and shops and presidents and directors and—and lots of things."

"Presidents and directors!" said Regan, in surprise. "What did you tell him about them?"

"I told him what you said—that they was fools, and you knew, 'cause you'd seen them."

Regan whistled softly.

"And," continued Bunty, "he laughed, and when I asked him what he was laughing at, he gave me a piece of paper and told me to give it to you, and you'd tell me."

Regan groaned. "Guess it's my time all right," he muttered. "Where's the paper, Bunty?"

"He putted it in my pocket."

Regan drew the chair with Bunty's clothing on it toward him, and began a hurried search. He fished out a narrow slip of paper and unfolded it on his knee. It was a check for one thousand dollars payable to Master Bunty Regan, and signed by the President of the road.

III
"IF A MAN DIE"

East and West now, the Transcontinental is double-tracked, all except the Hill Division and—that, in the nature of things, probably never will be. If you know the mountains, you know the Hill Division. From the divisional point, Big Cloud, that snuggles at the eastern foothills, the right of way, like the trail of a great sinewy serpent, twists and curves through the mountains, through the Rockies, through the Sierras, and finally emerges to link its steel with a sister division, that stretches onward to the great blue of the Pacific Ocean.

It is a stupendous piece of track. It has cost fabulous sums, and the lives of many men; it has made the fame of some, and been the graveyard of more. The history of the world, in big things, in little things, in battles, in strife, in sudden death, in peace, in progress, and in achievement, has its counterpart, in miniature, in the history of the Hill Division. There is a page in that history that belongs to "Angel" Breen. This is Breen's story.

It has been written much, and said oftener, that men in every walk of life, save one, may make mistakes and live them down, but that the dispatcher who falls once is damned forever. And it is true. I am a dispatcher. I know.

Where he got the nickname "Angel" from, is more than I can tell you, and I've wondered at it often enough myself. Contrast, I guess it was. Contrast with the boisterous, rough and ready men around him, for this happened back in the early days when men were what a life of hardship and no comfort made them. No, Breen wasn't soft—far from it. He was just quiet and mild-mannered. It must have been that—contrast. Anyway, he was "Angel" when I first knew him, and you can draw your own conclusions as to what he is now—I'm not saying anything at all about that.

Where did he come from? What was he before he came here? I don't know. I don't believe anybody knew, or ever gave the matter a thought. That sort of question was never asked—it was too delicate and pointed in the majority of cases. A man was what he was out here, not what he had been; he made good, or he didn't. Not that I mean to imply that there was anything crooked or anything wrong with Breen's past, I'm sure there wasn't for that matter, but I'm just trying to make you understand that when I say Breen had the night trick in the dispatcher's office here in Big Cloud, I'm beginning at the beginning.

Breen wasn't popular. He wasn't a good enough mixer for that. Personally, it isn't anything I'd hold up against him, or any other man. Popularity is too often cheap, and being a "good fellow" isn't always a license for a man to puff out his chest—though most of them do it, and that's the high sign that what I say is right. No, I'm not moralizing, I'm telling a story, you'll see what I mean before I get through. I say Breen wasn't popular. He got the reputation of thinking himself a little above the rank and file of those around him, stuck-up, to put it in cold English, and that's where they did him an injustice. It was the man's nature, unobtrusive, retiring—different from theirs, if you get my point, and they couldn't understand just because it was different. The limitations weren't all up to Breen.

If they had known, or taken the trouble to know, as much about him as they could have known before passing judgment on him, perhaps things might have been a little different; perhaps not, I won't say, for it's pretty generally accepted in railroad law that a dispatcher's slip is a capital offense, and there's no court of appeal, no stay of execution, no anything, and to all intents and purposes he's dead from the moment that slip is made. There have been lots of cases like that, lots of them, and there's no class of men I pity more—a slip, and damned for the rest of their lives! I don't say that because I'm a dispatcher myself. We're only human, aren't we? Mistakes like that, God knows, aren't made intentionally. Sometimes a man is overworked, sometimes queer brain kinks happen to him just as they do to every other man. We're ranked as human in everything but our work. I'm not saying it's not right. In the last analysis I suppose it has to be that way. It's part of the game, and we know the rules when we "sit in." We've no reason to complain, only I get a shiver every time I read a newspaper headline that I know, besides being a death-warrant, is tearing the heart out of some poor devil. You've seen the kind I mean, read scores of them— "Dispatcher's Blunder Costs Many Lives"—or something to the same effect. Maybe you'll think it queer, but for days afterward I can't handle an order book or a train sheet when I'm on duty without my heart being in my mouth half the time.

What's this got to do with Breen? Well, in one way, it hasn't anything to do with him; and, then again, in another way, it has. I want you to know that a blunder means something to a dispatcher besides the loss of his job. Do you think they're a cold-blooded, calloused lot? I want you to know that they *care*. Oh, yes, they're human. They've got a heart and they've got a soul; the one to break, the other to sear. My God! think of it—a slip. That's the ghastly horror of it all—a *slip!* Don't you think they can *feel?* Don't you think their own agony of mind is punishment enough without the added reproach, and worse, of their fellows? But let it go, it's the Law of the Game.

I said they didn't know much about Breen out here then except that he was a pretty good dispatcher, but as far as that goes it didn't help him any, rather the reverse, when the smash came. The better the man the harder the fall, what? It's generally that way, isn't it? Perhaps you're wondering what *I* know about him. I'll tell you. If any one knew Breen, I knew him. I was only a kid then, I'm a man now. I hadn't even a coat—Breen gave me one. I'm a dispatcher—Breen taught me, and no better man on the "key" than Breen ever lived, a better man than I could ever hope to be, yet he slipped. Do you wonder I shiver when I read those things? I'm not a religious man, but I've asked God on my bended knees, over and over again, to keep me from the horror, the suffering, the blasted life that came to Breen and many another man—through a slip. Yes, if any one knew Breen, I did. All I know, all I've got, everything in this whole wide world, I owe to Breen—"Angel" Breen.

You probably read of the Elktail wreck at the time it happened, but you've forgotten about it by now. Those things don't live long in the mind unless they come pretty close home to you; there's too many other things happening every hour in this big pulsing world to make it anything more than the sensation of the moment. But out here the details have cause enough to be fixed in the minds of most of us, not only of the wreck itself, but of what happened afterward as well — and I don't know which of the two was the worse. You can judge for yourself.

I'm not going into technicalities. You'll understand better if I don't. You'll remember I said that the Hill Division is only single-tracked. That means, I don't need to tell you, that it's up to the dispatcher every second, and all that stands between the trains and eternity is the bit of tissue tucked in the engineer's blouse and its duplicate crammed in the conductor's side pocket. Orders, meeting points, single track, you understand? The dispatcher holds them all, every last one of them, for life or death, men, women and children, train crews and company property, all — and Breen slipped!

No one knows to this day how it happened. I daresay some eminent authority on psychology might explain it, but the explanation would be too high-browed and too far over my head to understand it even if he did. I only know the facts and the result. Breen sent out a lap order on Number One, the Imperial Limited, westbound, and Number Eighty-Two, a fast freight, perishable, streaking east. Both were off schedule, and he was nursing them along for every second he could squeeze. Back through the mountains, both ways, all through the night, he'd given them the best of everything — the Imperial clear rights, and Eighty-Two pretty nearly, if not quite, as good. Then he fixed the meeting point for the two trains.

I read a story once where the dispatcher sent out a lap order on two trains and his mistake was staring at him all the time from his order book. I guess that was a slip of the pen, and he never noticed it. That was queer enough, but what Breen did was queerer still. His order book showed straight as a string. The freight was to hold at Muddy Lake, ten miles west of Elktail, for Number One. Number One, of course, as I told you, running free. Somehow, I don't know how, it's one of those things you can't explain, a subconscious break between the mind and the mechanical, physical action, you've noticed it in little things you've done yourself, Breen wired the word "Elktail" instead of "Muddy Lake"—and never knew it—never had a hint that anything was wrong—never caught it on the repeat, and gave back his O. K. The order, the written order in the book, was exactly as it should be. It read Muddy Lake—that was right, Muddy Lake. You see what happened? There wasn't time for the freight to make Elktail, but she got within three miles of it—and that's as far as she ever got! In a nasty piece of track, full of trestles and gorges, where the right of way bends worse than the letter S, they met, the two of them, head on—Number One and Number Eighty-Two!

And Breen didn't know what he had done even after the details began to pour in. How could he know? What was Eighty-Two doing east of Muddy Lake? She should have been waiting there for Number One to pass her. The order book showed that plain enough. And all through the rest of that night, while he worked like a madman clearing the line, getting up hospital relief, and wrecking trains—with Carleton, he was super then, gray-faced and haggard, like the master of a storm-tossed liner on his bridge giving orders, pacing the room, cursing at times at his own impotency—Breen didn't know, neither of them knew, where the blame lay. But the horror of the thing had Breen in its grip even then. I was there that night, and I can see him now bent over under the green-shaded lamp—I can see Carleton's face, and it wasn't a pleasant face to see. One thing I remember Breen said. Once, as the sounder pitilessly clicked a message more ghastly than any that had gone before, adding to the number of those whose lives had gone out forever, adding to the tale of the wounded, to the wild, mad story of chaos and ruin, Breen lifted his head from the key for a moment, pushed his hair out of his eyes with a nervous, shaky sweep of his hand, and looked at Carleton.

"It's horrible, horrible," he whispered; "*but think of the man who did it*. Death would be easy compared to what he must feel. It makes me as weak as a kitten to think of it, Carleton. My God, man, don't you see! I, or any other dispatcher, might do this same thing to-morrow, the next day, or the day after. Tell me again, Carleton, tell me again, that order's straight."

"Don't lose your nerve," Carleton answered sharply. "Whoever has blundered, it's not you."

Irony? No. It's beyond all that, isn't it? It's getting about as near to the tragedy of a man's life as you can get. It's getting as deep and tapping as near bed-rock as we'll ever do this side of the Great Divide. Think of it! Think of Breen that night—it's too big to get, isn't it? God pity him! Those words of his have rung in my ears all these years, and that scene I can see over again in every detail every time I close my eyes.

In the few hours left before dawn that morning, there wasn't time to give much attention to the cause. There was enough else to think of, enough to give every last man on the division from car tink to superintendent all, and more, than they could handle—the investigation could come later. But it never came. There was no need for one. How did they find out? It came like the crack of doom, and Breen got it—got it—and it seemed to burst the floodgates of his memory open, seemed to touch that dormant chord, and he knew, knew as he knew that he had a God, what he had done.

They found the order that made the meeting point Elktail tucked in Mooney's jumper when, after they got the crane at work, they hauled him out from under his engine. Who was Mooney? Engineer of the freight. They found him before they did any of his train crew, or his fireman either, for that matter. Dead? Yes. I'm a dispatcher, look at it from the other side if you want to, it's only fair. That bit of tissue cleared Mooney, of course—but it sent him to his death. Yes, I know, good God, don't you think I *know* what it means—to slip?

It was just before Davis, Breen's relief, came on for the morning trick, in fact Davis was in the room, when Breen got the report. He scribbled it on a pad, word by word as it came in, for Carleton to see. For a minute it didn't seem to mean anything to him, and then, as I say, he got it. I never saw such a look on a man's face before, and I pray God I never may again. He seemed to wither up, blasted as the oak is blasted by a lightning stroke. The horror, the despair, the agony in his eyes are beyond any words of mine to describe, and you wouldn't want to hear it if I could tell you. He held out his arms pitifully like a pleading child. His lips moved, but he had to try over and over again before any sound came from them. There was no thought of throwing the blame on anybody else. Breen wasn't that kind. Oh, yes, he could have done it. He could have put the blunder on the night man at the Gap where Mooney received his Elktail holding order, and Breen's order book would have left it an open question as to which of the two had made the mistake—would probably have let him out and damned the other. You say from the way he acted he didn't think of that and therefore the temptation didn't come to him. Yes, I know what you mean. Not so much to Breen's credit, what? Well, I don't know, it depends on the way you look at it. I'd rather believe the thought didn't come because the man's soul was too *clean*. It was clean them—no matter what he did afterward.

There have been death scenes of dispatchers before, many of them—there will be others in the days to come, many of them. So long as there are railroads and so long as men are frail as men, lacking the infallibility of a higher power, just so long will they be inevitable. But no death scene of a dispatcher's career was ever as this one was. Breen was his own judge, his own jury, his own executioner. Do you think I could ever forget his words? He pointed his hand toward the window that faced the western stretch of track, toward the foothills, toward the mighty peaks of the Rockies that towered beyond them, and the life, the being of the man was in his voice. They came slowly, those words, wrenched from a broken heart, torn from a shuddering soul.

"I wish to God that it were me in their stead. Christ be merciful! I did it, Carleton. I don't know how. I did it."

No one answered him. No one spoke. For a moment that seemed like all eternity there was silence, then Breen, his arms still held out before him, walked across the room as a blind man walks in his own utter darkness, walked to the door and passed out—alone. Those few steps across the room—alone! I've thought of that pretty often since—they seemed so horribly, grimly, significantly in keeping with what there was of life left for the stricken man—*alone*. It's a pretty hard word, that, sometimes, and sometimes it brings the tears.

I don't know how I let him go like that. I was too stunned to move I guess, but I reached him at the foot of the stairs as he stepped out onto the platform. There wasn't anything I could say, was there? What would you have said?

No man knew better than Breen himself what this would mean to him. He was wrecked, wrecked worse than that other wreck, for his was a living death. There weren't any grand jurys or things of that kind out here then, not that it would have made any difference to Breen if there had been. You can't put any more water in a pail when it's already full, can you? You can't add to the maximum, can you? Don't you think Breen's punishment was beyond the reach of man or men to add to, or, for that matter, to abate by so much as the smallest fraction? It was, God knows it was — all except one final twinge, that I believe now settled him, though I'll say here that whatever it did to Breen it's not for me to judge her. Who am I, that I should? It is between her and her Maker. I'll come to that in a minute.

Yes, Breen knew well enough what it meant to him, but his thoughts that morning as we walked up the street weren't, I know right well, on himself — he was thinking of those others. And I, well, I was thinking of Breen. Wouldn't you? I told you I owed Breen everything I had in the world. Neither of us said a word all the way up to his boarding-house. It was almost as though I wasn't with him for all the attention he paid to me. But he knew I was there just the same. I like to think of that. I wasn't very old then — I'm not offering that as an excuse, for I'm not ashamed to admit that I was near to tears — if I'd been older perhaps I could have said or done something to help. As it was, all I could do was to turn that one black thought over and over and over again in my mind. Breen's living death, death, death, death. That's the way it hit me, the way it caught me, and the word clung and repeated itself as I kept step beside him.

He was dead, dead to hope, ambition, future, everything, as dead as though he lay outstretched before me in his coffin. It seemed as if I could see him that way. And then, don't ask me why, I don't know, I only know such things happen, come upon you unconsciously, suddenly, there flashed into my mind that bit of verse from the Bible, you know it—"if a man die, shall he live again?" I must have said it out loud without knowing it, for he whirled upon me quick as lightning, placed his two hands upon my shoulders, and stared with a startled gaze into my eyes. I say startled. It was, but there was more. There seemed for a second a gleam of hope awakened, hungry, oh, how hungry, pitiful in its yearning, and then the uselessness, the futility of that hope crushed it back, stamped it out, and the light in his eyes grew dull and died away.

We had halted at the door of his boarding-house and I made as though to go upstairs with him to his room, but he stopped me.

"Not now, Charlie, boy," he said, shaking his head and trying to smile; "not now. I want to be alone."

And so I left him.

Alone! *He wanted to be alone.* Were ever words more full of cruel mockery! It seems hard to understand sometimes, doesn't it? And we get to questioning things we'd far better leave alone. I know at first I used to wonder why Almighty God ever let Breen make that slip. He could have stopped it, couldn't He? But that's not right. We're running on train orders from the Great Dispatcher, and the finite can't span the infinite.

Maybe you'll think it queer that I left Breen like that, let him go to his room alone. You're thinking that in his condition he might do himself harm—end it all, to put it bluntly. Well, that thought didn't come to me then, it did afterward, but not then. Why? It must have been just the innate consciousness that he wouldn't do that sort of thing. Some men face things one way, some face them another. It's a question of individuality and temperament. I don't think Breen could have done anything like that, I know he seemed so far apart from it in my mind that, as I say, the thought didn't come to me. He was too big a man, big enough to have faced what was before him, faced conditions, faced the men, though God knows they treated him like skulking coyote, if it had not been for her. I want to stand right on this. Breen would never have done what he did if she had acted differently. That much I know. But, I want to say it again, I've no right to judge her.

Perhaps you've read that story of Kipling's about the Black Tyrone Regiment that saw their dead? Well, Breen, as I told you, at the beginning, wasn't popular, and the boys had seen their dead. Do you understand? Pariah, outcast, what you like, they made him, all except pity they gave him, and I say he would have taken it all, accepted it all, only there are some things too heavy for a man to bear, aren't there? Load limit, the engineers call it when they build their bridge. Well, there's a load limit on the heart and brain and soul of a man just as there is on a bridge; and while one, strained beyond the breaking point, goes crashing in a horrid mass of twisted wreckage to the bottom of the cañon, to the bottom of the gorge, into the rushing, boiling waters of the river beneath, the other crashes, a damned soul, to the bottom of hell. Kitty Mooney had seen her dead. Kitty Mooney, the engineer's sister! And Breen loved her, was going to marry her. That's all.

How do I know? How do you know? Perhaps it was grief, perhaps it was hysteria, perhaps it was according to the light God gave her and she couldn't understand, perhaps it was only wild, unreasoning, frantic passion. I don't know. I only know she called him—a *murderer*. She couldn't have loved him, you say. Perhaps no, perhaps yes. Does it make any difference? Breen thought she did, and Breen loved *her*. I don't know. I only know that where he looked for a ray of mercy, *her* mercy, to light the blackened depths, for the touch, *her* touch, that would have held him back from the brink, for the word of comfort, *her* word, that would have bid him stand like a gallant soldier facing untold odds, he received, instead, a condemnation more terrible than any that had gone before, and a bleeding heart dried bitter as gall, a patient, grief-stricken man became a vicious snapping wolf, and "Angel" Breen—a devil.

Would I have been a stronger man than Breen? Would you? Would I have done differently than Kitty Mooney did if I had been in her place? Would you? We don't know, do we? No one knows. God keep us from ever knowing. The poor devil in the gutters, the wretched, ruined lives of women who have lost their grip and drunk the dregs, the human, stranded, battered wrecks we see around us, were once like you and me. We don't know, do we? God pity them! God keep us from the sneer! Our strength has never been measured. It may be no greater than theirs. To-morrow it may be you or I.

It was pretty lawless out here in those days. We had the riff-raff of the East, and worse; and there was nothing to restrain them, nothing much to keep them in check, and they did about as they liked. They brought the touch into the picture of the West that the West hasn't lived down yet, and I'm not sure ever will. The brawling, gambling, gun-handling type, the thief, the desperado, the bad man, rotten bad, bad to the core. They've been stamped out now most of them, but it was different then. *They* didn't turn a cold shoulder to Breen. Why should they? They were outcasts and pariahs, too, weren't they? And Breen, well, I guess you understand as well as I do, and you know as I know that when a man like that goes he goes the limit. There's no middle course for some men, they're not made that way.

Whatever holds them for good, or whatever holds them for bad, it holds them all, either way, all, body, mind and spirit, all. And that is true in spite of the fact that, often enough, there's some one thing, it may be a little thing, it may be a big thing, but some *one* thing that the worst of us balk at, can't do. It's not morality, it's not conscience, a man gets way beyond all that; it's a memory of the past perhaps, a something bred in him from babyhood. I don't know. You can't treat human nature like a specimen on the glass slide under a microscope. There is no specimen. As there are millions of people, so is each one in some way different from the other. You can't classify, you can't tabulate the different kinks into a list and learn it by heart, can you? The man who says he knows human nature says he is as wise as the God who made him, and that man is a poor fool. That's right, isn't it? And so I say that, strange as it may seem, in the worst of us, fall as low as we will, there's generally some one thing our soul, what's left of it, revolts at doing. Breen was a railroad man. Railroading was in his blood. I want you to get that. It was part of him. Any man that's worth his salt in this business is that way. It's in the blood or it isn't; you're a railroad man or you're not.

Breen disappeared from Big Cloud and I didn't see him from the day Kitty Mooney turned him from her door until the night—but I'm coming to that—that's the end. There's a word or two that goes before—so that you'll understand. He disappeared from Big Cloud, but he didn't leave the mountains. Maybe back of it all, an almost impossible theory if you like, but I can understand it, a something in him wouldn't let him run away. He did run away, you say. Yes, but there's the queer brain kink again. Perhaps he temporized. You temporize. I temporize. We try to fool and delude sometimes, snatch at loopholes, snatch at straws, to bolster up our self-respect, don't we? That's what I mean when I say it's possible he couldn't run away. He clung to the straw, the loophole, that running away was measured in *miles*. I don't say that was it, for I don't know. It's possible. We heard of him from time to time as the months went by, and the things we heard weren't pleasant things to hear. He drifted from bad to worse, until that something that he couldn't do brought him to a halt—brought the end.

Don't ask me when Breen threw in his lot with Black Dempsey and the band of fiends that called him leader—the ugliest, soul-blackened set of fiends that ever polluted the West, and that's using pretty strong language. Don't ask me how Breen got to Big Cloud that night away from the others waiting to begin their hellish work. Don't ask me. I don't know. *Why* he did it—is different. That, I can tell you. What they wanted him to do, to have a part in, was that one thing I was speaking about, the one thing he *couldn't* do. Breen was a railroad man, railroading was in his blood, that's all—but it's everything—railroading was in his blood. As for the rest, maybe he didn't know what they were really up to until the last moment, and then stole away from them. Maybe they found it out, suspected him, and some of them followed him, tried to stop him, tried to keep him from reaching here. But what's the use of speculating? I never knew, I never will know. Breen can't tell me, can he? And all that I can tell you is what I saw and heard that night.

I had the night trick then—Breen's job—they gave me Breen's job. It seemed somehow at first like sacrilege to take it—as though I was *robbing* him of it, taking it away from him, wronging, stripping, impoverishing the man to whom I owed even the knowledge that made me fit, that made it possible, to hold down a key—his key. Of course, that was only sensitiveness, but you understand, don't you? It caught me hard when I first "sat in," but gradually the feeling wore off; not that I ever forgot, I haven't yet for that matter, only time blunts the sharp edges, and routine, habit, and custom do the rest. I don't need to tell you that I remember that night. Remember it! That was before this station was built, and in those days we had an old wooden shack here that did duty for freight house, station, division headquarters, and everything else all rolled into one. The dispatcher's room was upstairs.

Things were moving slick as a whistle that night. No extra traffic, no road troubles, in—out, in—out, all along the line the trains were running like clockwork from one end of the division to the other. If there was anything on my mind at all it was the Limited, Number Two, eastbound. We were handling a good deal of gold in those days, there was a lot of it being shipped East then—is still, from the Klondyke now, you know—and we were getting a fair share of the business away from the southern competition. We hadn't had any trouble, weren't looking for any, but it was pretty generally understood that all shipments of that kind were to get special attention. Number Two was carrying an extra express car with a consignment for the mint that night, so, naturally, I had kept my eye on her more closely than usual all the way through the mountains from the time I got her from the Pacific Division. At the time I'm speaking about, four o'clock in the morning, I was almost clear of her, for she wasn't much west of Coyote Bend, fifteen miles from here, and she had rights all the way in. Half an hour more at the most, and she would be off my hands and up to the dispatchers of the Prairie Division. She had held her schedule to the tick every foot of the way, and all I was waiting for was the call from Coyote Bend that would report her in and out again into the clear for Big Cloud. Coyote Bend is the first station west of here, you understand? There's nothing between. She was due at Coyote at 4.05, and I want you to remember this—I said it before, but I want to repeat it. I want you to get it *hard*—she had run to the second all through the night.

My watch was open on the table before me, and I watched the minute hand creep round the dial. 4.03, 4.04, 4.05, 4.06, 4.07, 4.08. I was alone in the office. The night caller had gone out perhaps ten minutes before to call the train crew of the five o'clock local. There wasn't anything to be nervous about. I don't put it down to that. Three minutes wasn't anything. Perhaps it was just impatience, fretfulness. You know how it is when you're waiting for something to happen, and I was expecting the sounder to break every second with that report from Coyote Bend. Anyway, put it down to what you like, though I didn't want a drink particularly I pushed back my chair, got up, and walked over to the water cooler. The dispatcher's table was on the east side of the room, the door opened on the south side, and the water cooler was over in the opposite corner. I'm explaining this so that you'll understand that the door was *between* the water cooler and the table. That old shack was rough and ready, and I've wondered more than once what ever kept it from falling to pieces. It didn't take more than a breath of wind to set every window-sash in the outfit rattling like a corps of snare drums. That's why, I guess, I didn't hear any one coming up the stairs. It was blowing pretty hard that night. But I heard the door open. I thought it was the caller back again, and I wondered how he'd made his rounds in such quick time. With the tumbler half up to my lips I turned around—then the glass slipped from my fingers and crashed into slivers on the floor. My mouth went dry, my heart seemed to stop. I couldn't speak, couldn't move. It was Breen—"Angel" Breen!

I saw him start at the noise of the splintering glass, but he didn't look at me. He clung swaying to the door jamb for an instant, his face chalky white, then he reeled across the room—*and dropped into his old chair.* I saw him glance at my watch and his face seemed to go whiter than before, then he snatched at the train sheet and a smile—no, it wasn't exactly a smile, you couldn't call it that, his whole face seemed to change, light up, and his lips moved—I know now in a prayer of gratitude. You understand, don't you? He knew the time-card, knew that Number Two, after he had seen my watch, should have been *out* of Coyote Bend four, perhaps five, minutes before, but the train sheet showed her still unreported. His fingers closed on the key and he began to make the Coyote Bend call. Over and over, quick, sharp, clear, incisive, with all the old masterful touch of his sending Breen was rattling the call—cc,cx—cc,cx—cc,cx—cc,cx.

And then I found my voice.

"God in Heaven, Breen!" I stammered, and started toward him. "You! What——"

The sounder broke. Coyote Bend answered. And on the instant Breen flashed this order over the wire.

"Hold Number Two. Hold Number Two"—twice the sender spelled out the words.

Then Coyote Bend repeated the order, and Breen gave back the O. K.

"*Breen!*" I shouted. "What are you doing? Are you crazy! What are you doing here? Speak, man, what——"

He had straightened in his chair, and a sort of low, catchy gasp came from his lips. It seemed as though it took all his power, all his strength, to lift his eyes to mine. I sprang for the key, but he jerked himself suddenly forward and pushed me desperately away. And then he called me by the old name, not much above a whisper, I could hardly catch the words, and I didn't understand, didn't know, that the man before me was a wounded, *dying man*. My brain was whirling, full of that other night, full of the days and months that had followed. I couldn't think. I——

"Charlie boy, it's all right. Black Dempsey in the Cut. I was afraid I was too late—too late. They shot—me—here"—he was tearing with his fingers at his waistcoat.

And then I understood—too late. As I reached for him, he swayed forward and toppled over, a huddled heap, over the key, over the order book, over the train sheet that once had taken his life and now had given it back to him—dead.

What is there to say? Whatever he may have done, however far he may have fallen, back of it all, through it all, bigger than himself, stronger than any other bond was the railroading that was in his blood. Breen was a railroad man.

I don't know why, do I? You don't know why, after Number Two had run to schedule all that night, it happened just when it did. It might have happened at some other time — but it didn't. Luck or chance if you like, more than that if you'd rather think of it in another way, but just a few miles west of Coyote Bend something went wrong in the cab of Number Two. Nothing much, I don't remember now what it was, don't know that I ever knew, nothing much. Just enough to hold her back a few minutes, the few minutes that let Breen sit in again on the night dispatcher's trick, sit in again at the key, hold down his old job once more before he quit railroading forever with the order that he gave his life to send, to keep Number Two from rushing to death and destruction against the rocks and boulders Black Dempsey and his gang had piled across the track in the Cut five miles east of Coyote Bend.

I don't know. "If a man die, shall he live again?" I leave it to you. I only know that they think a lot of him out here, think a lot of Breen, "Angel" Breen — now.

IV
SPITZER

Spitzer was just naturally born diffident. Sometimes that sort of thing wears off as one grows older, sometimes it doesn't. When it doesn't, it is worse than the most virulent disease—it had been virulent with Spitzer for all of his twenty-two years.

Spitzer wasn't much to look at, neither was he of much account on the Hill Division. Some men rise to occasions, others don't; as for Spitzer—well, he was a snubby-nosed, peaked-faced, touzled-haired little fellow with washed-out blue eyes that always seemed to carry around an apology in their depths that their owner existed, and this idea was backed up a good bit by Spitzer's voice. Spitzer had a weak voice and that militated against him. The ordinary voice of the ordinary man on the Hill Division was not weak—it was assertive. Spitzer suffered thereby because everybody crawled over him. Nobody thought anything of Spitzer. They all knew him, of course, that is, those whose duties brought them within the zone of Spitzer's orbit, which was restricted to Big Cloud or, rather, to the roundhouse at Big Cloud. Nobody ever gave him credit for courage enough to call his soul his own. Even when it came to pay day he took his check as though it was a mistake and that it really wasn't meant for him. He just dubbed along, doing his work day after day like a faithful dog, only he was a hanged sight less obtrusive. Summed up in a word, Spitzer ranked as a nonentity, physically, mentally, professionally.

Of course he never got ahead. He just kept on sweeping out the roundhouse and puttering around playing bell-boy to every Tom, Dick and Harry that lifted a finger at him. Year in, year out, he swept and wiped in the roundhouse. As far as seniority went he was it, but when it came to promotion he wasn't. Promotion and Spitzer were so obviously, so ostentatiously at variance with each other that no one ever thought of such a thing. When there was a vacancy others got it. Spitzer saw them move along, firing, driving spare, up to full-fledged regulars on the right-hand side of the cabs, men that had started after he did; but Spitzer still wiped and swept out the roundhouse.

Carleton, the super, called him a landmark, and that hit the bull's-eye. Summer, winter, fall, spring, good weather, bad weather, five-foot-five-with-his-boots-on Spitzer, lugging a little tin dinner-pail, trudged down Main Street in Big Cloud as regular as clockwork, and reported at the roundhouse at precisely the same hour every morning—five minutes of seven. Never a miss, never a slip—five minutes of seven. The train crews got to setting their watches by him, and the dispatchers wired the meteorological observatory every time their chronometers didn't tally—that is, tally with Spitzer—and the meteorological crowd put Spitzer first across the tape every shot.

It was just the same at night, only then Spitzer went by the six o'clock whistle. Ten hours a day, Sundays off—sometimes—wiping, sweeping, sweeping, wiping, from his boarding-house to the roundhouse in the morning, from the roundhouse to his boarding-house at night—that was Spitzer, self-effaced, self-obliterated, innocuous, modest Spitzer.

Night times? Spitzer didn't exist, there was no Spitzer—it wasn't expected of him! If any one had been asked they would have looked their amazement, but then no one ever was asked—or asked, which is the same thing the other way. Spitzer was like a tool laid away after the day's work and forgotten absolutely and profoundly until the following morning. No one knew anything about Spitzer after the six o'clock whistle blew, no one knew and cared less—that is, none of the railroad crowd knew, and they, when all is said and done, were Big Cloud, they owned it, ran it, absorbed it, and properly so, since Big Cloud was the divisional point on the Hill Division.

In the ineffable perversity of things is the spice and variety of life. Tommy Regan, the master mechanic, was a man not easily jolted, not easily disturbed. He was very short, very broad, with little black eyes, and a long, scraggly, drooping-at-the-corners, brown mustache. Also, he was blessed with a well-defined, well-nourished paunch—which is a sign irrefutable of contentment, a calm and placid outlook upon life in general and particular, and a freedom from the ills of haste and worry. A man with a paunch is a man apart and greatly to be envied, even when that paunch, as was the case with Regan, is of Irish extraction, for then the accompanying touch of Celtic temper makes him more like an ordinary, cross-grained, irritable, everyday mortal and less of a temperamental curiosity. Regan was justly proud of both—his paunch and his nationality. Regan put it the other way—his nationality and his paunch. That, however, is a matter for individual decision and the relative importance of things is as one sees it; the main thing is that one permitted him to use fiery words on occasion, and the other enabled him to preserve, ordinarily, a much to be commended state of equanimity.

Perversity of perversities! It was Spitzer that jolted Regan—not once, more than once. And before he got through, jolted him so hard that Regan hasn't got over the wonder of it yet.

"Think of it," he'll say, when the subject is brought up. "Think of it! You know Spitzer, h'm? Well, *think* of it! SPITZER!" And if it's summer he'll mop his beady brow, and if it's winter he'll twiddle his thumbs with his fingers laced over his *embonpoint*, which is to say over the lower button of his waistcoat.

Regan's first jolt came to him one morning as, after a critical inspection of his pets in the roundhouse—big six- and eight-wheeled mountain engines—he strolled out and leaned against the push-bar on the turntable, mentally debating the respective merits of a rust-joint and a straight patch as specifically applied to number 583 that had been run into the shops the day before for repairs.

A figure emerged from the engine doors at the far end of the roundhouse and came toward him. Regan's eyes, attracted, barely glanced in that direction, and then went down again in meditation, as he kicked a little hole in the cinders with the toe of his boot—it was only Spitzer.

When he looked up again Spitzer was nearer, quite near. Spitzer had halted before him and was standing there patiently, an embarrassed flush on his cheeks, wiping his hands nervously on an exceedingly dirty piece of packing which in his abstraction, for Spitzer was plainly abstracted, he had picked up for a piece of waste.

"Huh!" said Regan, staring at Spitzer's hands, "what you trying to do? Black up for a minstrel show?"

Spitzer dropped the packing as though it had been a handful of thistles, and rubbed his hands up and down the legs of his overalls.

"Well?" Regan invited.

Spitzer began to talk, rapidly, hurriedly—that is, his lips moved rapidly, hurriedly.

Regan listened attentively and with a strained and hopeless expression, as he strove to catch a word and hence the drift of Spitzer's remarks.

"How?" he demanded, when he saw Spitzer was at an end. "Speak out, man. You won't wake the baby up."

Spitzer began all over again. This time he did a little better.

"A dollar twenty-five," repeated the master mechanic numbly.

Spitzer brightened visibly, and nodded.

Regan stared, bewildered and dumfounded. Gradually, impossible, incomprehensible, incongruous as it appeared, it dawned on him that Spitzer, even Spitzer, *Spitzer* was asking for a *raise!*

"A dollar twenty-five," was all Regan could repeat over again, and the words came away with a gasp.

Spitzer, misinterpreting the tone, his face grew rueful and full of trouble. He was appalled at his own temerity in broaching the subject in the first place, but now he had overstepped the bounds—he had asked for too much!

"A dollar twenty," he ventured, in timid compromise—Spitzer was getting a dollar fifteen.

"How long you been working here?" inquired Regan, recovering a little and beginning to get a grip on himself.

"Four years," said Spitzer faintly.

"Good Lord!" mumbled Regan. "Four years. A dollar twenty-five, h'm? Well, I dunno, I guess we can manage that." And then, as a new thought suddenly struck him: "What the blazes would *you* do with more money, h'm?"

But Spitzer only grinned sheepishly as, after murmuring his thanks, he walked back and disappeared in the roundhouse.

"Good Lord!" muttered Regan, looking after him. "Four years, and a dollar and a quarter, *and* Spitzer! Good Lord!"

Regan went around more or less dazed all that day. He ordered the patch on 583 when he had definitely decided on the rust-joint as the best tonic for the engine's complaint, and he figured out how much one dollar and fifteen cents a day came to for a year barring Sundays, then he did the same with a dollar twenty-five as the multiplicand and compared the results. Spitzer's demand was not exorbitant, and it wasn't much to upset any man—that was just it—it was Spitzer, and Spitzer wasn't much. Effect, psychological or otherwise, is by no manner of means to be measured by the mere magnitude of the cause, it is the phenomenal and unusual that is to be treated with wholesome respect, and for safe handling requires a double-tracked, block system with the cautionary signals up from start to finish—the master mechanic found it that way anyhow, and he ought to know.

He unburdened himself that night after supper to Carleton and a few of the others over at division headquarters, which had been moved upstairs over the station, where the chiefs used to meet regularly each evening for a pipe, with a round of pedro thrown in to liven things up a bit—Big Cloud not being blessed with many attractions in the amusement line.

Carleton grinned.

"Bad company," he suggested. "Hard lot, that of yours over in the roundhouse, Tommy. They're spoiling his manners. Been a long time in coming, but you know the old story of the water and the stone. What?"

"What in blazes would *he* do with more money?" inquired Spence, the chief dispatcher, in unfeigned astonishment.

Regan glared disdainfully. He had put precisely the same question to Spitzer himself, but since then he had been brushing up his mathematics.

"Do with it!" he choked. "Thirty dollars and eighty cents—*a year*. Hell of a problem, ain't it?"

"Well, you needn't run off your schedule," said Spence, a little tartly. "You're the one that's making most of the fuss over it."

"Tell you what, Tommy," remarked Carleton, still grinning, "you want to look out for Spitzer from now on. I guess his emancipation has begun—nothing like a start. Before you know it he'll be running roughshod over the motive power department, including the master mechanic."

"I give him the raise," said Regan, more to himself than aloud. "'Twas coming to him, what? Four years, and the first time I ever heard a yip out of him."

"You'll hear more," prophesied Carleton; "even if he doesn't talk very loud."

"Think so?" said Regan, puckering up his eyes.

"I do," said Carleton.

And Regan did.

Not at once, not for several weeks. But in the meantime a change came over Spitzer. He swept and wiped and reported at five minutes of seven every morning and kept himself just as much in the background, just as much out of everybody's way, just as unobtrusive as he had before, but Spitzer was none the less changed.

It began the day after he got his raise. It was an indefinite, elusive, negative sort of a change, not the kind you could lay your hand on and describe in so many words. Regan tried to, and gave it up. The nearest he came to anything concrete was one day when he came around the tail-end of a tender and, unexpectedly, upon Spitzer. Spitzer was sweeping as usual, but Spitzer was also whistling—which was not usual. Regan, it is true, couldn't puzzle very much out of that, but then Regan had his limitations.

Mindful of Carleton's words, Regan kept his eye in a mildly curious kind of a way on the little faded, blue-eyed drudge, and as he noticed the first change without being able to define it, he now, after a week or so, noticed a second, with the difference that this time the diagnosis was painfully obvious—Spitzer's return to Spitzer's normal self. Spitzer stopped whistling.

Regan began to catch Spitzer's eyes fixed on him with a hesitating, irresolute, anxious gaze about every time he entered the roundhouse. And though he didn't quite grasp it, something of the truth came to him. Spitzer was screwing up his courage to the sticking point preparatory to another step onward in his belated march toward emancipation.

It was a month to the day from the first interview when Spitzer tackled the master mechanic again, and as before, out by the turntable in front of the roundhouse, and, if anything, in a manner even more nervous and ill at ease than on the former occasion. He stammered once or twice in an effort to begin—and his effort was utter failure.

Regan eyed him in profound distrust. Once in four years wasn't so much, and after all, even Spitzer, now that the shock was over, might be expected to do that. But again in a month—and from Spitzer! Something was wrong—perhaps Carleton was right.

"Well," he snapped, "you got your raise. Ain't you satisfied?"

Spitzer nodded dumbly.

"Well, then, what's the matter with you if you're satisfied?" exploded the master mechanic.

"I want to get——" the last word trailed off into tremulous, quavering incoherency.

"You want to get what?" growled Regan. "Don't sputter as though you'd swallowed your teeth. What is it you want to get?"

"Firing," blurted Spitzer after a desperate struggle.

Regan gasped for his breath. Spitzer! SPITZER—in a cab! He couldn't have heard straight.

"Say it again," whispered the master mechanic.

"Firing," repeated Spitzer, with more confidence now that the plunge was taken.

"Yes," said Regan weakly to himself. "That's it. I got it right—firing! He wants to get *firing!*"

"I—I can do it," faltered Spitzer. "I 'got *to.*"

"Eh? What's that? " said Regan. "You got to? Say, you, Spitzer, what the devil's the matter with you anyway?"

Spitzer wriggled like a worm on a hook, and his face went the color of a semaphore arm—a deep red one. Spitzer was suffering acutely.

"Well, well," prodded Regan. "Release the air! Take the brakes off!"

"I'm," began Spitzer shamefacedly, "I'm——" He gulped down his Adam's apple hard, twice, and then it came away with a rush: "I'm going to get married to Merla Swenson."

Regan's jaw sagged like the broken limb of a tree, and his eyes fairly popped out and hung down over the roll of his cheeks. Then gradually, very gradually, he began to double up and unhandsome contortions afflicted his facial muscles. Spitzer! Spitzer was enough! But Spitzer *and* Merla Swenson! Six-foot-heavy-boned-long-armed Swedish-maiden Merla! Oh, contrariety, variety, perversity of life!

"Haw!" he roared suddenly. "Haw, haw! Haw, haw, haw!" And again——only louder. The turner and a helper or two poked their noses out of the roundhouse doors to get a line on the disturbance.

Can a stone float? Can a feather sink? Astonishing, bewildering, dumfounding, impossible, oh, yes; but it was also very funny. It was the funniest thing that Regan had ever heard in his life.

"Haw, haw!" he screamed. "Ho, ho! Haw, haw!"

His paunch shook like jelly, and he held both hands to his sides to ease the pain. He straightened up preparatory to going off into another burst of guffaws, and then, with his mouth already opened to begin, he stopped as though he had been stunned. Spitzer was still standing before him, and Spitzer's head was turned away, but Regan caught it, caught the two big tears that rolled slowly down the grimy cheeks. And in that moment he realized what neither he nor any other man on the Hill Division had ever realized before—that Spitzer, too, was *human*.

Regan coughed, choked, and cleared his throat. Here was Spitzer in a new light, but the Spitzer of years was not so readily to be consigned to the background of oblivion. Spitzer in a cab was as much an anomaly as ever, conjugal aspirations to the contrary.

"Firing?" said he, with grave consideration that he meant, by contrast, should serve as palliation for the sting of his mirth. "Firing? I'm afraid not. You're not fit for it. You're not big enough."

Spitzer dashed his hands across his eyes.

"I *can* fire," he announced with a surprising show of spirit, "an' I *got* to. There's smaller ones than me doing it."

"What do you mean by 'got to'?" demanded the master mechanic.

Spitzer shifted uneasily and kicked at the ground.

"Merla an' me's been making up for quite a while," he stammered: "but she wouldn't say nothing one way or the other till I got a raise."

"Well, you got it," said Regan.

Spitzer nodded miserably.

"Yes, an' now she says 'tain't enough to get married on, an—an' we'll have to wait till I get firing."

"Good Lord!" murmured Regan, and he mopped his brow in deep perplexity. The destiny of mortals was in his hands—but so was the motive power department of the Hill Division. He could no more see Spitzer in a cab than he could see the time-honored camel passing through the eye of a needle. Then inspiration came to him.

"Look here, Spitzer," said he, soothingly. "There ain't any use talking about firing, and I ain't going to let you build up any false hopes. But I'll tell you what, you don't need to feel glum about it. She loves you, don't she?"

Spitzer's lips moved.

"H'm?" inquired Regan solicitously, bending forward.

"Yes; she says she does," repeated Spitzer in thin tones.

"Yes; well then, when you know women, and as much about 'em as I do, you'll know that nothing else counts—nothing but the love, I mean. It's their nature, and they're all alike. That's the way it is with all of 'em"—Regan waved his hand expansively. "It'll be all right. You'll see. She won't hold out on that line."

Some men profit much by little experience, others profit little by much experience. Spitzer, possibly, had had little, very little, but the dejected droop of his shoulders, as he started back for the roundhouse, intimated that in the matter of knowledge as applied to the eternal feminine he was perhaps, in so far as it lay between himself and the master mechanic, the better qualified of the two to speak. And that, certainly, when concretely applied, which is to say applied to Merla Swenson.

Regan couldn't have kept the story back to save his life, and it didn't take long for the division to get it. They all got it—train crews and engine crews on way freights, stray freights, locals, extras and regulars, the staff, the shop hands, the track-walkers and the section gangs down to the last car-tink. At first the division looked incredulous, then it grinned, and then it howled, and its howl was the one word "Spitzer!" with seventeen exclamation points after it to make the tempo and rhythm hang out in a manner befitting and commensurate with the occasion.

It's an ill wind that blows nobody good. Dutchy Damrosch did the business of his life—he did more business than he had ever dreamed of doing in his wildest flights of imagination, for Dutchy had the lunch counter rights at Big Cloud. What's that got to do with Spitzer and his marital ambition? Well, a whole lot! Merla Swenson was second girl in Dutchy's establishment, and Merla was the "fee-ancy" of Spitzer—which was a rotten bad pun of Spider Kelly's, the conductor, and due more to the brogue-like twist of his tongue than to any malice aforethought.

To see any girl that was in love with Spitzer was worth the price of coffee and sinkers any old time. The lunch counter took on the air of a dime museum, and the visitors questioned Merla anxiously, a little suspicious that after all there might be a nigger in the woodpile somewhere in the shape of a "frame-up" with the hoax on themselves.

Merla settled all doubts on that score. Unruffled, calmly, stoically, dispassionately she answered the same question fifty times a day, and each time in the same way.

"Yah, I ban love Spitzer," was her infallible reply, in a tone that made the bare possibility that she could have done anything else seem the very acme of absurdity. Merla's inflexion struck deep at the root of things inevitable.

After that there was nothing to be said. A few, very few, and as the days went by their numbers thinned with amazing rapidity, had the temerity to snicker audibly. They only did it once, as with arms akimbo and hands on hips Merla advanced to the edge of the counter with a look in her steadfast, blue eyes, that was far from inviting, and inquired:

"Him ban goot mans, I tank?"

It was put in the form of a question, it is true, but the "put" was of such cold uncompromise that the result was always the same. The offender hastily buried his nose in his coffee-cup, dug for a dime to square his account—with Dutchy—and made for the platform.

This was all very well, but unless Regan died and some one with a little less—or a little more, depending on how you look at it—imagination took his place, Spitzer's chances of getting into a cab were as good as ever, which is to say that they were about as good as the goodness of a plugged nickel. And the trouble was that, as far as Spitzer could see, the master mechanic wasn't sprouting out with any visible signs of premature decay. Furthermore, as he had suspicioned and now discovered, Regan *wasn't* the last word on women; not, perhaps, that Merla put firing before love, only she was uncommonly strong on firing. Spitzer was unhappy.

All things come to those who wait, they say. So they do, perhaps; but the way of their coming is sometimes not to be understood or fathomed. The story of a man who fell from the eighteenth story window of an office building, and, incidentally, broke his neck has no place here except in a general way. A friend who took a passing interest in the event was curious enough to investigate the cause, and he traced it back step by step, logically, surely, inevitably, beyond the possibility of refutation, to the fact that the second hook from the top on the back of the man's wife's dress—not the man's dress, the dress of the man's wife—was missing on the morning of the day of his untimely decease. The man—not the man's friend—was an inventor. But no matter. It just shows. Regan being still alive, the chances are better than a thousand to one that Spitzer would have known a cold and forlorn old age, as Robert Louis puts it, and Merla would never have had a second edition of herself if it hadn't been for a few measly, unripe crab-apples. What? Yes, that's it—crab-apples. That's the way Spitzer got where he is to-day—just crab-apples. Funny how things happen sometimes when you come to think of it, isn't it? Spitzer and the man who broke his neck aren't the only ones who've had their ups and downs that way, not by several. There isn't any moral to this except that here and there you'll find a man who isn't as modest about his own ability as he ought to be!

Spitzer's nocturnal habits, that were a matter of so much unconcern and of which the railroad crowd at Big Cloud were so densely in ignorance, have a part in this. The truth is that between the lunch-counter and the station is the baggage and freight-shed, and behind the freight-shed it is very dark; and also, not less pertinent, is the fact that Merla was possessed of no other quarters than those shared by her sister-in-arms in Dutchy's employ—which were neither propitious nor commodious. Hence—but the connection is obvious.

On Merla's night off at eight o'clock, Spitzer sneaked down through the fields and across the platform, weather permitting, and on those nights Merla donned her bonnet "for a walk"—at the same hour. When the station-clock struck ten and, coincidentally, Number One's mellow chime sounded down the gorge, Merla retraced her steps to the upstairs rear of the lunch-counter, and Spitzer retraced his across the platform to the fields in the direction of the town and his boarding-house; only, of late, Spitzer had taken to lingering on the platform way up at the far end where it was also very dark and equally as deserted.

Here he would gaze wistfully at the big mogul with valves popping and the steam drumming at her gauges, as she waited on the siding just in front of him—Big Cloud being a divisional point where the engines were changed—to back down onto Number One for the first stretch of the mountain run—Burke's run with 503, and big Jim MacAloon looking after the shovel end of it.

There wasn't anything novel in the sight, but it didn't seem to strike Spitzer as monotonous although, when it was all over and he watched the vanishing tail lights, he always sighed. It was just the same performance each time. Ten minutes or so before Number One, westbound, was due, MacAloon would run 503 out of the roundhouse, over the turntable, up the line, and back onto the siding. Then Burke would appear on the scene, light a torch, and poke around with a long-spouted oil can.

Spitzer would usually reach his position up the platform in time to see the engineer's final jab with the torch between the drivers or into the link-motion before swinging himself through the gangway into the cab, as the Limited with snapping trucks and screeching brake-shoes rolled into the station; but one night it fell out a little differently. The station clock had struck ten, Merla had hastened to her domicile, and Spitzer to the far end of the platform as usual, but Number One was late.

Suddenly Spitzer jumped and his heart seemed to shoot into his mouth. There was a wild, piercing scream of agony. It came again. The blood left Spitzer's cheeks. He saw Burke fly around the end of the pilot, the torch dancing in his hand, and make for the cab. Spitzer involuntarily leaped from the platform to the track and ran in the same direction, then the safety-valve popped with a terrific roar, drowning out all other sounds. He clambered cautiously into the cab. On the floor MacAloon was going through a performance that would have beggared the efforts of a writhing python, and the while he groaned and yelled.

As Spitzer watched, Burke, who was bending over MacAloon with an anxious face, suddenly reached forward and picked up a little round object that rolled from the pocket of the fireman's jumper, then another and another. Spitzer instinctively craned forward, and in so doing attracted Burke's notice for the first time. Burke's look of anxiety gave way to a grin and he held out the objects to Spitzer, just as if it wasn't Spitzer at all but an ordinary man — humor, like death, is a great leveler, but no matter, let that go. Burke held them out to Spitzer, Spitzer took them, and even Spitzer grinned. It didn't need any doctor to diagnose MacAloon's complaint and the complaint wasn't poetic! Cramps, old-fashioned, unadulterated cramps — just plain cramps and green crab-apples! Some things lay a man out worse perhaps — but there aren't many.

Burke's grin didn't last long, for at that moment came Number One's long, clear siren note, and back over the tender a streak of light shot out in a wide circle from around a butte and then danced along the rails and began to light up the platform, as the Limited thundered, five minutes late, into the straight stretch.

"Holy fishplates!" yelled Burke. "I've got to get a man to fire. Spitzer, you run like hell to the roundhouse and——"

Burke stopped. Spitzer stopped him. There are moments in everybody's life when they rise above themselves, above habit, above environment, above everything, if even for only a brief instant. A chance like this would never come again. If he could fire one trip maybe Regan would change his mind. Spitzer grasped at it frantically, despairingly.

"Burke, I *can* fire," he fairly screamed. "Give me a chance, Burke. I'll never get one if you don't."

Burke gasped for a moment like a man with his breath knocked out of him, then something like a dry chuckle sounded in his throat. No one knows but Burke what decided him. It might have been either of two things, or a combination of them both—Spitzer's pleading face, or the desire to take a rise out of Regan—Burke and Regan not having been on the best of terms since the last general elections. Be that as it may, Burke pointed at the squirming fireman.

"Take his feet," he grunted.

Together they lifted and dragged the stricken MacAloon out of the cab and to the ground. 1108, pulling Number One, had come to a stop abreast of them by now, and Burke shouted at the engine crew.

"Here!" he bawled. "Lend a hand!"

And as both men stuck their heads out of the gangway, he and Spitzer boosted the fireman up to them.

"Got cramps," explained Burke tersely. "You'll be able to fix him up in the roundhouse. Five minutes late, h'm? Well, hurry, you're clear. There's your 'go-ahead.' Pull out and let me get hold."

Burke turned to Spitzer, as 1108 slipped away from the baggage-car and moved up the track, and pointed to the gangway of his own engine.

"Get in," he said grimly. "You'll get a chance to fire, and, take it from me, you'll never get a chance to do that or anything else again this side of the happy hunting-grounds, my bucko, if you throw me down."

And while Regan quarreled amiably over a game of pedro upstairs in the station with Carleton, 503, with Spitzer, touzled-haired, mild-eyed, heart-beating-like-a-trip-hammer Spitzer, in the cab, backed down on the Imperial Limited and coupled on for the mountain run. There was a quick testing of the "air," a hurried running up and down the platform, and then Burke, leaning from the window with his arms stretched out inside the cab and fingers on the throttle, opened a notch, and the platform began to slide past them.

Spitzer wrinkled his face and stared at the gauge needle — two hundred and ten pounds, all the way, all the time — two hundred and ten pounds. It was up to him. With a jerk of the chain, he swung the furnace door wide and a shovelful of coal shot, neatly scattered, over the grate.

There is art in all things; there is the quintessence of art in the prosaic and laborious task of firing an engine. Spitzer was not without art, for in a way he had had years of experience; but banking a fire in the roundhouse, and nursing a roaring pit of flame to its highest degree of efficiency in a swaying, lurching cab, are two different and distinct operations that are in no way to be confounded. 503 began to lurch and sway. Notch by notch Burke was opening her out, and the bark of her exhaust was coming like the quick crackle of a gatling. Five minutes late in the mountains on a time schedule already marked up to a dizzy height that called for more chances than the passengers paid for is — well, it's five minutes, just *five minutes*, that's all. Some men would have left it for the Pacific Division crowd the next day on a level track and a straight sweep — but not Burke.

Spitzer's initiation was in ample form and he got the full benefit of all the rites and ceremonies with every detail of the ritual worked in—and no favors shown. So far all was well, the rough country was all in front of the pilot, and Spitzer was all business. His pulse was beating in tune to only one thing—the dancing needle on the gauge. Again he swung the door open, and the red flare lighted up the heavens and played on features that Regan would never have known for Spitzer's—they were set, grim and determined, covered with little sweat beads that glistened like diamonds. The singing sweep of the wind was in his ears as he poised his shovel. There was a sickening slur. 503 shot round a tangent—and the shovelful of coal shot like bullets all over the cab, and, including Burke, hit about everything in sight but the objective point aimed at. Simultaneously, Spitzer promptly performed a gyration that resembled something like a back hand-spring and landed well up on the tender, to roll back to the floor of the cab again with an accompanying avalanche of coal.

He picked himself up and glanced apprehensively at the engineer. There was not a scowl, not even a grin on Burke's face, just an encouraging flirt of the hand—but the flirt was momentous. Wise and full of guile was Burke, for with that little act Spitzer, biblically speaking, girded up his loins and got his second wind.

They were well into the foothills now, and the right of way was an amazing wonder. Diving, twisting, curving, it circled and bored and trestled its way, and buttes, cañons, gorges and coulees roared past like flights of fancy.

The speed was terrific. To Spitzer it was all a wild, mad medley of things he had never known before, of things that had neither beginning nor end. The giddy slew as the big mountain racer hit the curves, the crunching grind of the flanges as for an instant she lifted from her wheel-base, the pitch, the roll, the staggering reel, the gasp for breath, the beat of the trucks, the whir of the racing drivers, the rush of the wind, the echoing thunder of the flying coaches behind — it was all there, all separate, all welded into one, a creation, new, vernal, life, the life of the rail, that beat at his eardrums and quickened the pounding throb of his heart.

At first, from time to time, Burke leaned over his levers to glance at the pressure gauge, but after a bit he crouched a little further forward in his seat and his eyes held on the track ahead where the beam of the electric headlight flooded the glittering ribbons of steel. He was getting what MacAloon or no other man had ever given him before — two hundred and ten pounds *all* the way. SPITZER was firing Number One, the Imperial Limited, westbound, on the mountain run, *three* minutes late!

The sweat was rolling in streams from the little fellow now, and he clung in the gangway for a moment's breathing spell, leaning out, staring ahead at a few shining lights in the distance. Came the hoarse scream of the whistle, the clattering crash as they shattered the yard switches, a blurred vision of dark outlines dotted with tiny scintillating points, and station, yard, lights, switches and all were behind him.

Spitzer drew his sleeve across his forehead, and turned again to his work as they thundered over a long steel trestle—Thief Creek. Spitzer knew the road well enough at second hand, if not from personal experience. Just ahead was The Pass—Sucker Pass—straight enough for its quarter-mile stretch, but where the rock walls rose up on either side so close as to almost scratch the paint off the rolling stock. Eased for a moment in scant deference to switches and trestle just passed, Spitzer felt the forward leap of the racer as Burke threw her wide open again. He bent for his shovel—and then, quick as the winking of an eye, sudden as doom, came a tearing, rending crash, a scream from Burke, and the right-hand side of the cab seemed literally torn in two.

A flying piece of woodwork that struck him across the eyes, a terrific jolt as the engine lifted and fell back, sent Spitzer headlong to the floor of the cab. Dazed, half mad with the pain, the blood streaming from his forehead, he staggered to his feet. Burke lay coiled in an inert heap just in front of him by the furnace door. A whizzing piece of steel rose up, crunched, slithered, gashed a track of ruin for itself, and was gone. It had missed Burke only by a hair's-breadth—next time there might not be even that limit of safety. With a cry, Spitzer leaped forward and dragged the unconscious engineer across the cab. Again the jolt, the slur, the stagger, the desperate wrench. It seemed like years, like eternity to Spitzer. He was living a lifetime in the passing of a second—it had been no more than that, no more than two or three at most.

There are some things worse, much worse, in railroading than a broken crank-pin and a rod amuck, but not when it comes in The Pass, where derailment at their racing speed spelt death, quick and sudden. There was just one chance for the trailing string of coaches, just one for every last soul aboard—Spitzer. But between Spitzer and the throttle and the air-latch was a thing of steel that rose and fell, now swinging a splintering, murderous arc through the shattered side of the cab, now grinding into the ties and roadbed, threatening with every revolution to pitch 503 and the train behind her headlong from the rails to crumple like flimsy eggshells against the narrow rocky walls that lined The Pass. Just one chance for the train crew and passengers—*just one in a thousand for Spitzer*. And little five-foot-five Spitzer, diffident, retiring, self-effaced, unobtrusive Spitzer, with a dry, choking sob in his throat, flung himself forward to stop the train. His hands clutched desperately at the levers, there was a hiss, the vicious bite of the brake-shoes, then a blinding light before his eyes as the rod caught him and he pitched, senseless, half out through the front window of the cab, head down on the running-board.

The last word is a woman's—it is her inalienable right. Said Merla to Regan with a world of suggestion in the cadence of her voice, when Spitzer was getting well enough to think about going to work again:

"I ban love Spitzer."

"Well," said Regan, squinting at her round, steadfast, blue eyes, "there ain't anything I know of to keep you waiting. He can name any run he wants. And then, the wonder of it being still heavy upon him, he exclaimed with the air of one invoking the universe: "Now, wouldn't that get you! What do you think, h'm?"

All English to Merla was literal.

"Him ban goot mans, I tank," she said.

V
SHANLEY'S LUCK

Generally speaking, Carleton, the super, was a pretty good judge of human nature, and he wasn't in the habit of making many breaks when it came to sizing up a man—not many. He did sometimes, but not often. However——

Shanley came out from the East, third class, colonist coach, billed through to Bubble Creek, B. C. Not that Shanley had any relatives or friends there, nor, for that matter, any particular reason for wanting to go there—it was simply a question of how far his money would go in yards of pink-colored paper, about two and one-half inches wide, stamped, printed, countersigned, and signed again to obviate any possible misunderstanding that might arise touching the company's liability for baggage, the act of God, dangers foreseen and unforeseen, personal effects or resultant personal defects whether due to negligence or not—it was all one. The colonist ticket was a bill of lading, and the "goods" went through "O. R.," owner's risk.

This possibly may not be strictly legal, but it is strictly safe—for the company. Furthermore, the directors didn't have to sit up very late at night to figure out that if they got the colonists' money first there would be none left for legal advice in case of eventualities, and that's the way it was with about nine hundred and ninety-nine out of every thousand colonists. The company, of course, did take *some* risk—they took a chance on the one-thousandth man. The company had sporting blood.

If Shanley had only known what was going to happen, he could have saved some of his money on that ticket. As it stands now, he has still got transportation coming to him from Little Dance on the Hill Division to Bubble Creek, B. C. That may be an asset, or it may not—Shanley never asked for it.

Third class, colonist, no stop over allowed, red-haired, freckle-faced, an uptilt to the nose, a jaw as square as the side of a house, shoulders like a bull's, and a fist that would fell an ox — that was Shanley. That was Shanley until the sprung rail that ditched the train at Little Dance caused him the loss of two things — his erstwhile status in the general passenger agent's department, and a well-beloved and reeking brier.

Both were lost forever — his status partly on account of the reasons before mentioned, and partly because Shanley wasn't particularly interested in Bubble Creek; his brier because it became a part, an integral part, of that memorable wreck, as Shanley, who was peacefully smoking in the front-end compartment of the colonist coach when the trouble happened, left the pipe behind while he catapulted through the open door — it was summer and sizzling hot — and landed, a very much dazed, bewildered, but not otherwise hurt Shanley, halfway up the embankment on the off side of a scene of most amazing disorder.

The potentialties that lie in a sprung rail are something to marvel at. Up ahead, the engine had promptly turned turtle, and, as promptly giving vent to its displeasure at the indignity heaped upon it, had incased itself in an angry, hissing cloud of steam; behind, the baggage and mail cars seemed to have vied with each other in affectionate regard for the tender. Only the brass-polished, nickel-plated Pullmans at the rear still held the rails; the rest was just a crazy, slewed-edgeways, up-canted, toppled-over string of cars, already beginning to smoke as the flames licked into them.

The shouts of those who had made their escape, the screams of those still imprisoned within the wreckage, the sight of others crawling through the doors and windows brought Shanley back to his senses. He rose to his feet, blinked furiously, as was his habit on all untoward occasions, and the next instant he was down the embankment and into the game — to begin his career as a railroad man. That's where he started — in the wreck at Little Dance.

In and out of the blazing pyre, after a woman or a child; the crash of his ax through splintering woodwork; the scorching heat; prying away some poor devil wedged down beneath the débris; tinkling glass as the heat cracked the windows or he beat through a pane with his fist—it was all hazy, all a dream to Shanley as, hours afterward, a grim, gaunt figure with blackened, bleeding face, his clothes hanging in ribbons, he rode into the Big Cloud yards on the derrick car.

Some men would have hit up the claim agent for a stake; Shanley hit up Carleton for a job. But for modesty's sake, previous to presenting himself before the superintendent's desk, he borrowed from one of the wrecking crew the only available article of wearing apparel at hand—a very dirty and disreputable pair of overalls. Dirty and disreputable, but—whole.

"I want a job, Mr. Carleton," said he bluntly, when he had gained admittance to the super.

"You do, eh?" replied Carleton, looking him up and down. "You do, eh? You're a pretty hard-looking nut, h'm?"

Shanley blinked, but, being painfully aware that he undoubtedly did look all if not more than that, and being, too, not quite sure what to make of the super, he contented himself with the remark:

"I ain't a picture, I suppose."

"H'm!" said Carleton. "Been up at the wreck, I hear—what?"

"Yes," said Shanley shortly. No long story, no tale of what he'd done, no anything—just "Yes," and that was what caught Carleton.

"What can you do?" demanded the super.

"Anything. I'm not fussy," replied Chanley.

"H'm!" said Carleton. "You don't look it." And he favored Shanley with another prolonged stare.

Shanley, at first uncomfortable, shifted nervously from one foot to the other; then, as the stare continued, he began to get irritated.

"Look here," he flung out suddenly. "I ain't on exhibition." I come for a job. I ain't got any letters of recommendation from pastors of churches in the East. I ain't got anything. My name's Shanley, an' I haven't even got anything to prove *that*."

"You've got your nerve," said Carleton, leaning back in his swivel chair and tucking a thumb in the armhole of his vest. "Ever worked on a railroad?"

"No," answered Shanley, a little less assertively, as he saw his chances of a job vanishing into thin air, and already regretting his hasty speech — a few odd nickels wasn't a very big stake for a man starting out in a new country, and that represented the sum total of Shanley's worldly wealth. "No, I never worked on a railroad."

"H'm," continued Carleton. "Well, my friend, you can report to the trainmaster in the morning and tell him I said to put you on breaking. Get out!"

It came so suddenly and unexpectedly that it took Shanley's breath. Carleton's ways were not Shanley's ways, or ways that Shanley by any peradventure had been accustomed to. A moment before he wouldn't have exchanged one of his nickels for his chances of a job, therefore his reply resolved itself into a sheepish grin; moreover — but of this hereafter — Shanley back East was decidedly more in the habit of having his applications refused with scant ceremony than he was to receiving favorable consideration, which was another reason for his failure to rise to the occasion with appropriate words of thanks.

Incidentally, Shanley, like a select few of his fellow creatures, had his failings; concretely, his particular strayings from the straight and narrow way, not having been hidden under a bushel, were responsible, with the advice and assistance of a distant relative or two—advice being always cheap, and assistance, in this case, a marked-down bargain—for his migration to the West, as far West as the funds in hand would take him—Bubble Creek, B. C, the distant relatives saw to that. They bought the ticket.

Shanley, still smiling sheepishly and in obedience to the super's instruction to "get out," was halfway to the door when Carleton halted him.

"Shanley!"

"Yes, sir?" said Shanley, finding his voice and swinging around.

"Got any money?"

Shanley's hand mechanically dove through the overalls and rummaged in the pocket of his torn and ribboned trousers—the pocket had not been spared—the nickels, every last one of them, were gone. The look on his face evidently needed no interpretation.

Carleton was holding out two bills—two tens.

"Cleaned out, eh? Well, I wouldn't blame any one if they asked you for your board bill in advance. Here, I guess you'll need this. You can pay it back later on. There's a fellow keeps a clothing store up the street that it wouldn't do you any harm to visit—h'm?"

With gratitude in his heart and the best of resolutions exuding from every pore—he was always long on resolutions—Shanley being embarrassed, and therefore awkward, made a somewhat ungraceful exit from the super's presence.

But neither gratitude nor resolutions, even of steel-plate, double-riveted variety, are of much avail against circumstances and conditions over which one has absolutely, undeniably, and emphatically no control. If Dinkelman's clothing emporium had occupied a site between the station and MacGuire's Blazing Star saloon, instead of the said Blazing Star saloon occupying that altogether inappropriate position itself, and if Spider Kelly, the conductor of the wrecked train, had not run into Shanley before he had fairly got ten yards from the super's office, things undoubtedly would have been very different. Shanley took that view of it afterward, and certainly he was justified. It is on record that he had no hand in the laying out of Big Cloud nor in the control of its real estate, rentals, or leases.

Railroad men are by no stretch of the imagination to be regarded as hero worshipers, but if a man does a decent thing they are not averse to telling him so. Shanley had done several very decent things at the wreck. Spider Kelly invited him into the Blazing Star.

Shanley demurred. "I've got to get some clothes," he explained.

"Get 'em afterward," said Kelly; "plenty of time. Come on; it's just supper-time, and there'll be a lot of the boys in there. They'll be glad to meet you. If you're hungry you'll find the best free layout on the division. There's nothing small about MacGuire."

Shanley hesitated, and, proverbially, was lost.

An intimate and particular description of the events of that night are on no account to be written. They would not have shocked, surprised, or astonished Stanley's distant relatives—but everybody is not a distant relative. Shanley remembered it in spots—only in spots. He fought and whipped Spider Kelly, who was a much bigger man than himself, and thereby cemented an undying friendship; he partook of the hospitality showered upon him and returned it with a lavish hand—as long as Carleton's twenty lasted; he made speeches, many of them, touching wrecks and the nature of wrecks and his own particular participation therein—which was seemly, since at the end, about three o'clock in the morning, he slid with some dignity under the table, and, with the fond belief that he was once more clutching an ax and doing heroic and noble service, wound his arms grimly, remorselessly, tenaciously, like an octopus, around the table leg—and slept.

MacGuire before bolting the front door studied the situation carefully, and left him there—for the sake of the table.

The sunlight next morning was not charitable to Shanley. Where yesterday he had borne the marks of one wreck, he now bore the marks of two—his own on top of the company's. Up the street Dinkelman's clothing emporium flaunted a canvas sign announcing unusual bargains in men's apparel. This seemed to Shanley an unkindly act that could be expressed in no better terms than "rubbing it in." He gazed at the sign with an aggrieved expression on his face, blinked furiously, and started, with a step that lacked something of assurance, for the railroad yards and the trainmaster's office.

He was by no means confident of the reception that awaited him. If there is one characteristic over and above any other that is common to human nature, it is the faculty, though that's rather an imposing word, of worrying like sin over something that *may* happen but never does. Shanley might just as well have saved himself the mental worry anent the trainmaster's possible attitude. He did not report to the trainmaster that morning, never saw that gentleman until long, very long afterward. Instead, he reported to Carleton — — at the latter's urgent solicitation in the shape of a grinning call-boy, who intercepted his march of progress toward the station.

"Hi, you, there, cherub face!" bawled the urchin politely. "The super wants you — on the hop!"

Shanley stopped short, and, resorting to his favorite habit, blinked.

"Carleton. Get it? Carleton," repeated the messenger, evidently by no means sure that he was thoroughly understood; and then, for a parting shot as he sailed gayly up the street: "Gee, but you're pretty!"

Carleton! Shanley had forgotten all about Carleton for the moment. His hand instinctively went into his pocket — and then he groaned. He remembered Carleton. But worst of all, he remembered Carleton's twenty.

There were two courses open to him. He could sneak out of town with all possible modesty and dispatch, or he could face the music. Not that Shanley debated the question — the occasion had never yet arisen when he hadn't faced the music — he simply experienced the temptation to "crawl," that was all.

"It looks to me," he ruminated ruefully, "as though I was up against it for fair. Just my luck, just my blasted luck, always the same kind of luck, that's what. 'Tain't my fault neither, is it? *I* ain't responsible for that darned wreck—if 'twasn't for that I wouldn't be here. An' Kelly, Spider he said his name was, if 'twasn't for him I wouldn't be here neither. What the blazes did *I* have to do with it? I always have to stand for the other cuss. That's me every time, I guess. An' that's logic."

It was. Neither was there any flaw in it as at first sight might appear, for the last test of logic is its power of conviction. Shanley, from being a man with some reasonable cause for qualms of conscience, became, in his own mind, one deeply sinned against, one injured and crushed down by the load of others he was forced to bear.

He explained this to Carleton while the thought of his burning wrongs was still at white heat, and before the super had a chance to get in a word. He began as he opened the office door, continued as he crossed the room, and finished as he stood before the super's desk.

The scowl that had settled on Carleton's face, as he looked up at the other's entrance, gradually gave way to a hint of humor lurking around the corners of his mouth, and he leaned back in his chair and listened with an exaggerated air of profound attention.

"Just so, just so," said he, when Shanley finally came to a breathless halt. "Now perhaps you will allow *me* to say a word. It may not have occurred to you that I sent for you in order that *I* might do the talking—h'm?"

This really seemed to require no answer, so Shanley made none.

"Yesterday," went on Carleton, "you came to me for a job, and I gave you one, didn't I?"

"Yes," admitted Shanley, licking his lips.

"Just so," said Carleton mildly. "I hired you then. I fire you now. Pretty quick work, what?"

"You're the doctor," said Shanley evenly enough. He had, for all his logic, expected no more nor less — he was too firm a believer in his own particular and exclusive brand of luck. "You're the doctor," he repeated. "There's a matter of twenty bucks———"

"I was coming to that," interrupted Carleton; "but I'm glad *you* mentioned it. I'll be honest enough to admit that I hardly expected you would. A man who acts as you've acted doesn't generally — h'm? "

"I told you 'twasn't my fault," said Shanley stubbornly.

Carleton reached for his pipe, and struck a match, surveying Shanley the while with a gaze that was half perplexed, half quizzical.

"You're a queer card," he remarked at last. "Why don't you cut out the booze?"

"'Twasn't my fault, I tell you," persisted Shanley.

"You're a pretty good hand with your fists, what?" said Carleton irrelevantly. "Kelly's no slouch himself."

Shanley blinked. It appeared that the super was as intimately posted on the events of the preceding evening as he was himself. The remark suggested an inspection of the fists in question. They were grimy and dirty, and most of the knuckles were barked; closed, they resembled a pair of miniature battering-rams.

"Pretty good," he admitted modestly.

"H'm! About that twenty. You intend to pay it back, don't you?"

"I'm not a thief, whatever else I am," snapped Shanley. "Of course, I'll pay it back. You needn't worry."

"When?" insisted Carleton coolly.

"When I get a job."

"I'll give you one," said Carleton — "Royal" Carleton the boys called him, the squarest man that ever held down a division. "I'll give you one where your fists will be kept out of mischief, and where you can't hit the high joints quite as hard as you did last night. But I want you to understand this, Shanley, and understand it good and plenty and once for all, it's your last chance. You made a fool of yourself last night, but you acted like a man yesterday — that's why you're getting a new deal. You're going up to Glacier Cañon with McCann on the construction work. You won't find it anyways luxurious, and maybe you'll like McCann and maybe you won't — he's been squealing for a white man to live with. You can help him boss Italians at one seventy-five a day, and you can go up on Twenty-nine this morning, that'll take care of your transportation. What do you say?"

Shanley couldn't say anything. He looked at the super and blinked; then he looked at his fists speculatively — and blinked.

Carleton was scribbling on a piece of paper.

"All right, h'm?" he said, looking up and handing over the paper. "There's an order on Dinkelman, only get some one else to show you the way this time, and take the other side of the street going up. Understand?"

"Mr. Carleton," Shanley blurted out, "if ever I get full again, you——"

"I will!" said Carleton grimly. "I'll fire you so hard and fast you'll be out of breath for a month. Don't make any mistake about that. No man gets more than two chances with me. The next time you get drunk will finish your railroad career for keeps, I promise you that."

"Yes," said Shanley humbly; and then, after a moment's nervous hesitation: "About Kelly, Mr. Carleton. I don't want to get him in bad on this. You see, it was this way. He left early — that's what started the fight. I called him a — a — quitter — or something like that."

"H'm, yes; or something like that," repeated Carleton dryly. "So I believe. I've had a talk with Kelly. You needn't let the incomprehensible workings of that conscience of yours prick you any on his account. Kelly knows when to stop. His record is O. K. in this office. Kelly doesn't get drunk. If he did, he'd be fired just as fast as you will be if it ever happens again."

"If I'm never fired for anything but that," exclaimed Shanley in a burst of fervent emotion, "I've got a job for life. I'll prove it to you, Mr. Carleton. I'm going to make good. You see if I don't."

"Very well," said Carleton. "I hope you will. That's all, Shanley. I'll let McCann know you're coming."

Shanley's second exit from the super's presence was different from the first. He walked out with a firm tread and squared shoulders. He was rejuvenated and buoyant. He was on his mettle—quite another matter, entirely another matter, and distinctly apart from the paltry consideration of a mere job. He had told Carleton that he would make good. Well, he would—and he did. Carleton himself said so, and Carleton wasn't in the habit of making many breaks when it came to sizing up a man—not many. He did sometimes, but not often.

Shanley did not take the other side of the street on the way to Dinkelman's—by no means. He deliberately passed as close to the Blazing Star saloon as he could, passed with contemptuous disregard, passed boastfully in the knowledge of his own strength. A sixteen-hundred class engine with her four pairs of forty-six-inch drivers can pull countless cars up a mountain grade steep enough to make one dizzy, but Shanley would have backed himself to win against her in a tug of war over the scant few inches that separated him from MacGuire's dispensary as he brushed by. None of MacGuire's for him. Not at all. Red-headed, freckle-faced, barked-knuckled, bulwarked-and-armor-cased-against-temptation Shanley dealt that morning with Mr. Dinkelman, purveyor of bargains in men's apparel.

The dealings were liberal—on the part of both men. On Shanley's part because he needed much; on Mr. Dinkelman's part because it was Mr. Dinkelman's business, and his nature, to sell much—if he could—safely. This was eminently safe. Carleton's name in the mountains stood higher than guaranteed, gilt-edged gold bonds any time.

The business finally concluded, Shanley boarded Twenty-nine, local freight, west, and in due time, well on in the afternoon, righteously sober, straight as a string, cleaned, groomed, and resplendent in a new suit, swung off from the caboose at Glacier Cañon as the train considerately slackened speed enough to give him a fighting chance for life and limb.

He landed safely, however, in the midst of a jabbering Italian labor gang, who received his sudden advent with patience and some awe. A short, squint-faced man greeted him with a grin.

"Me name's McCann," said he of the squint face. "This is Glacier Cañon, fwhat yez see av ut. Them's the Eyetalians. Yon's fwhere I roost an' by the same token, fwhere yez'll roost, too, from now on. Above is the shack av the men. Are yez plased wid yer introduction? 'Tis wan hell av a hole ye've come to. Shanley's the name, eh? A good wan, an' I'm proud to make the acquaintance."

Shanley blinked as he stretched out his hand and made friends with his superior, and blinked again as he looked first one way and then another in an effort to follow and absorb the other's graphic description of the surroundings.

The road foreman's summary was beyond dispute. Glacier Cañon was as wild a piece of track as the Hill Division boasted, which was going some. The right of way hugged the bald gray rock of the mountains that rose up at one side in a sheer sweep, and the trains crawled along for all the world like huge flies at the base of a wall. On the other side was the Glacier River with its treacherous sandy bed that had been the subject of more reports and engineers' gray hairs than all the rest of the system put together. The construction camp lay just to the east of the Cañon, and at the foot of a long, stiff, two-mile, four-per-cent grade. That was the reason the camp was there—that grade.

Locking the stable door when the horse is gone is a procedure that is very old. It did not originate with the directors of the Transcontinental—they never claimed it did. But their fixed policy, if properly presented before a court of arbitration, would have gone a long way toward establishing a clear title to it. If they had built a switchback at the foot of the grade in the first place, Extra Number Eighty-three, when she lost control of herself near the bottom coming down, would have demonstrated just as clearly the necessity for one being there as she demonstrated most forcibly what would happen when there wasn't. All of which is by way of saying that rock or no rock, expense or no expense, the door was now to be locked, and McCann and his men were there to lock it.

McCann explained this to Shanley as he walked him around, up the track to the men's shanties, over the work, and back again down the track to inspect the interior of the dwelling they were to share in common—a relic of deceased Extra Number Eighty-three in the shape of a truckless box-car with dinted and bulging sides—dinted one side and bulged the other, that is.

"But," said Shanley, "I dunno what a switchback is."

"Who expected it av ye?" inquired McCann.

"An' fwhat difference does ut make? Carleton sint word ye were green. Ye've no need to know. So's ye can do as yez are told an' make them geesers do as they are told, *an'* can play forty-foive at night—that's the point, the main point wid me, an' it's me yez av to get along wid—'twill be all right. Since Meegan, him that was helpin' me, tuk sick a week back, I've been alone. Begad, playin' solytare is——"

"I can play forty-five," said Shanley.

McCann's face brightened.

"The powers be praised!" he exclaimed. "I'll enlighten ye, then, on the matter av switchbacks, me son, so as ye'll have an intilligent conception av the work. A switchback is a bit av a spur track that sticks out loike the quills av a porkypine at intervuls on a bad grade such as the wan forninst ye. 'Tis run off the main line, d'ye mind, an' up contrariwise to the dip av the grade. Whin a train comin' down gets beyond control an' so expresses herself by means av her whistle, she's switched off an' given a chance to run uphill by way av variety until she stops. An' the same holds true if she breaks loose goin' up. Is ut clear?"

"It is," said Shanley. "When do I begin work?"

"In the mornin'. 'Tis near six now, an' the bhoys'll be quittin' for the night. Forty-foive is a grand game. We'll play ut to-night to our better acquaintance. I contind 'tis the national game av the ould sod."

Whether McCann's contention is borne out by fact, or by the even more weighty consideration of public opinion, is of little importance. Shanley played forty-five with McCann that night and for many nights thereafter. He lost a figure or two off the pay check that was to come, but he won the golden opinion of the little road boss, which ethically, and in this case practically, was of far greater value.

"He's a bright jool av a lad," wrote McCann across the foot of a weekly report.

And Carleton, seeing it, was much gratified, for Carleton wasn't in the habit of making many breaks when it came to sizing up a man—not many. He did sometimes, but not often. Shanley was making good. Carleton was much gratified.

Of the three weeks that followed Shanley's advent to Glacier Cañon, this story has little to do in a detailed way; but, as a whole, those three weeks are pointed, eloquent, and important—very important.

Italian laborers have many failings, but likewise they have many virtues. They are simple, demonstrative, and their capacity for adoration—of both men and things—is very great.

From Jacko, the water boy, to Pietro Maraschino, the padrone, they adored Shanley, and enthroned him as an idol in their hearts, for the very simple reason that Shanley, not being a professional slave-driver by trade, established new and heretofore undreamed-of relations with them. Shanley was very green, very ignorant, very inexperienced—he treated them like human beings. That was the long and short of it. Shanley became popular beyond the popularity of any man, before or since, who was ever called upon to handle the "foreign element" on the Hill Division.

And the work progressed. Day by day the cut bored deeper into the stubborn mountain-side; day by day the Glacier River gurgled peacefully along over its treacherous sandy bed, one of the prettiest scenic effects on the system, so pretty that the company used it in the magazines; day by day regulars and extras, freights and passengers, east and west, snorted up and down the grade, the only visitations from the outside world; night after night Shanley played forty-five with McCann in the smoky, truckless box-car.

Also the camp was dry, very dry, dryer than a sanatorium—that is, than *some* sanatoriums. Carleton had been quite right. There was no opportunity for Shanley to hit the high joints quite as hard as he had that night in Big Cloud—there was no opportunity for him to hit the high joints *at all*. Shanley had not seen a bottle for three weeks. Therefore Shanley felt virtuous, which was proper.

Some events follow others as the natural, logical outcome and conclusion of preceding ones; others, again, are apparently irrelevant, and the connection is not to be explained either by logic, conclusion, or otherwise. Rain, McCann's departure for Big Cloud, and Pietro Maraschino's birthday are an example of this.

When it settles down for a storm in the mountains, it is, if the elements are really in earnest, torrential, and prolonged, and has the effect of tying up construction work tighter than a supreme court injunction could come anywhere near doing it.

McCann had business in Big Cloud, whether personal or pertaining to the company is of no consequence, and the day the storm set in—the morning having demonstrated that its classification was not to be considered as transient—he seized the opportunity to flag the afternoon freight eastbound. This was natural and logical, and an opportunity not to be neglected.

That this day, however, should be the anniversary of the day the padrone's mother of blessed memory had given birth to Pietro Maraschino in sunny Naples fifty-three years before is, though apparently irrelevant, far from being so; and since its peculiar and coincident happening cannot be laid at the door of either logical, natural, scientific, or philosophical conclusions, and since it demands an explanation of some sort, it must, perforce, be attributed to the metaphysical— which is a name given to all things about which nobody knows anything.

"Yez are in charge," said McCann grandiloquently, waving his hand to Shanley as he swung into the caboose. "Yez are in charge av the work, me son. See to ut. I trust ye."

As the work at the moment was entirely at a standstill and bid fair to remain so until McCann's return on the morrow, this was very good of McCann. But all men like words of appreciation, most of them whether they deserve them or not, so Shanley went back into the box-car out of the rain to ponder over the tribute McCann had paid him, and to ponder, too, over the new responsibility that had fallen to his lot.

He did not ponder very long; indeed, the freight that was transporting McCann could hardly have been out of sight over the summit of the grade, when a knock at the door was followed by the entrance of the dripping figure of the padrone.

Shanley looked up anxiously.

"Hello, Pietro," he said nervously, for the weather wasn't the kind that would bring a man out for nothing, and he was keenly alive to that new responsibility. "Hello, Pietro," he repeated. "Anything wrong?"

Pietro grinned amiably, shook his head, unbuttoned his coat, and held out—a bottle.

Shanley stared in amazement, and then began to blink furiously.

"Here!" said he. "What's this?"

"Chianti," said Pietro, grinning harder than ever.

"Key-aunty." Shanley screwed up his face. "What the devil is key-aunty?"

"Ver' good wine from Italia," said the beaming padrone.

"It is, is it? Well, it's against the rules," asserted Shanley with conviction. "It's against the rules. McCann 'u'd skin you alive. He would. Where'd you get it? What's up, eh? It's against the rules. I'm in charge."

Pietro explained. It was his birthday. It was very bad weather. For the rest of the afternoon there would be no work. They would celebrate the birthday. Meester McCann had taken the train. As for the wine — Pietro shrugged his shoulders — his people adored wine. Unless they were very poor his people would have a little wine in their packs, perhaps. He was not quite sure where they had got it, but it was very thoughtful of them to remember his birthday. Each had presented him with a little wine. This bottle was an expression of their very great good estime of Meester Shanley. Perhaps, later, Meester Shanley would come himself to the shack.

"It's against the rules," blinked Shanley. "McCann 'u'd skin you alive. Maybe I'll drop in by and by. You can leave the bottle."

Pietro bobbed, grinned delightedly, handed over the bottle, and backed out into the storm.

Shanley, still blinking, placed the bottle on the table, and gazed at it thoughtfully for a few minutes — and his thoughts were of Carleton.

"If 'twere whisky," said he, "I'd have no part of it, not a drop, not even a smell. I would not. I would not touch it. But as it is———" Shanley uncorked the bottle.

Not at all. One does *not* get drunk on a bottle of Chianti wine. A single bottle of Chianti wine is very little. That is the trouble — it is *very* little. After three weeks of abstinence it is very little indeed — so little that it is positively tantalizing.

The afternoon waned rapidly — and so did the Chianti. Outside, the storm instead of abating grew worse — the thunder racketing through the mountains, the lightning cutting jagged streaks in the black sky, the rain coming down in sheets that set the culverts and sluiceways running full. It was settling down for a bad night in the mountains, which, in the Rockies, is not a thing to be ignored.

"'Tis no wonder McCann found it lonely," muttered Shanley, as he squeezed the last drop from the bottle. "'Tis very lonely, indeed"—he held the bottle upside down to make sure that it was thoroughly drained—"most uncommon lonely. It is that. Maybe those Eyetalians'll be thinkin' I'm stuck up, perhaps—which I am not. It's a queer name the stuff has, though it's against the rules, an' I can't get my tongue around it, but I've tasted worse. For the sake of courtesy I'll look in on the birthday party."

He incased himself in a pair of McCann's rubber boots, put on McCann's rubber coat, and started out.

"An' to think," said he, as he sloshed and buffeted his way up the two hundred yards of track to the construction shanties, "to think that Pietro came out in cruel bad weather like this all for to present his compliments an' ask me over! 'Twould be ungracious to refuse the invitation; besides my presence will keep them in due bounds an' restraint. I've heard that Eyetalians, being foreigners, do not practice restraint—but, being foreigners, 'tis not to be held against them. I'm in charge, an' I'll see to it."

Ihey greeted him in the largest of the three bunk-houses. They greeted him heartily, sincerely, uproariously, and with fervor. They were unfeignedly glad to see him, and if he had not been by nature a modest man he would have understood that his popularity was above the popularity ever before accorded to a boss. Likewise, their hospitality was without stint. If there was any shortage of stock—which is a matter decidedly open to question—they denied themselves that Shanley might not feel the pinch. Shanley was lifted from the mere plane of man—he became a king.

A little Chianti is a little; much Chianti is to be reckoned with and on no account to be despised. Shanley not only became a king, he became regally, imperially, royally, and majestically drunk. Also there came at last an end to the Chianti, at which stage of the proceedings Shanley, with extravagant dignity and appropriate words—an exhortation on restraint—waddled to the door to take his departure.

It was very dark outside, very dark, except when an intermittent flash of lightning made momentary daylight. Pietro Maraschino offered Shanley one of the many lanterns that, in honor of the festive occasion, they had commandeered, without regard to color, from the tool boxes, and had strung around the shack. Further, he offered to see Shanley on his way.

The offer of assistance touched Shanley—it touched him wrong. It implied a more or less acute condition of disability, which he repudiated with a hurt expression on his face and forceful words on his tongue. He refused it; and being aggrieved, refused also the lantern Pietro held out to him. He chose one for himself instead—the one nearest to his hand. That this was red made no difference. Blue, white, red, green, or purple, it was all one to Shanley. His fuddled brain did not differentiate. A light was a light, that was all there was to that.

The short distance from the shanty door to the right of way Shanley negotiated with finesse and aplomb, and then he started down the track. This, however, was another matter.

Railroad ties, at best, do not make the smoothest walking in the world, and to accomplish the feat under some conditions is decidedly worthy of note. Shanley's performance beggars the English language—there is no metaphor. For every ten feet he moved forward he covered twenty in laterals, and, considering that the laterals were limited to the paltry four feet, eight and one-half inches that made the gauge of the rails, the feat was incontestably more than worthy of mere note—it was something to wonder at. He clung grimly to the lantern, with the result that the gyrations of that little red light in the darkness would have put to shame an expert's exhibition with a luminous dumb-bell. The while Shanley spoke earnestly to himself.

"Queshun is am I drunk—thash's the queshun. If I'm drunk—lose my job. Thash what Carleton said—lose my job. If I'm not drunk—s'all right. Wish I knew wesser I'm drunk or not."

He relapsed into silent communion and debate. This lasted for a very long period, during which, marvelous to relate, he had not only reached a point opposite his box-car domicile, but, being oblivious of that fact, had kept on along the track. Progress, however, was becoming more and more difficult. Shanley was assuming a position that might be likened somewhat to the letter C, owing to the fact that the force of gravity seemed to be exerting an undue influence on his head. Shanley was coming to earth.

As a result of his communion with himself he began to talk again, and his words suggested that he had suspicions of the truth.

"Jus' my luck," said he bitterly. "Jus' my luck. Allus same kind of luck. What'd I have to do wis Peto Mara—Mars—Marscheeno's birthday? Nothing. Nothing 'tall. 'Twasn't my fault. Jus' my luck. Jus' my———"

Shanley came to earth. Also his head came into contact with the unyielding steel of the left-hand rail, and as a result he sprawled inertly full across the right of way, not ten yards west of where the Glacier River swings in to crowd the track close up against the mountain base.

Providence sometimes looks after those who are unable to look after themselves. By the law of probabilities the lantern should have met disaster quick and absolute; but, instead, when it fell from Shanley's hand, it landed right side up just outside the rail between two ties, and, apart from a momentary and hesitant flicker incident to the jolt, burned on serenely. And it was still burning when, five minutes later, above the swish of leaping waters from the Glacier River now a chattering, angry stream with swollen banks, above the moan of the wind and the roll of the thunder through the mountains, above the pelting splash of the steady rain, came the hoarse scream of Number One's whistle on the grade.

Sanderson, in the cab, caught the red against him on the right of way ahead, and whistled insistently for the track. This having no effect, he grunted, latched in the throttle, and applied the "air." The ray of the headlight crept along between the rails, hovered over a black object beside the lantern, passed on again and held, not on the glistening rain-wet rails—*they* had disappeared—but on a crumbling road-bed and a dark blotch of waters, as with a final screech from the grinding brake-shoes Number One came to a standstill.

"Holy MacCheesar!" exclaimed Sanderson, as he swung from the cab.

He made his way along past the drivers to where the pilot's nose was inquisitively poked against the lantern, picked up the lantern, and bent over Shanley.

"Holy MacCheesar!" he exclaimed again, straightening up after a moment's examination. "Holy MacCheesar!"

"What's wrong, Sandy?" snapped a voice behind him, the voice of Kelly, Spider Kelly, the conductor, who had hurried forward to investigate the unscheduled stop.

"Search me," replied Sanderson. "Looks like the Glacier was up to her old tricks. There's a washout ahead, and a bad one, I guess. But the meaning of this here is one beyond me. The fellow was curled up on the track just as you see him with the light burning alongside, that's what saved us, but he's as drunk as a lord."

As Kelly bent over the prostrate form, others of the train crew appeared on the scene. One glance he gave at Shanley's never-under-any-circumstances-to-be-forgotten homely countenance, and hastily ordered the men to go forward and investigate the washout ahead. Then he turned to the engineer.

"The man is not drunk, Sandy," said he.

"He is gloriously and magnificently drunk, Kelly," replied the engineer.

"What would he be doing here, then? He is not drunk."

"Sleeping it off. He is disgracefully drunk."

"Can ye not see the bash on his head where he must have stumbled in the dark trying to save the train and struck against the rail? He is *not* drunk."

"Can ye not *smell?*" retorted Sanderson. "He is dead drunk!"

"I have fought with him and he licked me. He is a man and a friend of mine" — Kelly shoved his lantern into Sanderson's face. "*He is not drunk.*"

"He is *not* drunk," said Sanderson. "He is a hero. What will we do with him?"

"We'll carry him, you and me, over to the construction shanty, it's only a few yards, and put him in his bunk. He works here, you know. McCann's in Big Cloud, for I saw him there. After that we'll run back to the Bend for orders and make our report."

"Hurry, then," said the engineer. "Take his legs. What are you laughing at?"

"I was thinking of Carleton," said Kelly.

"Carleton? What's Carleton got to do with it?"

"I'll tell you later when we get to the Bend. Come on."

"H'm," said Sanderson, as they staggered with their burden over to the box-car shack. "I've an idea that bash on the head is more dirt than hurt. He's making a speech, ain't he?"

"Jus' my luck," mumbled the reviving Shanley dolefully. "Jus' my luck. Allus same kind of luck."

"Possibly," said Kelly. "Set him down and slide back the door. That's right. In with him now. We haven't got time to make him very comfortable, but I guess he'll do. I can fix him up better at the Bend than I can here."

"At the Bend? What d'ye mean?" demanded Sanderson.

"You'll see," replied Kelly, with a grin. "You'll see."

And Sanderson saw. So did Carleton—in a way.

Kelly's report, when they got to the Bend, was a work of art. He disposed of the nature and extent of the washout in ten brief, well-chosen words, but the operator got a cramp before Kelly was through covering Shanley with glory. The passengers, packed in the little waiting-room clamoring for details, yelled deliriously as he read the message aloud—and promptly took up a collection, a very generous collection, because all collections are generous at psychological moments—that is to say, if not delayed too long to allow a recovery from hysteria.

At Big Cloud, the dispatcher, because the washout was a serious matter that not only threatened to tie up traffic, but *was* tying it up, sent a hurry call to Carleton's house that brought the super on the run to the office. By this time the collection had been counted, and the total wired in, as an additional detail—one hundred and forty dollars and thirty-three cents. The odd change being a contribution from a Swede in the colonist coach who could not speak English, and who paid because a man in uniform, a brakeman acting as canvasser, made the request. A Swede has a great respect for a uniform.

"H'm," said Carleton, when he had read it all. "I know a man when I see one. Tell Shanley to report here. I guess we can find something better for him to do than bossing laborers. What? Yes, send the letter up on the construction train. One hundred and forty, thirty-three, h'm? Tell him that, too. He'll feel good when he sees it in the morning."

But Shanley did not feel good when he saw it in the morning, for he was nursing a very bad headache and a stomach that had a tendency to squeamishness. The letter was lying on the floor, where some one had considerately chucked it in without disturbing him. His eyes fell on it as he struggled out of his bunk. He picked it up, opened it, read it—and blinked. His face set with a very blank and bewildered expression. He read it again, and again once more. Then he went to the door and looked out.

A construction train was on the line a little below him, and a gang of men, not his nor Pietro Maraschino's men, were busily at work. As he gazed, his face puckered. The problem that had so obsessed him on his return journey from the birthday celebration the night before was a problem no longer.

"I *was* drunk," said he, with conviction. "I *must* have been."

He went back to the letter and studied it again, scratching his head.

"Something," he muttered, "has happened. What it is, I dunno. I was drunk, an' I'm not fired. I was drunk, an' I'm promoted. I was drunk, an' I'm paid well for it, very well. I was drunk—an' I'll keep my mouth shut."

Which was exactly the advice Kelly took pains to give him half an hour later, when Number One crawled down to the Canon and halted for a few minutes opposite the dismantled box-car, while the construction train put the last few touches to its work.

VI
THE BUILDER

THERE are two sides to every story — which is a proverb so old that it is in the running with Father Time himself. It is repeated here because there must be *some* truth in it — anything that can stand the wear and tear of the ages, and the cynics, and the wise old philosophical owls without getting any knock-out dints punched in its vital spots must have some sort of merit fundamentally, what? Anyway, the company had their side, and the men's version differed — of course. Maybe each, in a way, was more or less right, and, equally, in a way, more or less wrong. Maybe, too, both sides lost their tempers and got their crown-sheets burned out before the arbitration pow-wow had a chance to get the line clear and give anybody rights, schedule or otherwise. However, be that as it may, whoever was right or whoever was wrong, one or the other, or both, it is the strike, not the ethics of it, that has to do with — but just a moment, we're over-running our holding orders.

From the time the last rail was spiked home and bridging the Rockies was a reality, not a dream from then to the present day, there isn't any very much better way of describing the Hill Division than to call it rough and ready. Coming right down to cases, the history of that piece of track, the history of the men who gave the last that was in them to make it, and the history of those who have operated it since isn't far from being a pretty typical and comprehensive example of the pulsing, dominating, dogged, go-forward spirit of a continent whose strides and progress are the marvel of the world; and, withal, it is an example so compact and concrete that through it one may see and view the larger picture in all its angles and in all its shades. Heroism and fame and death and failure—it has known them all—but ever, and above all else, it has known the indomitable patience, the indomitable perseverance, the indomitable determination against which no times, nor conditions, nor manners, nor customs, nor obstacles can stand—the spirit of the New Race and the Great New Land, the essence and the germ of it.

Building a road through the Rockies and tapping the Sierras to give zest to the finish wasn't an infant's performance; and operating it, single-track, on crazy-wild cuts and fills and tangents and curves and tunnels and trestles with nature to battle and fight against, isn't any infant's performance, either. The Hill Division was rough and ready. It always was, and it is now—just naturally so. And Big Cloud, the divisional point, snuggling amongst the buttes in the eastern foothills, is even more so. It boasts about every nationality classified in certain erudite editions of small books with big names, and, to top that, has an extra anomaly or two left over and up its sleeve for good measure; but, mostly, it is, or rather was—it has changed some with the years—composed of Indians, bad Americans, a scattering of Chinese, and an indescribable medley of humans from the four quarters of Europe, the Cockney, the Polack, the Swede, the Russian and the Italian—laborers on the construction gangs. Big Cloud was a little more than rough and ready—it wasn't exactly what you'd call a health resort for finnicky nerves.

So, take it by and large, the Hill Division, from one end to the other, wasn't the quietest or most peaceful locality on the map even before the trouble came. After that—well, mention the Big Strike to any of the old-timers and they'll talk fast enough and hard enough and say enough in a minute to set you wondering if the biographers hadn't got mixed on dates and if Dante hadn't got his material for that little hair-stiffener of his no further away than the Rockies, and no longer back than a few years ago. But no matter——

The story opens on the strike—*not* the ethics of it. There's some hard feeling yet—too much of it to take sides one way or the other. But then, apart from that, this is not the story of a strike, it is the story of men —a story that the boys tell at night in the darkened roundhouses in the shadow of the big ten-wheelers on the pits, while the steam purrs softly at the gauges and sometimes a pop- valve lifts with a catchy sob. They tell it, too, across the tracks at headquarters, or on the road and in construction camps; but they tell it better, somehow, in the roundhouse, though it is not an engineer's tale—and Clarihue, the night turner, tells it best of all. Set forth as it is here it takes no rank with him, — but all are not so fortunate as to have listened while Clarihue talked.

Just one word more to make sure that the red isn't against us anywhere and we'll get to Keating and Spirlaw— just a word to say that Carleton, "Royal" Carleton, was superintendent then, and Regan was master mechanic, Harvey was division engineer, Spence was chief dispatcher, and Riley was trainmaster. Pretty good men that little group, pretty good railroaders—there have never been better. Some of them are bigger now in the world's eyes, heads of systems instead of departments—and some of them will never railroad any more. However——

If you haven't forgotten Shanley you will recall the Glacier Cañon, and, most of all, you will recall the Glacier River with its treacherous sandy bed that snuggled close to the right of way and forced the track hard against the rocky walls of the mountain's base. The havoc the Glacier played with the operating department on the night of Shanley's memorable heroism was not the first time it had misbehaved itself, nor was it the last—that was the trouble. It washed out the road-bed with such consistent persistency, on so little provocation, and did it so effectually as to stir at last to resentment even the torpid blood of the directors down East. So they voted the sum, though it hurt, and solaced themselves with the thought that after all it was economy—which was true.

There was only one thing to do against that over-hospitable and affectionate little stream, and that was to get away from it; but, before proceeding to do so—in order to get elbow room to work so that the flyers and the fast mails and the traffic generally wouldn't be hung up every time a Polack swung a pick—they pushed the track out over the chattering river on a long, temporary, hybrid trestle of wood and steel. That done, the rest was up to Spirlaw—up to Spirlaw and Keating.

The plans called for the shaving down of the mountainside, the barbering, mostly, to be done with dynamite, for the beard of the Rockies is not the down of a youth. So, when the trestle was finished, Spirlaw with a gang of some thirty Polacks moved into construction camp, promptly tore up the old track, and set themselves to the task in hand. A little later, Keating joined them.

Spirlaw was a road boss, and the roughest of his kind. Physically he was a giant; and which of the three was the hardest, his face, his fist, or his tongue, would afford the sporting element a most excellent opportunity to indulge in a little book-making with the odds about even all round. His hair was a coarse mop of tawny brown that straggled over his eyes; and his eyes were all black, every bit of them—there didn't seem to be any pupil at all, which gave them a glint that was harder than a cold chisel. Take him summed up, Spirlaw looked a pretty tough proposition, and in some ways, most ways perhaps, he was—he never denied it.

"What the blue blinding blazes, d'ye think, h'm?" he would remark, reaching into his hip pocket for his "chewing," as he swept the other arm comprehensively over the particular crowd of sweating foreigners that happened to be under his particular jurisdiction at the time. "What d'ye think! You can't run cuts an' fills with an outfit like this on soft soap an' candy sticks, can you? Well then—h'm?"

That last "h'm" was more or less conclusive—very few cared to pursue the argument any further. At a safe distance, the Big Fellows on the division, as a salve to their consciences when humanitarian ideas were in the ascendancy, would bombard Spirlaw with telegrams which were forceful in tone and direful in threat—but that's all it ever amounted to. Spirlaw's work report for a day on anything, from bridging a cañon to punching a hole in the bitter hard rock of the mountain-side, was a report that no one else on the division had ever approached, let alone duplicated—and figures count perhaps just a little bit more in the operating department of a railroad than they do anywhere else in the world. Spirlaw used the telegrams as spills to light a pipe as hard-looking as himself, whose bowl was down at the heels on one side from much scraping, and on such occasions it was more than ordinarily unfortunate for the sour-visaged Polack who should chance to arouse his ire.

Some men possess the love of a fight and their natures are tempestuous by virtue of their nationality, because some nationalities are addicted that way. This may have been the case with Spirlaw—or it may not. There's no saying, for Spirlaw's nationality was a question mark. He never delivered himself on the subject, and, certainly, there was no figuring it out from the derivation of his name—*that* could have been most anything, and could have come from most anywhere.

To say that "opposites attract" isn't any more original, any less gray-bearded, than the words at the head of these pages. Generally, that sort of thing is figured in the worn-out, stale, familiarity-breeds-contempt realm of platitude, and at its unctuous repetition one comes to turn up his nose; but, once in a while, life has a habit of getting in a kink or a twist that gives you a jolt and a different side-light, and then, somehow, a thing like that rings as fresh and virile as though you had just heard it for the first time. As far as any one ever knew, Keating was the only one that ever got inside of Spirlaw's shell, the only one that the road boss ever showed the slightest symptoms of caring a hang about—and yet, on the surface, between the two there was nothing in common. Where one was polished the other was rough; where one was weak the other was strong. Keating was small, thin, pale-faced, and he had a cough—a cough that had sent him West in a hurry without waiting for the other year that would have given him his engineer's diploma from the college in the East.

When the boy, he wasn't much more than a boy, dropped off at Big Cloud, and Carleton read the letter he brought from one of the big Eastern operators, the super raised his eyebrows a little, looked him over and sent him out to Spirlaw. Afterwards, he spoke to Regan about him.

"I didn't know what to do with him, Tommy; but I had to do something, what? Any one with half an eye could tell that he had to be kept out of doors. Thought he might be able to help Spirlaw out a little as assistant, h'm? Guess he'll pick up the work quick enough. He don't look strong."

"Mabbe it's just as well," grinned the master mechanic. "He won't be able to batter the gang any. One man doing that is enough—when it's Spirlaw."

Spirlaw heard about it before he saw Keating, and he swore fervently.

"What the hell!" he growled. "Think I'm runnin' a nursery or an outdoor sanatorium? I guess I've got enough to do without lookin' after sick kids, I guess I have. Fat lot of help he'll be—help my eye! I don't need no help."

But for all that, somehow, from the first minute when Keating got off the local freight, that stopped for him at the camp, and shoved out his hand to Spirlaw it was different—after that it was *all* Keating as far as the road boss was concerned.

Queer the way things go. Keating looked about the last man on earth you would expect to find rubbing elbows with an iron-fisted foreman whose tongue was rougher than a barbed-wire fence; the last man to hold his own with a slave-driven gang of ugly Polacks. He seemed too quiet, too shy, too utterly unfit, physically, for that sort of thing. The blood was all out of the boy—he got rid of it faster than he could make it. But his training stood him in good stead, and, within his limitations, he took hold like an old hand. That was what caught Spirlaw. He did what he was told, and he did what he could—did a little more than he could at times, which would lay him up for a bad two or three days of it.

"Good man," Spirlaw scribbled across the bottom of a report one day—a day that was about equally divided between barking his knuckles on a Polack's head and feeding cracked ice to Keating in his bunk. Cracked ice? No, it wasn't on the regular camp bill of fare—but the company supplied it for all that. Spirlaw, with supreme contempt for the dispatchers and their schedules and their train sheets, held up Number Twelve and the porter of the Pullman for a goodly share of the commodity possessed by that colored gentleman. That's what Spirlaw thought of Keating.

For the first few weeks after he struck the camp Keating didn't have very much to say about himself, or anything else for that matter; but after he got a little nearer to Spirlaw and the mutual liking grew stronger, he began to open up at nights when he and the road boss sat outside the door of the construction shanty and watched the sun lose itself behind the mighty peaks, creep again with a wondrous golden-tinted glow between a rift in the range, and finally sink with ensuing twilight out of sight. Keating could talk then.

"Don't see what you ever took up engineerin' for," remarked Spirlaw one evening. "It's about the roughest kind of a life I know of, an' you——"

"I know, I know," Keating smiled. "You think I'm not strong enough for it. Why, another year out here in the West and I'll be like a horse."

"Sure, you will," agreed Spirlaw, hastily. "I didn't mean just that." Then he sucked his briar hard. Spirlaw wasn't much up on therapeutics, he knew more about blasting rock, but down in his heart there wasn't much doubt about another year in the West for the boy, and another and another, *all of them*—only they would be over the Great Divide that one only crosses once when it is crossed forever. Six months, four, three,—just months, not years, was what he read in Keating's face. "What I meant," he amended, "was that you don't have to. From what you've said, I figur' your folks back there would be willin' to stake you in most any line you picked out, h'm?"

"No, I don't have to," Keating answered, and his face lighted up as he leaned over and touched the road boss on the sleeve. "But, Spirlaw, it's the greatest thing in all the world. Don't you see? A man does something. *He builds*. I'm going to be a builder—a builder of bridges and roads and things like that. I want to do something some day—something that will be worth while. That's why I'm going to be an engineer; because, all over the world from the beginning, the engineers have led the way and—and they've left something behind them. I think that's the biggest thing they can say of any man when he dies—that he was a builder, that he left something behind him. I'd like to have them say that about me. Well, after I put in another year out here—I'm a heap better even now than when I came—I'm going back to finish my course, and then—well, you understand what I want to do, don't you?"

There were lots of talks like that, evening after evening, and they all of them ended in the same way—Spirlaw would knock out his pipe against a stone or his boot heel, and "figur' he'd stroll up the camp a bit an' make sure all was right for the night."

A pretty hard man Spirlaw was, but under the rough and the brutal, the horny, thick-shelled exterior was another self, a strange side of self that he had never known until he had known Keating. It got into him pretty deep and pretty hard, the boy and his ambitions; and the irony of it, grim and bitter, deepened his pity and roused, too, a sense of fierce, hot resentment against the fate that mocked in its pitiless might so defenseless and puny a victim. To himself he came to call Keating "The Builder," and one day when Harvey came down on an inspection trip, he told the division engineer about it—that's how it got around.

Carleton, when he heard it, didn't say anything—just crammed the dottle in his pipe down with his forefinger and stared out at the switches in the yards. They were used to seeing the surface of things plowed up and the corners turned back in the mountains, there weren't many days went by when something that showed the raw didn't happen in one way or another, but it never brought callousness or indifference, only, perhaps, a truer sense of values.

They had been blasting in the Cañon for a matter of two months when the first signs of trouble began to show themselves, and the beginning was when the shop hands at Big Cloud went out—the boiler-makers and the blacksmiths, the painters, the carpenters and the fitters. The construction camp, that is Spirlaw, didn't worry very much about this for the very simple reason that there didn't appear to be any reason why it, or he, should—that was Regan's hunt. But when the train crews followed suit and stray rumors of a fight or two at Big Cloud began to come in, with the likelihood of more hard on the heels of the first, it put a different complexion on things; for the rioting, what there had been of it, lay, not at the door of the railroad boys, but with the town's loafers and hangers-on, these and the foreign element—particularly the foreign element—the brothers and the cousins of the Polacks who were swinging the picks and the shovels under the iron hand of Spirlaw, their temporary lord and master—the Polacks, as pungently ungentle, when amuck, as starved pumas.

Then the Brotherhood said "quit," and the engine crews followed the trainmen. Things began to look black, and headquarters began to find it pretty hard to move anything. The train schedule past the Cañon was cut better than in half, and the faces of the men in the cabs and the cabooses were new faces to those in camp—the faces of the men the company were bringing in on hurry calls from wherever they could get them, from the plains East or the coast West.

Every day brought reports of trouble from one end of the line to the other, more rioting, more disorder at Big Cloud; and, in an effort to nip as much of it in the bud as possible, Carleton issued orders to stop all construction work—all except the work in Glacier Cañon, for there the temporary trestle lay uneasy on his mind.

The day the stop orders went out elsewhere a letter went out to Spirlaw. Spirlaw read it and his face set like a thunder cloud. He handed it to Keating.

Keating read it—and looked serious.

"I guess things aren't any too rosy down there," he commented; then slowly: "I've noticed our men seemed a bit sullen lately. They don't care anything much about the strike, it must be a sort of sympathetic movement with the rest of their crowd that's running wild at Big Cloud—only I don't just figure how they can know very much about what's going on. We don't ourselves, for that matter."

Spirlaw smiled grimly.

"I'll tell you how," he said. "I caught a Polack in the camp last night that didn't belong here—and I broke his head for the second time, see? He used to work for me about a year ago—that's when I broke it the first time. He's one of their influential citizens—name's Kuryla. Sneaked in here to stir up trouble—guess he's sorry for it, I guess he is."

"That's the first I've heard of it," said Keating, his eyes opening a little wider in surprise.

"You was asleep," explained Spirlaw tersely.

Keating stared curiously at the road boss for a minute, then he glanced again at the super's letter which he still held in his hand.

"Carleton says he is depending on you to put this work through if it's a possible thing. You don't really think we'll have any serious trouble here though, do you?"

Spirlaw bit deeply into his plug before he answered.

"Yes, son; I do," he said at last. "And there's a good many reasons why we will, too. Once start 'em goin' an' there's no worse hellions on earth than the breed we're livin' next door to. Furthermore they don't *love* me—they're just afraid of me as, by the holy razoo, I mean 'em to be. Let 'em once get a smell of the upper hand an' it would be all day *an'* good-by. Let 'em get goin' good at Big Cloud an' they'll get goin' good here—they'll kind of figur' then that there ain't any law to bother 'em—an', unless I miss my guess, Big Cloud's in for the hottest celebration in its history, which will be goin' some for it's had a few before that weren't tame by a damn sight."

"Well," inquired Keating, "what do you intend to do?"

"H'm-m," drawled Spirlaw reflectively, and there was a speculative look in his eyes as they roved over his assistant. "That's what I've been chewin' over since I caught that skunk Kuryla last night. As far as I can figur' it the chance of trouble here depends on how far those cusses go at Big Cloud. If I knew that, I'd know what to expect, h'm? I thought I'd send you up to headquarters for a day. You could have a talk with the super, tell him just where we stand here, an' size things up there generally. What do you say?"

"Why, of course. All right, if you want me to," agreed Keating readily.

"That's the boy," said Spirlaw, heartily. "Number Twelve will be along in half an hour. I'll flag her, an' you can go an' get ready now. I'll give you a letter to take along to Carleton."

As Keating, with a nod of assent, turned briskly away, Spirlaw watched him out of sight—and the hint of a smile played over the lips of the road boss. He pulled a report sheet from his pocket, and on the back of it scrawled laboriously a letter to the superintendent of the Hill Division. It wasn't a very long letter even with the P. S. included. His smile hardened as he read it over.

"Supt., Big Cloud," it ran. "Dear Sir:—Replying to yours 8th inst, please send a couple of good ·45s, and *plenty of stuffing*. ('Plenty of stuffing' was heavily underscored.) Yrs. Resp., H. Spirlaw. P.S. *Keep the boy up there out of this*." (The P. S. was even more heavily underscored than the other.)

Wise and learned in the ways of men—and Polacks—was Spirlaw. Spirlaw was not dealing with the *possibility* of trouble—it was simply a question of how long it would be before it started. He folded the letter, sealed it in one of the company's manilas, and, as he watched Number Twelve disappear around the bend steaming east for Big Cloud with Keating aboard her and the epistle reposing in Keating's pocket, he stretched out his arms that were big as derrick booms and drew in a long breath like a man from whose shoulders has dropped a heavy load.

That day Spirlaw talked from his heart to the men, and they listened in sullen, stupid silence, leaning on their picks and shovels.

"You know me," he snapped, and his eyes starting at the right of the group rested for a bare second on each individual face as they swept down the line. "You know *me*. You've been actin' like sulky dogs lately—don't think I haven't spotted it. You saw what happened to that coyote friend of yours that sneaked in here last night. I meant it as a lesson for the bunch of you as well as him. The yarns he was fillin' you full of are mostly lies, an' if they ain't it's none of your business, anyhow. It won't pay you to look for trouble, I promise you that. You can take it from me that I'll bash the first man to powder that tries it. Get that? Well then, wiggle them picks a bit an' get busy!"

"The man that hits first," said Spirlaw to himself, as he walked away, "is the man that usually comes out on top. I guess them there few kind words of mine'll give 'em a little something to chew on till Carleton sends that hardware down, I guess they will, h'm?"

The camp was pretty quiet that night—quieter than usual. The cook-house and the three bunk-houses, that lay a few hundred yards east of the trestle, might have been occupied by dead men for all the sounds that came from them. Occasionally, Spirlaw, sitting out as usual in front of his own shanty, that was between the trestle and the gang's quarters, saw a Polack or two skulk from one of the bunk-houses to the other—and he scowled savagely as he divided his glances between them and the sky. It looked like a storm in the mountains, and a storm in the mountains is never by any possibility to be desired—least of all was it to be desired just then. The men at work was one thing; the men cooped up for a day, or two days, of enforced idleness with the temper they were in was another—Spirlaw turned in that night with the low, ominous roll of distant thunder for a lullaby.

Once in the night he woke suddenly at the sound of a splitting crash, and once, twice, and again, like a fierce, winking stream of flame, the lightning filled the shack bright as day, while on the roof the rain beat steadily like the tattoo of a corps of snare drums. Spirlaw smiled grimly as the darkness shut down on him again.

"Got the little builder out just about the right time, h'm?" he remarked to himself; and, turning over in his bunk, went to sleep again—but even in his sleep the grim smile lingered on his lips.

The morning broke with the steady downpour unabated. Everything ran water, and the rock cut was filled with it. Work was out of the question. Spirlaw ate his breakfast, that the dripping camp cook brought him, and then, putting on his rubber boots and coat, started over for the track. Number Eleven was due at the Cañon at seven-thirty, and she would have the package of "hardware" he had asked Carleton for.

But though seven-thirty came, Number Eleven did not — neither did any other train, east or west. The hours passed from a long morning to drag through a longer afternoon. Something was wrong somewhere — and badly wrong at that. Spirlaw's face was blacker than the storm. Twice, once in the morning and once in the afternoon, he started down the track in the direction of Keefer's Siding, which was just what its name proclaimed it to be — a siding, no more, no less, only there was an operator there. Each time, however, he changed his mind after getting no further than a few yards. The Polacks could be no less alive to the fact than himself that something out of the ordinary was in the air, and second considerations swung strongly to the advisability of sticking close to the camp, so that his presence might have the effect of dampening the ardor of any mischief that might be brewing.

It was not until well on toward eight o'clock in the evening and the last of the twilight that the hoarse screech of a whistle sounded down the cañon grade — a long blast and three short ones. It was belated Number Eleven whistling for the camp — she wouldn't stop, just slow down to transact her business. Spirlaw, who was in his shanty at the time, snatched up his hat, dashed out of the door, and headed for the bend of the track. As he did so, out of the tail of his eye, he caught sight of the Polacks clustered with out-poked heads from the open doors of the bunk-houses.

As he reached the line, Number Eleven came round the curve, and the door of the express car swung back. The messenger dropped a package into his hand that the road boss received with a grim smile, and a word into his ear that caused Spirlaw's jaw to drop — nor was that all that dropped, for, from the rear end, as the train rolled by — dropped Keating.

White-faced and shaky the boy looked—more so than usual. Spirlaw stared as though he had seen an apparition, stared for a minute in silence before he could lay tongue to words—then they came like the out-spout of a volcano..

"What the hell's the meanin' of this?" he roared. "Who in the double-blanked blazes let you out of Big Cloud, h'm? I'll have some——"

"Let's get in out of the wet," broke in Keating, smiling through a spell of coughing that racked him at that moment. "You can growl your head off then, if you like"—and he started on a run for the shack.

Once inside, Spirlaw rounded on the boy again, and he stopped only when he was out of breath.

"Didn't Carleton tell you to stay where you was?" he finished bitterly.

"Oh yes," said Keating, "that's about the first thing he *did* say after he had read your letter, when I gave it to him yesterday. Then I tumbled to why you had sent me out of camp. You're about as square as they make them, Spirlaw. You needn't blame Carleton, *he* had about all he could do without paying any attention to me or any one else. Had any wires or news in here?"

Spirlaw shook his head.

"No; but I knew something was up, because Number Eleven is the first train in or out to-day. The express messenger just said they'd cut loose in Big Cloud and wrecked about everything in sight, but I guess he was puttin' it on a bit."

"He didn't put on anything," said Keating slowly. "My God, Spirlaw, it was an awful night! The freight-house and the shops and the roundhouse, what's left of them, are ashes. They cut all the wires and then they cut loose themselves—the Polacks and that crowd, you know. Yes, they wrecked everything in sight, and there's a dozen lives gone out to pay for it." Keating stopped suddenly, and again began to cough.

Spirlaw looked at the boy uneasily, and mechanically fumbled with the cords of the package he had laid upon the table. By the time he had removed the wrappers and disclosed two ugly, businesslike looking ·45s and a half-dozen boxes of cartridges, Keating's paroxysm had passed.

"I guess it was exciting enough for *me*, anyhow" — Keating tried hard to make his laugh ring true. "I'm a little weak from it yet."

"If you weren't sick," Spirlaw burst out, "I'd make you sick for comin' back here. You know well enough we'll get it next — you knew so well you came back to help———"

"I told Carleton he ought to send some help down here," Keating interrupted hastily; "and he just looked at me like a crazy man — he was half mad anyhow with the ruin of things. 'Help!' he flung out at me. 'Where's it coming from? Let Spirlaw yank up his stakes and pull out if things get looking bad!'"

"Pull out!" shouted Spirlaw, in a sudden roar. "Pull out! *Me!* Not for all the cross-eyed, hamstrung Polacks on the system!"

"I think you'd better," said Keating quietly. "After what I saw last night, I think you'd better. There was no holding them—they were like savages, and the further they went the worse they got. They were backed up by whisky and the worst element in town. I was in the station with Carleton, Regan, Harvey, Riley and Spence and some of the other dispatchers. It was a regular pitched battle, and in spite of their revolvers the station would have gone with the rest if, along toward morning, the striking trainmen and the Brotherhood hadn't taken a hand and helped us out. I don't know that it's over yet, that it won't break out again to-night; though I heard Carleton say there'd be a detachment of the police in town by four o'clock. I wish you would pull out, Spirlaw. You said yourself that all these fellows here needed to start them sticking their claws into you was a little encouragement from the other end. They've been afraid of you, but they hate you like poison. Once started, they'll be worse than the crowd at Big Cloud for hate is a harder driver than whisky. Then besides, I really think you'd be of more use in Big Cloud. You could do some good there no matter what the end was, while here you're alone and you stand to lose everything and gain nothing. I wish you would pull out, Spirlaw, won't you?"

Spirlaw reached out his hand and laid it on Keating's shoulder, as he shook his head.

"I've got a whole *lot* to lose," he answered, his hard face softening a little. "A whole lot. I can't say things the way you do, but I guess you'll understand. You got something that means a whole lot to you, that you'd risk anything for—what you want to do and what you want to leave behind you when it comes along time to cash in. Well, I guess most of us have in one way or another, though mabbe it don't rank anywheres up to that. I reckon, too, a whole lot of us don't never think to put it in words, an' a whole lot of us couldn't if we tried to, but it's there with any man that's any good. I'd rather go out for keeps than pull out—I'd rather they'd plant me. D'ye think I'd want to live an' have to cross the street because I couldn't look *even a Polack* in the eyes—a man would be better dead, what?"

For a moment Keating did not answer, he seemed to be weighing the possibility of still shaking the determination of the road boss before accepting it as irrevocable: then, evidently coming to the conclusion that it was useless to argue further, he pointed to the revolvers.

"Then the sooner you load those the better," he jerked out.

Spirlaw looked at him curiously, questioningly.

"Because," went on Keating, answering the unspoken interrogation, "when I dropped off the train I saw that fellow Kuryla—he was pointed out to me in Big Cloud yesterday—and three or four more drop off on the other side. I didn't know they were on the train until then, of course, or I would have had them put off. There isn't much doubt about what they are here for, is there?"

"So that's it, is it?" Spirlaw ripped out with an oath. "No, there ain't much doubt!"

He snatched up a cartridge-box, slit the paper band with his thumb nail, and, breaking the revolvers, began to cram the cartridges into the cylinders. His face was twitching and the red that flushed it shaded to a deep purple. Not another word came from him—just a deadly quiet. He thrust the weapons into his pockets, strode to the door, opened it, stepped over the threshold—and stopped. An instant he hung there in indecision, then he came back, shut the door behind him, sat down on the edge of his bunk, and looked at Keating grimly.

"There's been one train along, there'll be another," he snapped. "An' the first one that comes you'll get aboard of. I hate to keep those whinin' coyotes waitin', but——"

"I'll take no train," Keating cut in coolly; "but I'll take a revolver."

Spirlaw growled and shook his head.

"Why didn't you tell me about Kuryla at first?" he demanded abruptly.

"You know why as well as I do," smiled Keating. "I wanted to get you away from here if I could. There wouldn't have been any use trying at all if I'd begun by telling you that. Wild horses wouldn't have budged you then. As for a train, what's the use of talking about it, there probably won't be another one along under an hour. In the meantime, give me one of the guns."

"Not m——"

Spirlaw's refusal died half uttered on his lips, as he sprang suddenly to his feet; then he whipped out the revolvers and shoved one quickly into Keating's hand.

Carried down with the sweep of the wind came the sound of many voices raised in shouts and discordant song. It grew louder, swelled, and broke into a high-pitched, defiant yell.

"Whisky!" gritted Spirlaw between his teeth. "That devil Kuryla and the coyotes that came with him knew the best an' quickest way to start the ball rollin'. Well, son, I reckon we're in for it. The only thing I'm sorry about is that you're here; but that can't be helped now. You were white clean through to come — Holy Mother, listen to that!" — another yell broke louder, fiercer than before over the roar of the storm.

Spirlaw stepped to the door and peered out. It was already getting dark. The rain still poured in sheets, and the wind howled down the gorge in wild, furious, spasmodic gusts. Thin streaks of light strayed out from the doors of the bunk-houses, and around the doors were gathered shadowy groups. A moment more and the shadowy groups welded into a single dark mass. Came a mad, exultant yell from a single throat. It was caught up, flung back, echoed and re-echoed by a score of voices — and the dark mass began to move.

"Guess you'd better put out that light, son," said Spirlaw coolly. "There's no use makin' targets of our———"

Before he ended, before Keating had more than taken a step forward, a lump of rock shivered the little window and crashed into the lamp — it was out for keeps. A howl followed this exhibition of marksmanship, and, following that, a volley of stones smashed against the side of the shack thick and fast as hail — then the onrush of feet.

Spirlaw's revolver cut the black with a long, blinding flash, then another, and another. Screams and shrieks answered him, but it did not halt the Polacks. In a mob they rushed the door. Spirlaw sprang back, trying to close it after him; instead, a dozen hands grasped and half wrenched it from its hinges.

"Lie down on the floor, Spirlaw, *quick!*" — it was Keating's voice, punctuated with a cough. The next instant his gun barked, playing through the doorway like a gatling.

From the floor the road boss joined in. The mob wavered, pitched swaying this way and that, then broke and ran, struggling with each other to get out of the line of fire.

"Hurrah!" cried Keating. "I guess that will hold them."

"'Tain't begun," was Spirlaw's grim response. "Where's them cartridges?"

"On the table — got them?"

"Yes," said Spirlaw, after a minute's groping. "Here, put a box in your pocket."

"What are they up to now?" asked Keating as, in the silence that had fallen, they reloaded and listened.

"God knows," growled Spirlaw; "but I guess we'll find out quick enough."

As he spoke, from a little distance away, came the splintering crash of woodwork — then silence again.

"That's the storehouse," Spirlaw snarled. "They're after the bars an' anything else they can lay their hands on. Guess they weren't countin' on our havin' anything more than our fists to fight with, guess they weren't."

Keating's only reply was a cough.

The minutes passed, two, three, five of them. Once outside sounded what might have been the stealthy scuffle of feet or only a storm-sound so construed by the imagination. Then, from the direction of the river-bed, sudden, sharp, came a terrific roar.

"My God!" yelled Spirlaw. "There's the trestle gone — they've blown it up! They're sure to have laid a fuse here, too. Get out of here quick! Fool that I was, I might have known it was the *dynamite* they were after."

Both men were scrambling for the door as he spoke. They reached it not an instant too soon. The ground behind them lifted, heaved; the walls, the roof of the shack rose, cracked like eggshells, and scattered in flying pieces — and the mighty, deafening detonation of the explosion echoed up and down the gorge, echoed again — and died away.

The mob caught sight of them as they ran and, foiled for the moment, sent up a yell of rage — then started in pursuit.

"Make for the cut," shouted Spirlaw. "We can hold them off there behind the rocks."

Keating had no breath for words. Panting, sick, his head swimming, a fleck of blood upon his lips, he struggled after the giant form of the road boss; while, behind, coming ever closer, ringing in his ears, were the wild cries of the maddened Polacks. The splash of water revived him a little as they plunged along the old right of way where the river, flooded by the storm, had again claimed its own. The worst of it was up to his armpits. A grip on his shoulder and a pull from Spirlaw helped him over. They gained the other side with a bare two yards separating them from the mob behind, went on again—and then Spirlaw caught his foot, tripped and pitched headlong, causing Keating, at his heels, to stumble and fall over him.

Like wild beasts the Polacks surged upon them. Keating tried to regain his feet—but he got no further than his knees as a swinging blow from a pick-handle aught him on his head. Half-stunned, he sank back and, as consciousness left him, he heard Spirlaw's great voice roar out like the maddened bellow of a bull, saw the giant form rise with, it seemed, a dozen Polacks clinging to neck and shoulders, legs and body, saw him shake them off and the massive arms rise and fall—and all was a blur, all darkness.

The road boss lay stretched out a yard away from him when he opened his eyes. He was very weak. He raised himself on his elbow. From the camp down the line he could see the lights in the bunk-houses, hear drunken, chorused shouts. He crept to Spirlaw, called him, shook him—the big road boss never moved. The Polacks had evidently left both of them for dead—and one, it seemed, was. He slid his hand inside the other's vest for the heart beat. So faint it was at first he could not feel it, then he got it, and, realizing that Spirlaw was still alive he straightened up and looked helplessly around—and, in a flash, like the knell of doom, Spirlaw's words came back to him: *"There's the trestle gone!"*

Sick the boy was with his clotting lungs, deathly sick, weak from the blow on his head, dizzy, and his brain swam. "*There's the trestle gone!*" — he coughed it out between blue lips.

"*There's the trestle gone!*"

Keefer's Siding was a mile away. Somehow he must reach it, must get the word along the line that the *trestle was out*, get the word along before the stalled traffic moved, before the first train east or west crashed through to death, before more wreck and ruin was added to the tale that had gone before. He bent to Spirlaw's ear and three times called him frantically: "Spirlaw! Spirlaw! *Spirlaw!*" There was no response. He tried to lift him, tried to drag him — the great bulk was far beyond his strength. And the minutes were flying by, each marking the one perhaps when it would be too late, too late to warn any one that the trestle was out.

Just up past the rock cut, a bare twenty yards away where the leads to the temporary track swung into the straight of the main line, was the platform handcar they had used for carrying tools and the odds and ends of supplies between the storehouse and the work — if he could only get Spirlaw there!

He called him again, shook him, breathing a prayer for help. The road boss stirred, raised himself a little, and sank down again with a moan.

"Spirlaw, *Spirlaw*, for God's sake, man, try to get up! I'll help you. You must, do you hear, *you must!*" — he was dragging at the road boss's collar.

Keating's voice seemed to reach the other's consciousness, for, weakly, dazed, without sense, blindly, Spirlaw got upon his knees, then to his feet, and, staggering, reeling like a drunken man, his arm around Keating's neck, his weight almost crushing to the ground the one sicker than himself, the two stumbled, pitched, and, at the end, *crawled* those twenty yards.

"The handcar, Spirlaw, the handcar!" gasped Keating. "Get on it. You must! Try! Try!"

Spirlaw straightened, lurched forward, and fell half across the car with out-flung arms—unconscious again.

The rest Keating managed somehow, enough so that the dangling legs freed the ground by a few inches; then, with bursting lungs, far spent, he unblocked the wheels, pushed the car down the little spur, swung the switch, dragged himself aboard, and began to pump his way west toward Keefer's Siding.

No man may tell the details of that mile, every inch of which was wrung from blood that oozed from parted, quivering lips; no man may question from Whom came the strength to the frail body, where strength was not; the reprieve to the broken lungs, that long since should have done their worst—only Keating knew that the years were ended forever, that with every stroke of the pump-handle the time was shorter. The few minutes to win through—that was the last stake!

At the end he choked—fighting for his consciousness, as, like dancing points, switch lights swam before him. He checked with the brake, reeled from the car, fell, tried to rise and fell back again. Then, on his hands and knees, he crept toward the station door. It had come at last. The hemorrhage that he had fought back with all his strength was upon him. He beat upon the door. It opened, a lantern was flashed upon him, and he fell inside.

"The trestle's out at the Glacier—hold trains both ways—Polacks—Spirlaw on—handcar—I——"

That was all. Keating never spoke again.

"I dunno as you'd call him a builder," says Clarihue, the night turner, when *he* tells the story in the darkened roundhouse in the shadow of the big ten-wheelers on the pits, while the steam purrs softly at the gauges and sometimes a pop-valve lifts with a catchy sob, "I dunno as you would. It depends on the way you look at it. Accordin' to him, he was. He left something behind him, what?"

VII
THE GUARDIAN OF THE DEVIL'S SLIDE

There is one bad piece of track on the Hill Division, particularly bad, which is the same as saying that it is the worst piece of track, bar none, on the American Continent. Not that the engineers were to blame—they weren't. It was Dame Nature in the shape of the Rockies—Dame Nature and the directors.

Sir Ivers Clayborn, gray-haired and grizzled, a man schooled in the practical school of many lands and many years, who was chief consulting engineer when the road was building, advised a double-looped tunnel that, according to his sketch, looked something like the figure 8 canted over sideways. The directors poised their glasses and examined the sketch with interest until they caught sight of the penciled estimate in the corner. That settled it. They did not even take the trouble to vote. They asked for an alternative—and they got it. They got the Devil's Slide.

First and last, it has euchred more money out of the treasury of the Transcontinental than it would have taken to build things Sir Ivers' way to begin with; and it has taken some years, a good many of them, for the directors to learn their lesson. The old board never did, for that matter; but, thanks perhaps to younger blood, they've begun now to build as they should have built in the first place. It isn't finished yet, that double-looped tunnel, it won't be for years, but, no matter, it's begun, and some day a good many more than a few men will sleep the easier because of it.

From Carleton, the super, to the last section hand and track-walker, the Devil's Slide was a nightmare. The dispatchers, under their green-shaded lamps, cursed it in the gray hours of dawn; the traffic department cursed it spasmodically, but at such times so whole-heartedly and with such genuine fervor and abandon that its occasional lapses into silence were overlooked; the motive power department in the shape of Regan, the master mechanic, cursed it all the time, and did it breathlessly. It had only one friend — the passenger agent's department. The passenger agent's department swore *by* it — on account of the scenery.

"Scenery!" gulped the dispatchers, and the white showed under their nail tips as their fingers tightened on their keys.

"Scenery!" howled the traffic department, and reached for the claim file.

"Scenery!" — Regan didn't say it — he choked. Just choked, and spat the exclamation point in a stream of black-strap.

"Scenery!" murmured Mr. General Passenger Agent esthetically, waving a soft and diamond bedecked hand from the platform of Carleton's private car. "Wonderful! Grand! Magnificent! We've got them all beaten into a coma. No other road has anything like it anywhere in the world."

"They have not," agreed Carleton, and the bitterness of his soul was in his words.

Everybody was right.

The general passenger agent was right — the scenic grandeur was beyond compare, and he made the most of it in booklets, in leaflets, in pamphlets, and in a score of pages in a score of different magazines.

The others were right—the Devil's Slide was everything that the ethics of engineering said it shouldn't be. It was neither level nor straight. In its marvelous two miles from the summit of the pass to the canon below, its nearest approach to the ethical was three percent drop. There wasn't much of that—most of it was a straight five! It twisted, it turned, it slid, it slithered, and it dove around projecting mountain-sides at scandalous tangents and with indecent abruptness.

Chick Coogan swore, with a grin, that he could see his own headlight coming at him about half the time every trip he made up or down. That, of course, is exaggerating a little—but not much! Coogan sized up the Devil's Slide pretty well when he said that, all things considered, pretty well—there wasn't much chance to mistake what he meant, or what the Devil's Slide was, or what he thought of it. Anyway, be that as it may, Coogan's description gave the division the only chance they ever had to crack a smile when the Devil's Slide was in question.

They smiled then, those railroaders of the Rockies, but they'll look at you queerly now if you mention the two together—Coogan and the Devil's Slide. Fate is a pretty grim player sometimes.

Any one on the Hill Division can tell you the story—they've reason to know it, and they do—to the last man. If you'd rather get it first hand in a roundhouse, or between trains from the operator at some lone station that's no more than a siding, or in the caboose of a way freight—if you are a big enough man to ride there, and that means being bigger than most men—or anywhere your choice or circumstance leads you from the super's office to a track-walker's shanty; if you'd rather get it that way, and you'll get it better, far better, than you will here, don't try any jolly business to make the boys talk—just say a good word for Coogan, Chick Coogan. That's the "open sesame"—and the only one.

There's no use talking about the logical or the illogical, the rational or the irrational, when it comes to Coogan's story. Coogan's story is just Coogan's story, that's all there is to it. What one man does another doesn't. You can't cancel the human equation because there's nothing to cancel it with; it's there all the time swaying, compelling, dominating every act in a man's life. The higher branches of mathematics go far, and to some men three dimensions are but elemental, but there is one problem even they have never solved and never will solve — the human equation. What Coogan did, you might not do — or you might.

Coogan didn't come to the Transcontinental a full-blown engineer from some other road as a good many of the boys have, though that's nothing against them; Coogan was a product of the Hill Division pure and simple. He began as a kid almost before the steel was spiked home, and certainly before the right of way was shaken down enough to begin to look like business. He started at the bottom and he went up. Call-boy, sweeper, wiper, fireman — one after the other. Promotion came fast in the early days, for, the Rockies once bridged, business came fast, too; and Coogan had his engine at twenty-one, and at twenty-four he was pulling the Imperial Limited.

"Good goods," said Regan. "That's what he is. The best ever."

Nobody questioned that, not only because there was no one on the division who could put anything over Coogan in a cab, but also because, and perhaps even more pertinent a reason, every one liked Coogan — some of them did more than that.

Straight as a string, clean as a whistle was Coogan, six feet in his stockings with a body that played up to every inch of his height, black hair, jet black, black eyes that laughed with you, never *at* you, a smile and a cheery nod always — the kind of a man that makes you feel every time you see them that the world isn't such an eternal dismal grind after all. That was Chick Coogan — all except his heart. Coogan had a heart like a woman's, and a hard luck story from a 'bo stealing a ride, a railroad man, or any one else for that matter, never failed to make him poorer by a generous percentage of what happened to be in his pocket at the time. Who wouldn't like him! Queer how things happen.

It was the day Coogan got married that Regan gave him 505 and the Limited run as a sort of wedding present; and that night Big Cloud turned itself completely inside out doing honor and justice to the occasion.

Big Cloud has had other celebrations, before and since, but none quite so unanimous as that one. Restraint never did run an overwhelmingly strong favorite with the town, but that night it was hung up higher than the arms on the telegraph poles. Men that the community used to hide behind and push forward as hostages of righteousness, when it was on its good behavior and wanted to put on a front, cut loose and outshone the best — or the worst, if you like that better — of the crowd that never made any bones about being on the other side of the fence. They burned red flares, very many of them, that Carleton neglected to imagine had any connection with the storekeeper and the supply account; they committed indiscretions, mostly of a liquid nature, that any one but the trainmaster, who was temporarily blind in both eyes, could have seen; and, as a result, the Hill Division the next day was an eminently paralytic and feeble affair. This is a very general description of the event, because sometimes it is not wise to particularize this is a case in point.

Coogan's send-off was a send-off no other man, be he king, prince, president, sho-gun, or high mucky-muck of whatever degree, could have got—except Coogan. Coogan got it because he was Coogan, just Coogan—and the night was a night to wonder at.

Regan summarized it the next evening over the usual game of pedro with Carleton, upstairs over the station in the super's office.

"Apart from Coogan and me," said the master mechanic, in a voice that was still suspiciously husky, "apart from Coogan and me and *mabb* the minister"—the rest was a wave of his hand. Regan could wave his hand with a wealth of eloquence that was astounding.

"Quite so," agreed Carleton, with a grin. "Too bad to drag *them* into it, though. Both 'peds' to me, Tommy. It's a good thing for the discipline of the division that bigamy is against the law, what?"

"They'll be talking of it," said Regan reminiscently, "when you and me are on the scrap heap, Carleton."

"I guess that's right," admitted the super. "Play on, Tommy."

But it wasn't. They only talked of Coogan's wedding for about a year—no, they don't talk about it now. We'll get to that presently.

The Imperial Limited was the star run on the division—Regan gave Coogan the thirty-third degree when he gave him that—that and 505, which was the last word in machine design. And Coogan took them, took them and the schedule rights that pertained thereto, which were a clear and a clean-swept track, and day after day, up hill and down, Number One or Number Two, as the case might be, pulled into division on the dot. Coogan's stock soared—if that were possible; but not Coogan. The youngest engineer on the road and top of them all, would have been excuse enough for him to show his oats and, within decent limits, no one would have thought the worse of him for it—Coogan never turned a hair. He was still the friend of the 'bo and the man in trouble, still the Coogan that had been a wiper in the roundhouse; and yet, perhaps, not quite the same, for two new loves had come into his life—his love for Annie Coogan, and his love, the love of the master craftsman, for 505. In the little house at home he talked to Annie of the big mountain racer and Annie, being an engineer's daughter as well as an engineer's wife, listened with understanding and a smile, and in the smile was pride and love; in the cab Coogan talked of Annie, always Annie, and one day he told his fireman a secret that made big Jim Dahleen grin sheepishly and stick out a grimy paw.

Fate is a pretty grim player sometimes—and always, it seems, the cards are stacked.

The days and the weeks and the months went by, and then there came a morning when a sober-, serious-faced group of men stood gathered in the super's office, as Number Two's whistle, in from the Eastbound run, sounded down the gorge. They looked at Regan. Slowly, the master mechanic turned, went out of the room and down the stairs to the platform, as 505 shot round the bend and rolled into the station. For a moment Regan stood irresolute, then he started for the front-end. He went no further than the colonist coach, that was coupled behind the mail car. Here he stopped, made a step forward, changed his mind, climbed over the colonist's platform, dropped down on the other side of the track, and began to walk toward the roundhouse — they changed engines at Big Cloud and 505, already uncoupled, was scooting up for the spur to back down for the 'table.

The soles of Regan's boots seemed like plates of lead as he went along, and he mopped his forehead nervously. There was a general air of desertion about the roundhouse. The 'table was set and ready for 505, but there wasn't a soul in sight. Regan nodded to himself in sympathetic understanding. He crossed the turntable, walked around the half circle, and entered the roundhouse through the engine doors by the far pit — the one next to that which belonged to 505. Here, just inside, he waited, as the big mogul came slowly down the track, took the 'table with a slight jolt, and stopped. He saw Coogan, big, brawny, swing out of the cab like an athlete, and then he heard the engineer speak to his fireman.

"Looks like a graveyard around here, Jim. Wonder where the boys are. I won't wait to swing the 'table, they'll be around in a minute, I guess. I want to get up to the little woman."

"All right," Dahleen answered. "Leave her to me, I'll run her in. Good luck to you, Chick."

Coogan was starting across the yards with a stride that was almost a run. Regan opened his mouth to shout—and swallowed a lump in his throat instead. Twice he made as though to follow the engineer, and twice something stronger than himself held him back; and then, as though he had been a thief, the master mechanic stole out from behind the doors, went back across the tracks, climbed the stairs to Carleton's room with lagging steps, and entered.

The rest were still there: Carleton in his swivel chair, Harvey, the division engineer, Spence, the chief dispatcher, and Riley, the trainmaster. Regan shook his head and dropped into a seat.

"I couldn't," he said in a husky voice. "My God, *I couldn't,*" he repeated, and swept out his arms.

A bitter oath sprang from Carleton's lips, lips that were not often profane, and his teeth snapped through the amber of his briar. The others just looked out of the window.

Mac Vicar, a spare man, took the Limited out that night, and it was three days before Coogan reported again. Maybe it was the fit of the black store-clothes and perhaps the coat didn't hang just right, but as he entered the roundhouse he didn't look as straight as he used to look and there was a queer inward slope to his shoulders and he walked like a man who didn't see anything. The springy swing through the gangway was gone. He climbed to the cab as an old man climbs—painfully. The boys hung back and didn't say anything, just swore under their breaths with full hearts as men do. There wasn't anything *to* say—nothing that would do any good.

Coogan took 505 and the Limited out that night, took it out the night after and the nights that followed, only he didn't talk any more, and the slope of the shoulders got a little more pronounced, a little more noticeable, a little beyond the cut of any coat. And on the afternoons of the lay-overs at Big Cloud, Coogan walked out behind the town to where on the slope of the butte were two fresh mounds—one larger than the other. That was all.

Regan, short, paunchy, big-hearted Regan, tackled Jim Dahleen, Coogan's fireman.

"What's he say on the run, Jim, h'm?"

"He ain't talkative," Dahleen answered shortly.

"What the hell," growled the master mechanic deep in his throat, to conceal his emotion. "'Tain't doing him any good going up there afternoons. God knows it's natural enough, but 'tain't doing him any good, not a mite—nor them either, as far as I can see, h'm? You got to *make* him talk, Jim. Wake him up."

"Why don't you talk to him?" demanded the fireman.

"H'm, yes. So I will. I sure will," Regan answered.

And he meant to, meant to, honestly. But, somehow, Coogan's eyes and Coogan's face said "no" to him as they did to every other man, and as the days passed, almost a month of them, Regan shook his head, perplexed and troubled, for he was fond of Coogan.

Then, one night, it happened.

Regan and Carleton were alone over their pedro at headquarters, except for Spence, the dispatcher, in the next room. It was getting close on to eleven-thirty. The Imperial Limited, West-bound, with Coogan in the cab, had pulled out on time an hour and a half before. The game was lagging, and, as usual, the conversation had got around to the engineer, introduced, as it always was, by the master mechanic.

"I sure don't know what to do for the boy," said he. "I'd like to do something. Talking don't amount to anything, does it, h'm?—even if you *can* talk. I can't talk to him, what?"

"A man's got to work a thing like that out for himself, Tommy," Carleton answered, "and it takes time. That's the only thing that will ever help him — time. I know you're pretty fond of Coogan, even more than the rest of us and that's saying a good deal, but you're thinking too much about it yourself."

Regan shook his head.

"I can't help it, Carleton. It's got *me*. Time, and that sort of thing, may be all right, but it ain't very promising when a man broods the way he does. I ain't superstitious or anything like that, but I've a feeling I can't just explain that somehow something's going to break. Kind of premonition. Ever have anything like that? It gets on your mind and you can't shake it off. It's on me to-night worse than it's ever been."

"Nonsense," Carleton laughed. "Premonitions are out of date, because they've been traced back to their origin. Out here, I should say it was a case of too much of Dutchy's lunch-counter pie. You ought to diet anyway, Tommy, you're getting too fat. Hand over that fine-cut of yours, I——"

He stopped as a sharp cry came from the dispatcher's room, followed by an instant's silence, then the crash of a chair sounded as, hastily pushed back, it fell to the floor. Quick steps echoed across the room, and the next moment Spence, with a white face and holding a sheet of tissue in his hand, burst in upon them.

Carleton sprang to his feet.

"What's the matter, Spence?" he demanded sharply.

"Number One," the dispatcher jerked out, and extended the sheet on which he had scribbled the message as it came in off the sounder.

Carleton snatched the paper, and Regan, leaping from his chair, looked over his shoulder.

"Number One, engine 505, jumped track east of switch-back number two in Devil's Slide. Report three known to be killed, others missing. Engineer Coogan and fireman Dahleen both hurt," they read.

Carleton was ever the man of action, and his voice rang hard as chilled steel.

"Clear the line, Spence. Get your relief and wrecker out at once. Wire Dreamer Butte for their wrecker as well, so they can work from both ends. Now then, Tommy—my God, what's the matter with you, are you crazy?"

Regan was leaning over the back of his chair, his face strained, his arm outstretched, finger pointing to the wall.

"I knew it," he muttered hoarsely. "I knew it. That's what it is."

Carleton's eyes traveled from the master mechanic to the wall and back again in amazed bewilderment, then he shook Regan by the shoulder.

"That's what, what is?" he questioned brusquely. "Are you mad, man?"

"The date," whispered Regan, still pointing to where a large single-day calendar with big figures on it hung behind the super's desk. "It's the twenty-eighth."

"I don't know what you mean, Tommy,"—Carleton's voice was quiet, restrained.

"Mean!" Regan burst out, with a hard laugh. "I don't mean anything, do I? 'Tain't anything to do with it, it's just coincidence, mabbe, and mabbe it's not. *It's a year ago to-night Coogan was married.*"

For a moment Carleton did not speak; like Regan, he stared at the wall.

"You think that——"

"No, I don't"—Regan caught him up roughly—" I don't think anything at all. I only know it's queer, ghastly queer."

Carleton nodded his head slowly. Steps were coming up the stairs. The voice of Flannagan, the wrecking boss, reached them, other voices excited and loud joined in. He slapped the master mechanic on the back.

"I don't wonder it caught you, Tommy," he said. "It's almost creepy. But there's no time for that now. Come on."

Regan laughed, the same hard laugh, as he followed the chief into the dispatcher's room.

"East of number two switch-back, eh?" he swore. "If there's any choice for hellishness anywhere on that cursed stretch of track, that's it. My God, it's come, and it's come good and hard—good and hard."

It had. It was a bad mess, a nasty mess—but, like everything else, it might have been worse. Instead of plunging to the right and dropping to the canon eighteen hundred feet below, 505 chose the inward side and rammed her nose into the gray mass of rock that made the mountain wall. The wreckers from Dreamer Butte and the wreckers from Big Cloud tell of it to this day. For twenty-four hours they worked and then they dropped—and fresh men took their places. There was no room to work—just the narrow ledge of the right of way on a circular sweep with the jutting cliff of Old Piebald Mountain sticking in between, hiding one of the gangs from the other, and around which the big wrecking cranes groped dangling arms and chains like fishers angling for a bite. It was a mauled and tangled snarl, and the worst of it went over the cañon's edge in pieces, as axes, sledges, wedges, bars and cranes ripped and tore their way to the heart of it. And as they worked, those hard-faced, grimy, sweating men of the wrecking crews, they wondered—wondered that any one had come out of it alive.

Back at headquarters in Big Cloud they wondered at it, too—and they wondered also at the cause. Every one that by any possible chance could throw any light upon it went on the carpet in the super's office. Everybody testified—everybody except Dahleen, the fireman, and Coogan, the engineer; and they didn't testify because they couldn't. Coogan was in the hospital with queer, inconsequent words upon his tongue and a welt across his forehead that had laid bare the bone from eye to the hair-line of his skull; and Dahleen was there also, not so bad, just generally jellied up, but still too bad to talk. And the testimony was of little use.

The tender of switch-back number one reported that the Limited had passed him at perhaps a little greater speed than usual — which was the speed of a man's walk, for trains crawl down the Devil's Slide with fear and caution — but not fast enough to cause him to think anything about it.

Hardy, the conductor, testified. Hardy said it was the "air;" that the train began to slide faster and faster after the first switch-back was passed and that her speed kept on increasing up to the moment that the crash came. He figured that it couldn't be anything else — just the "air" — it wouldn't work and the control of the train was lost. That was all he knew.

And while Regan swore and fumed, Carleton's face set grim and hard — and he waited for Dahleen.

It was a week before the fireman faced Carleton across the super's desk, but when that time came Carleton opened on him straight from the shoulder, not even a word of sympathy, not so much as "glad to see you're out again," just straight to the point, hard and quick.

"Dahleen," he snapped, "I want to know what happened in the cab that night, and I want a straight story. No other kind of talking will do you any good."

Dahleen's face, white with the pallor of his illness, flushed suddenly red.

"You're jumping a man pretty hard, aren't you, Mr. Carleton?" he said resentfully.

"Maybe I've reason to," replied Carleton. "Well, I'm waiting for that story."

"There is no story that I know of," said Dahleen evenly. "After we passed switch-back number one we lost control of the train — the 'air' wouldn't work."

"Do you expect me to believe that?"

"You don't seem to," retorted Dahleen, with a set jaw.

"What did you do to stop her?"

"What I could," said Dahleen, with terse finality.

Carleton sprang to his feet, and his fist crashed down upon the desk.

"You are lying!" he thundered. "That wreck and the lives that are lost are at your door, and if I could prove it!"—he shook his fist at the fireman. "As it is I can only fire you for violation of the rules. I thought at first it was Coogan and that he'd gone off his head a bit, and you are cur enough to let the blame go there if you could, to let me and every other man think so!"

Dahleen's fists clenched, and he took a step forward.

"That's enough!" he cried hoarsely. "Enough from you or any other man!"

Carleton rounded on him more furiously than before.

"I've given you a chance to tell a straight story and you wouldn't. God knows what you did that night. I believe you were fighting drunk. I believe that gash in Coogan's head wasn't from the wreck. If I knew I'd fix you." He wrenched open a drawer of his desk, whipped out a metal whisky flask, and shook it before Dahleen's eyes. "*When you were picked up this was in the pocket of your jumper!*"

The color fled from Dahleen's face leaving it whiter than when he had entered the room. He wet his lips with the tip of his tongue. All the bluster, all the fight was gone. He stared mutely, a startled, frightened look in his eyes, at the damning evidence in the super's hand.

"Forgotten about it, had you?" Carleton flung out grimly. "Well, have you anything to say?"

Dahleen shook his head.

"Ain't anything *to* say, is there?"—his voice was low with just a hint of the former defiance. "It's mine, but you can't *prove* anything. You can't prove I drank it. D'ye think I'd be fool enough to do anything but keep my mouth shut?"

"No; I can't *prove* it"—Carleton's voice was deadly cold. 'You're out! I'll give you twelve hours to get out of the mountains. The boys, for Coogan's sake alone if for no other, would tear you to pieces if they knew the story. No one knows it yet but the man who found this in your pocket and myself. I'm not going to tell you again what I think of you—*get out!*"

Dahleen, without a word, swung slowly on his heel and started for the door.

"Wait!" said Carleton suddenly. "Here's a pass East for you. I don't want your blood on my hands, as I would have if Coogan's friends, and that's every last soul out here, got hold of you. You've got twelve hours—after that they'll know—to set Coogan straight."

Dahleen hesitated, came back, took the slip of paper with a mirthless, half-choked laugh, turned again, and the door closed behind him.

Dahleen was out.

Carleton kept his word—twelve hours—and then from the division rose a cry like the cry of savage beasts; but Regan was like a madman.

"Curse him!" he swore bitterly, breaking into a seething torrent of oaths. "What did you let him go for, Carleton? You'd no business to. You should have held him until Coogan could talk, and then we'd have had him."

"Tommy"—Carleton laid his hand quietly on the master mechanic's shoulder—"we're too young out in this country for much law. I don't think Coogan knows or ever will know again what happened in the cab that night. The doctors don't seem quite able to call the turn on him themselves, so they've said to you and said to me. But whether he does or not, it doesn't make any difference as far as Dahleen goes. It would have been murder to keep him here. And if Coogan ever can talk he'll never put a mate in bad no matter what the consequences to himself. There's nothing against Dahleen except that he had liquor in his possession while on duty. That's what I fired him for—that's the only story that's gone out of this office. You and I and the rest are free to put the construction on it that suits us best, and there it ends. If I was wrong to let him go, I was wrong. I did what I thought was right—that's all I can ever do."

"Mabbe," growled Regan, "mabbe; but, damn him, he *ought* to be murdered. I'd like to have had 'em done it! It's that smash on the head put Coogan to the bad. You're right about one thing, I guess, he'll never be the same Coogan again."

And in a way this was so; in another it wasn't. It was not the wound that was to blame, the doctors were positive about that; but Coogan, it was pitifully evident, was not the same. Physically, at the end of a month, he left the hospital apparently as well as he had ever been in his life; but mentally, somewhere, a cog had slipped. His brain seemed warped and weakened, simple as a child's in its workings; his memory fogged and dazed, full of indefinite, intangible snatches, vague, indeterminate glimpses of his life before. One thing seemed to cling to him, to predominate, to sway him—the Devil's Slide.

Regan and Carleton talked to him, trying to guide his thoughts and stimulate his memory.

"You remember you used to drive an engine, don't you, Chick?" asked Carleton.

"Engine?" Coogan nodded. "Yes; in the Devil's Slide."

"505," said Regan quickly. "You know old 505."

Coogan shook his head.

Carleton tried another tack.

"You were in a bad accident, Coogan, one night. You were in the cab of the engine when she went to smash. Do you remember that?"

"The smash was on the Devil's Slide," said Coogan.

"That's it," cried Carleton. "I knew you'd remember."

"They're always there," said Coogan simply, "always there. It is a bad track. I'm a railroad man and I know. It's not properly guarded. I'm going to work there and take care of it."

"Work there?" said Regan, the tears almost in his eyes. "What kind of work? What do you want to do, Chick?"

"Just work there," said Coogan. "Take care of the Devil's Slide."

The super and the master mechanic looked at each other—and averted their eyes. Then they took Coogan up to his boarding-house, where he had moved after Annie and the little one died.

"He'll never put his finger on a throttle again," said Regan with a choke in his voice, as they came out. "The best man that ever pulled a latch, the best man that ever drew a pay-check on the Hill Division. It's hell, Carleton, that's what it is. I don't think he really knew you or me. He don't seem to remember much of anything, though he's natural enough and able enough to take care of himself in all other ways. Just kind of simple-like. It's queer the way that Devil's Slide has got him, what? We can't let him go out there."

"I wonder if he remembers Annie," said Carleton. "I was afraid to ask him. I didn't know what effect it might have. No; we can't let him go out on the Devil's Slide."

But the doctors said yes. They went further and said it was about the only chance he had. The thing was on his mind. It was better to humor him, and that, with the outdoor mountain life, in time might bring him around again.

And so, while Regan growled and swore, and Carleton knitted his brows in perplexed protest, the doctors had their way—and Coogan, Chick Coogan, went to the Devil's Slide. Officially, he was on the pay-roll as a section hand; but Millrae, the section boss, had his own orders.

"Let Coogan alone. Let him do what he likes, only see that he doesn't come to any harm," wired the super.

And Coogan, when Millrae asked him what he wanted to do, answered simply: "I'm going to take care of the Devil's Slide."

"All right, Chick," the section boss agreed cheerily. "It's up to you. Fire ahead."

At first no one understood, perhaps even at the end no one quite understood—possibly Coogan least of all. He may have done some good—or he may not. In time they came to call him the Guardian of the Devil's Slide—not slightingly, but as strong men talk, defiant of ridicule, with a gruff ring of assertion in their tones that brooked no question.

Up and down, down and up, two miles east, two miles west, Coogan patroled the Devil's Slide, and never a weakened rail, a sunken tie, a loosened spike escaped him—he may have done some good, or he may not.

He slept here and there in one of the switch-back tender's shanties, moved and governed by no other consideration than fatigue—day and night were as things apart. He ate with them, too; and scrupulously he paid his footing. Twenty-five cents for a meal, twenty-five cents for a bunk, or a blanket on the floor. They took his money because he forced it upon them, furiously angry at a hint of refusal; but mostly the coin would be slipped back unnoticed into the pocket of Coogan's coat—poor men and rough they were, nothing of veneer, nothing of polish, grimy, overalled, horny-fisted toilers, their hearts were big if their purses weren't.

At all hours, in the early dawn, at midday or late afternoon, the train crews and the engine crews on passsengers, specials and freights, passed Coogan up and down, always walking with his head bent forward, his eyes fastened on the right of way—passed with a cheery hail and the flirt of a hand from cab, caboose, or the ornate tail of a garish Pullman. And to the tourists he came to be more of an attraction than the scenic grandeur of the Rockies themselves; they stared from the observation car and listened, with a running fire of wondering comment, as the brass-buttoned, swelled-with-importance, colored porters told the story, until at last to have done the Rockies and have missed the Guardian of the Devil's Slide was to have done them not at all. It was natural enough, anything out of the ordinary ministers to and arouses the public's curiosity. Not very nice perhaps, no—but natural. The railroad men didn't like it, and that was natural, too; but their feelings or opinions, in the very nature of things, had little effect one way or the other.

Coogan grew neither better nor worse. The months passed, and he grew neither better nor worse. Winter came, and, with the trestle that went out in the big storm that year, Coogan went into Division for the last time, went over the Great Divide, the same simple, broken-minded Coogan that had begun his self-appointed task in the spring—he may have done some good, or he may not. They found him after two or three days, and sent him back to Big Cloud.

"He'd have chosen that himself if he could have chosen," said Carleton soberly. "God knows what the end would have been. The years would have been all alike, he'd never have got his mind back. It's all for the best, what?"

Regan did not answer. Philosophy and the master mechanic's heart did not always measure things alike.

The Brotherhood took charge of the arrangements, and Coogan's funeral was the biggest funeral Big Cloud ever had. Everybody wanted to march, so they held the service late in the afternoon and closed down the shops at half-past four: and the shop hands, from the boss fitter to the water boy, turned out to the last man—and so did every one else in town.

It was getting dark and already supper time when it was over, but Carleton, who had left some unfinished work on his desk, went back to his office instead of going home. He lighted the lamp, put on the chimney, but the match was still burning between his fingers when the door opened and a man, with his hat pulled far down over his face, stepped in and closed it behind him.

Carleton whirled around, the match dropped to the floor, and he leaned forward over his desk, a hard look settling on his face. The man had pushed back his hat. It was Dahleen, Coogan's fireman, Jim Dahleen.

For a moment neither man spoke. Bitter words rose to Carleton's tongue, but something in the other's face checked and held them back. It was Dahleen who spoke first.

"I heard about Chick—that he'd gone out," he said quietly. "I don't suppose it did him any good, but I kind of had to chip in on the good-by—Chick and me used to be pretty thick. I saw you come down here and I followed you. Don't stare at me like that, you'd have done the same. Have you got that flask yet?"

"Yes," Carleton answered mechanically, and as mechanically produced it from the drawer of his desk.

"Ever examine it particularly?"

"Examine it?"

"I guess that answers my question. I was afraid you might, and I wanted to ask you for it that day, only I thought you'd think it mighty funny, refuse, and well—well, get to looking it over on your own hook. Will you give it here for a minute?"

Carleton handed it over silently.

Dahleen took it, pulled off the lower half that served as drinking cup, laid his finger on the inside rim, and returned it to the super.

Carleton moved nearer to the light—then his face paled. *It was Coogan's flask!* The inscription, a little dulled, in fine engraving, was still plain enough. "To Chick from Jim, on the occasion of his wedding." Carleton's hand was trembling as he set it down.

"My God!" he said hoarsely. "It was Coogan who was drunk that night—not you."

"I figured that's the way you'd read it, you or any other railroad man," said Dahleen. "It was him or me and one of us drunk, in the eyes of any of the boys on the road, from the minute that flask showed up. There was only one thing would have made you believe different, and I couldn't tell you—then. I'd have taken the same stand you did. But you're wrong. Coogan wasn't drunk that night—he never touched a drop. I wouldn't be telling you this now, if he had, would I?"

"Sit down," said Carleton.

Dahleen took the chair beside the desk, and resting his feet on the window-sill stared out at the lights twinkling below him.

"Yes, I gave him the flask," he said slowly, as though picking up the thread of a story, "for a wedding present. The day he came back to his run after the little woman and the baby died he had it in his pocket, and he handed it to me. '*I'm afraid of it, Jimmy,*' he said. That was all, just that—only he *looked* at me. Then he got down out of the cab to oil round, me still holding it in my hand for the words kind of hit me—they meant a whole lot. Well, before he came back, I lifted up my seat and chucked it down in the box underneath. I don't want to make a long story of this. You know how he took to brooding. Sometimes he wouldn't say a word from one end of the run to the other. And once in a while he seemed to act a little queer. I didn't think much of it and I didn't say anything to anybody, figuring it would wear off. When we pulled out of Big Cloud the night of the wreck I didn't see anything out of the ordinary about him, I'd kind of got used to him by then and if there was any difference I didn't notice it. He never said a word all the way out until we hit the summit of the Devil's Slide and started down. I had the fire-box door open and was throwing coal when he says so sudden as almost to make me drop my shovel:

"'Jimmy, do you know what night this is?'"

"'Sure,' says I, never thinking, 'it's Thursday.'

"He laughed kind of softlike to himself.

"'It's my wedding night, Jimmy,' he says. 'My wedding night, and we're going to celebrate.'

"The light from the fire-box was full on his face, and he had the queerest look you ever saw on a man. He was white and his eyes were staring and he was pushing his hand through his hair and rocking in his seat. I was scart. I thought for a minute he was going to faint, then I remembered that whisky and jumped for my side of the cab, opened the seat and snatched it up. I went back to him with it in my hand. I don't think he ever saw it—I know he didn't. He was laughing that soft laugh again, kind of as though he was crooning, and he reached out his hand and pushed me away.

"'We're going to celebrate, Jimmy,' says he again. 'We're going to celebrate. It's my wedding night.'

"I felt the speed quicken a bit, we were on the Slide then, you know, and I saw his fingers tightening on the throttle. Then it got me, and my heart went into my mouth — Chick was clean off his head. I slipped the flask into my pocket, and tried to coax his hands away from the throttle.

"'Let me take her a spell, Chick,' says I, thinking my best chance was to humor him.

"He threw me off like I was a plaything. Then I tried to pull him away and he smashed me one between the eyes and sent me to the floor. All the time we was going faster and faster. I tackled him again, but I might as well have been a baby, and then — then — well, that wound in his head came from a long-handled union-wrench I grabbed out of the tool box. He went down like a felled ox — but it was too late. Before I could reach a lever we were in splinters."

Dahleen stopped. Carleton never stirred, he was leaning forward, his elbows on his desk, his chin in his hands, his face strained, eyes intently fastened on the other.

Dahleen fumbled a second with his watch chain, twisting it around his fingers, then he went on:

"While I laid in the hospital I turned the thing over in my mind pretty often, long before the doctors thought I knew my own name again, and I figured that, if it was ever known, old Coogan was down and out for fair even if when he got better his head turned out all right again, because he wouldn't be ever trusted in a cab under any circumstances, you understand? If he didn't come out straight why that ended it, of course; but I had it in my mind that it was only what they call a temporary aberration. I couldn't queer him if that was all, could I? So I said to myself, 'Jimmy, all you know is that the "air" wouldn't work.' That's what I told you that day; and then you sprang that flask on me. You were right, I *had* forgotten it. Whisky in the cab on the night of an accident is pretty near an open and shut game. It was him or me, and I couldn't tell you the story then without doing Coogan cold, but Coogan's gone now and it can't hurt him. That's all."

The tick of the clock on the wall, the click of the sounder from the dispatcher's room next door were the only sounds for a long minute, then Carleton's chair scraped and he stood up and put out his hand.

"Dahleen," he said huskily, "I'd give a good deal to be as white a man as you are."

Dahleen shook his head.

"Any one would have done it for Coogan," he said.

VIII
THE BLOOD OF KINGS

There never was, and there isn't now, anything elusive about the Hill Division, unless you get to talking about the mileage—when you strike the mileage you strike deep water, and the way of it is this. Most things that are big and vital and enduring develop with the years to their own maturity, and with maturity comes perfection—as nearly as anything is perfect. When the last rail that proclaimed man's mastery of the Rockies and the Sierras an accomplished fact was spiked to the ties with much ceremony and more eclat, to say nothing of the somewhat wobbly and uncertain blows with which the silk-hatted, very-important-national-personage performed this crowning act, while the rough-and-readys whose toil and sweat and grime and blood had bought the miles the orators were eulogizing, being no longer of the elect, looked on from a respectful distance—when all this was done the Hill Division, even then, was no more than the rough draft of a masterpiece.

In the years that followed came the pruning and the changes, the smoothing and the toning down—tunnels bored through the mountain-sides lessened the grades and lopped off winding miles around projecting spurs; trestles with long embankment approaches added their quota to this much-to-be-desired result; while in the foothills, instead of circling around and around, to the right and the left and the left and the right of an endless procession of buttes, the buttes themselves came to be bisected with mathematical precision. All told, many miles, very many miles, have been wiped out in this fashion—the elusive part of it is that, measured in the dollars and cents paid by the tourists for transportation and the shippers and consignees for freight hauls, the line is just as long as ever it was! And it would appear that a good deal of money had been spent with nothing to show for it; but then against this is the fact that the directors down East were never rated as imminent or near-imminent subjects for a lunacy commission. The mileage is elusive—let it go at that.

For the rest, the right of way from Big Cloud, the divisional point, just East of the mighty blue-blurred, snow-capped range that towers to the skyline North and South—from there to the rolling, undulating country that reaches West from the base of the Sierras, the Hill Division is, without question, the most marvelous piece of track ever conceived by man, and it stands a perpetual and enduring monument to the brains and the genius, ay, and the manhood, too, of those who built it.

Such is the Hill Division. You who know the Rockies know it for the grandeur of its scenery, know it for the glory of its conquest over obstacles seemingly insurmountable; but there is another side that you may not know, a side that the maps and plans and blueprints and the railroad folders and the windows of the observation cars, big as they are, do not show — and that side is the human side. It is full of tears and laughter, full of sorrow and joy, of dangers and death and mistakes and triumph — its history would fill many pages, but it is a history that will never be written, for the generals and the rank and file of its army have fought their battles without the blare of trumpets, have done their work and their duty as they saw it, simply and with few words, without thought of personal profit and, much less, of fame. They tell their own stories amongst themselves, and they hold in honor those entitled thereto — which is a meed beyond any recognition of governments or kings or principalities, because it is the tribute of man to man, without glamor and without pretense. If you are a man as they measure men, they will tell you the stories, too; and, if you care to smoke, they will offer you their black plugs with the heart-shaped tin tags that their favorite manufacturer imbeds therein and, further, they will hand you their clasp knives with which to slice it. If you are wise you will understand that you are honored above most men, and you will be becomingly humble and will listen. But if this, through circumstance and misfortune, has never been your lot, then, here and there, inadequately and meagerly, you may run across, in print, a stray breath from the Hill Division — this is a case in print — the story of "King" Gilleen.

Gilleen was a man you would never pass in a crowd without turning your head to look at him a second time, not even in a big crowd, for nature had dealt with Gilleen generously—or otherwise—whichever way it pleases you best to consider it. He had red hair of a shade that might be classified as brilliant, but which Regan, the master mechanic, described in metaphor. Said Regan: "You could see that head a mile away on the other side of a curve in a blizzard at night when he pokes it out of the cab window. You'll never get Gilleen on the carpet because his headlight's out, what?" Certainly, at any rate, Gilleen's hair was undeniably red. He had blue eyes, and a very small nose which, for all that, was, next to his hair, the most prominent feature he possessed—small noses with a slight up-cant to the tip *are* pronounced, mere size to the contrary. His face was freckled and so were his hands; also, he was no small chunk of a man, not so very tall, but the shoulders on him were something to envy if you were friendly with him, or to respect if you were not. That was Gilleen, all except the fact that he admitted with emphasis to the blood of some wild Irish race of kings coursing through his veins. This last point was never established—every one took Gilleen's word for it, that is every one but Regan, who was Irish himself and, more pertinent still, Gilleen's direct superior. On this point Regan, who was never averse to doing it, could get a rise out of Gilleen quicker than the bite of a hungry trout.

"By Christmas," Gilleen would sputter on such occasions, "I'll have you know I'm no liar, an' if 'twere not for the missus an' the six kids"—here Gilleen would always stop to count, owing to a possible arrival since the last clash, realizing that any slip would be instantly and mercilessly turned against him by the grinning master mechanic—"if 'twere not for them, Regan, you listen to me, I'd bash your face an' then ram the measly job you give me down your throat, I would that!"

"Well," Regan would return, "when you get to sitting on a dinky, gilded throne, sunk to the crown-sheet in the bogs though it will be, I'd ask no more nor as much from your hands as you get from mine—which is more than your deserts. Who but me would do as much for you? You ought to be back wiping. I've thought some seriously of it, h'm? Six, is it now?—well, it's a grand race!"

Whereupon Gilleen would say hot words and say them fervently, while he shook his fist at the master mechanic.

"I'll show you some day, Regan," was his final word. "I'll show you what kind of a race it is, an' don't you forget it!"

All of which is neither very interesting nor in any degree witty—it simply shows where Gilleen's nickname came from. Everybody on the division called him "King"—not to his face, they do now, but they didn't then. Queer the way a little thing like that acts on a man sometimes. Gilleen was well enough liked in a way, but no one ever really took him seriously in anything. Associate a man with a joke and henceforward and forever after, usually, the two are inseparable. He may have aspirations, ambitions, what you will, but he is given no credit for having them—with Gilleen it was that way. Just Gilleen, "King" Gilleen—and a grin.

The Lord only knows what possessed Gilleen to adhere with such stout-hearted loyalty to his ancestors—you may put an interrogation mark after that last word, if you like—it began with perhaps no more than a boyish boast when his official connection with the system was no further advanced than to the degree of holding down the job of assistant boiler-washer in the roundhouse. The more they guyed him the more stubbornly he stuck—it was a matter worth fighting for, and Gilleen fought. He threw pounds, reach, and other advantages to the winds and took on anybody and everybody. By the time he had moved up to firing he had fought all who cared to fight, who were not a few; and when, following that in the due course of promotion, he got his engine, he had by blows, not argument, established his assertion outwardly at least. At a safe distance the division, remembering broken noses and missing teeth and no longer denying him his royal blood, gave him his way, smiled tolerantly in self-solace and called him "nutty."

Regan, of course, still guyed—but Regan was master mechanic. Not that he did it by virtue of the immunity his official position afforded him, he never gave that a thought. He did it because he was Regan, and Regan was built that way. He could no more forego the chance of a laugh or an inward chuckle than he could forego the act of breathing—and live. A joke was a joke, just fun with him, that was all.

But with Gilleen it was different. Being unable to use his fists as was his wont, and being possessed of no other safety-valve, the pressure mounted steadily until it registered a point on his mental gauge that spoke eloquently of trouble to come.

And so matters stood when, following a rather dull summer, the fall business opened with a rush and a roar. Things moved with a jump, and the rails hummed under a constant stream of traffic east and west. Here, at least, was no joke—a rush on the Hill Division, single-track, through the mountains, never was. A month of it, and every one from cartink to superintendent began to show the effects of the strain. It was double up everywhere, extra duty, extra tricks. The dispatchers caught their share of it and their eyes grew red and heavy under the lamps at night, and the heads of the daymen ached as they figured a series of meeting points that had no beginning and no end; but, bad as it was for the men on the keys, it was worse for some of those in the cabs. Schedules went to smash. Perishables and flyers were given the best of it—the rights of the rest were the sidings. It was a case of crawl along, sneak from one to the other, with layout after layout, until the ordinary length of a day's duty lapped over into fifteen-hour stretches and sometimes to twenty-four. Sleep, what they could get of it, the engine crews snatched bolt upright in their seats while they waited for Number One's headlight to shoot streaming out of the East, or nodded until roused by the roar and thunder of a flying freight, cars and cars of it crammed with first-class ratings, streaking East, as it hurtled by with insolent disregard for every mortal thing on earth.

Maybe Gilleen got a little more of it than any one else on the throttles, maybe he did—or maybe he didn't. Gilleen thought he did anyhow, and naturally he put it own to Regan's account. Regan was head of the motive power department of the Hill Division—there was no one else *to* put it down to. It was Regan or imagination. Gilleen, not being strong on imagination, did not debate the question—he let it go at Regan.

In from one run, shot out on another—that was Gilleen's schedule. The little woman in the little house uptown off Main street got to be mostly a memory to Gilleen, and as for the six brick-headed scions of his kingly race he came to wonder if they really existed at all.

Things boomed and hummed on the Hill Division, and while everybody on it snarled and swore and nagged at each other, as weary, worn-out, dropping-with-fatigue men will do, the smiles broadened on the lips and spread over the faces of the directors down East, as they rubbed their palms beneficently, expectantly, scenting extra dividends and soaring stock.

It was noon one day when Gilleen, with a trailing string of slewing freights behind him, pulled into the Big Cloud yards, uncoupled, backed down the spur, crossed the 'table, and ran into the roundhouse. As he swung from the gangway, Regan came hurrying in through the engine doors of Gilleen's pit from the direction of headquarters, and walked up to the engineer.

"Gilleen," said he briskly, "you'll have to take out Special Eighty-three. 1603's ready with a full head on pit two."

"What's that?" snapped Gilleen. "Take out a special *now?*" You know damn well I'm just in from a run. I'm tired. You'll rub it in once too often, Regan."

"We're all tired, aren't we?" returned the master mechanic tartly. "Do you think you're the only one? As for rubbing it in, you'd better draw your fire, my bucko. There's no rubbing in being done except in your eye! Anyhow, that's enough talk. Special Eighty-three's carded on rush orders from down East, and she's been in here an hour now."

"Well, why didn't you let the crew that brought her in keep goin' then?" snarled Gilleen. It was a fool question and he knew it; but, as he had said, he was tired, and his temper, never angelic, was now pretty well on edge.

Regan glared at him a moment angrily. Regan, too, was tired and irritable, harassed beyond the limit that most men are harassed. The demand upon the motive power department for men and engines had kept him up more than one night trying to figure out a problem that was well-nigh impossible.

"Let 'em go on!" he snorted. "You know well enough I haven't anything on the Prairie Division men. You know that—what d'ye say it for, h'm? You're the first man in—and you go out first."

"It strikes me I'm *generally* the first man in these days," retorted Gilleen angrily; "an' I'm sick of gettin' the short end of it. I guess I won't go out this time."

It took a breathing spell before the master mechanic could explode adequately.

"You call yourself a railroad man!" he flung out furiously. "What are you whining about? Every man's got his shoulder to the wheel and pushing without talk. We haven't got any room here for quitters. I guess that blood of yours you're so pinhead-brained proud——"

Regan did not finish. With a bellow of rage the red-haired engineer went at the other like a charging bull, and the master mechanic promptly measured his length on the roundhouse floor from a wallop on the head that made him see stars.

Regan scrambled to his feet. His heart was the heart of a fighter, even if his build was not. Straight at Gilleen he flew, and the passes and lunges and jabs he made—while the engineer played on the master mechanic's paunch like a kettle-drum and delivered a second wallop on the head as a plaster for the first—are historic only for their infinitesimal coefficient of effectiveness. It is unquestionably certain that the master mechanic then and there would have proceeded to make up for some of his lost sleep, at least, if Gilleen's fireman and a wiper or two hadn't got in between the two men just when they did.

Gilleen was boiling mad.

"Well," he bawled, "got anything more to say about quittin' or that other thing? I guess I won't go out this time, what?"

Regan was equally mad. And as he felt tenderly of his forehead, where a lump was rapidly approximating the formation of a goose egg, he grew madder still.

"You won't go out, won't you?" he roared. "Well *I* guess you will; and, what's more, you'll go out now — and get your time! I fire you, understand?"

"You bet!" said "King" Gilleen — and that's all he said. He looked at the master mechanic for a minute, but didn't *say* anything more — just laughed and walked out of the roundhouse.

Naturally enough, the story got up and down the division, and everybody talked about it. With their rough and impartial justice they put both men in the wrong, but mostly Gilleen for insubordination. The affront Gilleen had suffered was not so big and momentous, a long way from being the vital thing in their eyes that it was in his. Gilleen was just nutty on that point, that was all there was to that. Regan's judgment had been bad and the moment he had seized for his thrust and fling was by no manner of means a psychological one; but, for all that, Gilleen had no business to strike the master mechanic. He had got what was coming to him — that was the verdict. He was out and out for good. It was pretty generally conceded that it would be a long while before he pulled a throttle on the Hill Division again.

What sympathy the engineer got, for he got some, wasn't on his own account. It was on account of his family — not the ancestral end of it, however. Six kids and a wife do not leave much change out of a pay-check even when it's padded by overtime; six kids and a wife with no pay-check is pretty stiff running.

Gilleen was too hot under the collar to give a thought to that when he marched out of the roundhouse that noon; but it wasn't many hours, after he had put in a few to make up for the sleep he hadn't had during the preceding weeks, that the problem was up to him for consideration with a vote for adjournment for once ruled out as not in order.

Mrs. Gilleen may or may not have shared her spouse's opinions on the subject of his illustrious descent—if she did she never put on any "airs" about it. Washing and dressing and cooking was about all one woman could manage for a household as big as hers. That's what she said anyway, whenever any one asked her about it. And one glance at the red-headed brood that filled the front yard and swung on the front gate, whose hinges creaked in loud and bitter protest, was enough to preclude any dispute on that score. Just a little bit of a woman she was physically; but bigger practically than the whole corps of leading lights in social and domestic economy—which, come to think of it, is damning Mrs. Gilleen with faint praise, whereas too much couldn't be said for her. However, let that go. Mrs. Gilleen *was* practical, and she had the matter up to the engineer almost before he had the sleep washed out of his eyes. No nagging, no reproach, nothing of that kind—Mrs. Gilleen wasn't that sort of a woman. "King," or not, Gilleen might have been, Katie Gilleen was a *queen*, not in looks perhaps, but a queen—that's flat. A fine woman is the finest thing in the world, and if that were said a little more often than it is maybe things generally wouldn't be any the worse for it—which is not a plank in the platform of the Suffragettes, though it may sound like it.

"Michael," said she, "you rowed with Mr. Regan, and he fired you. Will he take you back?"

Gilleen lowered the towel to his chin to catch the dripping water from his hair—he had just buried his head in the washbowl the minute before—and looked at his wife.

"I wouldn't *ask* him, Kate," he said shortly.

Mrs. Gilleen was proud, too—but for all that she sighed.

"What will you do, then, Michael?" she asked.

"I dunno yet, little woman. Some of the others will give me a job, I guess. Mabbe I'll try the train crews. I'll hit 'em up for something, anyway."

"But there's ever so much less money in that"—Mrs. Gilleen's tones were judicial, not plaintive.

"I know it," returned Gilleen; "but it'll tide us over an' keep the steam up till we get a chance to pull out for somewheres where a man can get an engine without a grinning fool of a master mechanic to double-cross him with the worst of it every chance he gets."

"I hope it will all come out right," said Mrs. Gilleen, a little wistfully.

"It will," Gilleen assured her. "Don't you worry. I'll get after a job right away as soon as I've had a bite."

It came easier even than Gilleen had figured it would—such as it was—and it was about the last job Gilleen had thought of as a possibility. Things have a peculiar way of working themselves out sometimes, and, curiously enough, by means which, on the surface, are, more often than not, apparently trivial and inconsequent. Certainly, if Gilleen, on his way to the station that morning, had not run into Gleason, the yard-master, why then—but he did.

"Call-boys kind of scarce around your diggin's since yesterday, ain't they, Gilleen?" was Gleason's greeting.

"Yes," said Gilleen. "I'm out."

"See you're headin' for the station," remarked Gleason tentatively. "Goin' down to patch it up?"

"No!" answered Gilleen with a hard ring in his voice—the "no" was emphatic.

Gleason stared at the engineer for a minute, then took a bite from his plug, and the motion of his head might have been a nod of understanding or merely a wrench or two to free his teeth from the black-strap in which they were imbedded.

"No," said Gilleen again; "I'm not. I'm goin' down for another job."

"What kind of a job?" inquired Gleason.

"Any kind from any one that will put me on—except Regan."

Gleason thought of his choked yards—the rush had in no way overlooked him. Men, men that knew a draw-bar and a switch-handle from a hunk of cheese, were as scarce in his department as they were in any of the others.

"Yards?" he queried—and blinked.

"D'y e mean it?" demanded Gilleen, taking him up short.

"Sure, I mean it."

"You're on," said Gilleen.

"Night switchman," amplified the yard-master. "You can begin to-night."

"All right, I'll be on deck," agreed Gilleen; "an' thanks, Gleason. I'm much obliged to you."

"Humph!" grunted Gleason. "'Tain't much of a stake compared with an engine, but it's yours, an' welcome."

It was quite true. Comparatively, it wasn't much of a stake, and even the first night of it was enough to throw the comparison into strong and bitter relief. If anything would have put a finishing touch on Gilleen's feelings anent the master mechanic it was that first night on yard switching, that and, of course, the nights that followed. It wasn't so much the work, though that was hard enough, and, being green, the engineer made about twice as much for himself as there was any need of, it was a not-to-be-denied tendency of his eyes to stray toward the roundhouse every time a gleaming headlight showed on the turn-table. If Gilleen had never known before how much he loved an engine he knew it in those dark hours while he swung a lantern from the roofs of a freight string, or hopped the foot-board of the switcher. Up and down the yards from dusk till dawn, to the accompaniment of the wheezing, grunting, coughing, foreshortened apology for a shunter, the clash of brake-beams, the bump and rattle, staccato, diminuendo, as a line of box-cars grumbled into motion, didn't take on any roseate hues from the angle Gilleen looked at it; nor did an occasional ten-wheeler, out or in, sailing grandly past him with impudent airs help any, either. Gilleen's language became as freckled as his face and hands and as fiery as his head. Even that grand old Irish race from which he sprang, that wild and untamed breed of kingly sires paled into insignificance—Gilleen was more occupied with Regan. What he thought he said, and said it aloud without making any bones about it—said it through his teeth, with his fists clenched.

Perhaps it was just as well Gilleen was on nights, for, ordinarily, the master mechanic had nothing to bring him around the yards, shops or roundhouse after sundown—Regan's evenings being spent with Carleton, the super, a pipe and a game of pedro upstairs over the station in the superintendent's office next door to the dispatcher's room—just as well for both their sakes; for Regan's physically; for Gilleen's because, little fond of his job as he was, there were certain necessities that even little Mrs. Gilleen with all her practicability and economy could not supply without money. Anyway, the days went by and the two men did not meet, though Gilleen's orations got around to Regan's ears fast enough. The master mechanic only laughed when he heard them.

"Gilleen," said he, "is like the parrot that said 'sic 'em!' and said it once too often. He talks too much. If he'd kept his mouth shut I'd have given him his run back, after a lay off to teach him manners. As it is, if he likes switching let him keep at it. Mabbe by the time he's tired the throne of his ancestors'll be ready for him, what?"

All this was enough to spell ructions in the air, and, ordinarily, the division to a man would have hung mildly expectant on the result of the final showdown. But the Hill Division just then wasn't hankering for anything more to liven it up—it was getting all of that sort of thing it wanted and a little besides. Attending strictly to business was about all it could do, a trifle beyond what it could do, and everything else was apart—the boom showed more signs of increasing than it did of being on the wane. There wasn't any let-up anywhere—things sizzled.

It never rains but it pours, they say; and that's one adage, at least, that the railroad men of Big Cloud, and the town itself for that matter, will swear by to this day. There are a few things that Big Cloud remembers vividly and with astounding minuteness for detail, but the night the shops went up tops them all.

When it was all over they decided that a slumbering forge-fire in the blacksmith shop was at the bottom of it—not that any one really knew, or knows now, but they put it down to that because it sounded reasonable and because there wasn't anything else *to* put it down to. However, whether that was the cause or whether it wasn't, on one point there was no possible opening for an argument—and that was the effect and the result.

If you knew Big Cloud in the old days, you know where the shops were and what they looked like; if you didn't, it won't take a minute to tell you. You could see them from the station platform across the tracks far up at the west end of the yards; and they looked more like a succession of barns nailed on to each other than anything else, except for the roofs which were low and flat—the buildings being all one-storied. What with the quarters of the boiler-makers, the carpenters, the machinists and the fitters, the old shops straggled out over a goodly length of ground, and a grimy, ramshackle, dirty, blackened, Godforsaken looking structure it was. To-day, thanks to that fire and the Big Strike when it came along, there's a modern affair of structural steel—and the rest is but a memory. However——

Night in the mountains in the Fall comes early, and by nine o'clock on the night the fire broke out it had shut down pitch dark. Nothing showed in the yards but the twinkling switch lights, the waving lamps of the men, and an occasional gleam from the shunter's headlight when it shot away from the end of a box-car. Across the tracks the station lights were like fireflies, and there was a glimmer or two showing from the roundhouse. Apart from the fact that a pretty strong west wind was brushing the yards, if you could count that as anything apart, there was nothing out of the ordinary, everything was going on as usual, when, suddenly without warning, a wicked fang of flame shot skyward, then another higher than the first. It was answered by a yell from the yardmen, caught up in the roundhouse, and then the switcher's whistle shrieked the alarm. A minute more, and everything with steam enough to lift a valve joined in. Dark forms began to run in the direction of the shops, and then the bell in the little English chapel uptown took a hand in the clamor. The alarm was unanimous enough and general enough when it came, there was never any doubt about that, but the fire must have got a pretty stiff start before it broke through the windows to fling its first challenge at the railroad men.

Gilleen and the rest of the yard crew were on the run for the scene when Gleason's voice, bawling over the din, halted them.

"Clean out three, four an' five, an' get 'em down to the bottom of the yards, an' look lively!" he yelled. "Leave that string of gondolas on six till the last. Jump now, boys! Eat 'em up!"

Oil-spattered floors and oil-smeared walls are a feeding ground for a fire than which there is no better. The flame tongues leaped higher and higher throwing a lurid glare down the yards, and throwing, too, as the wind caught them up and whirled them in gusts, a driving rain of sparks that threatened the long, dark lines of rolling stock, for the most part choked to the doors with freight—freight enough to total a sum in claim-checks that would blanch the cheeks of the most florid director on the board of the Transcontinental.

With Gleason in command, Gilleen and his mates went at their work heads down. There wasn't anything fancy or artistic about the way they banged those cars to safety—there wasn't time to be fussy. Behind them the south end of the shops was already a blazing mass. The little switcher took hold of first one string then another, shook it angrily for a minute as her exhaust roared into a quick crackle of reports and the drivers spun around like pin-wheels making the steel fly fire, then with a cough and a grunt and a final push she would snap the cars away from her, and the string would go sailing down the yard to bump and pound to a stop, with an echoing crash, into whatever might be at the other end. There was a car or two the next morning with front-ends and rear-ends and both ends at once, that looked as though they had been in a cyclone; and there was a claim-voucher or two put through for a consignment of nursing bottles and a sewing machine—not that the two necessarily go together, but no matter, they did then. Anyway, the record the yardmen made that night is the record to-day, and in no more than ten minutes there wasn't a car within three hundred yards of the shops.

But while the yard crew worked others were not idle. Regan and Carleton, both of them, had caught the first flash from the windows of the super's room, and they were down the stairs, across the yards and into the game from the start. Joined by the nightmen and the hostlers and the wide-eyed call-boys they tackled the blaze. By the time they had dragged and coupled the fifty-foot hose lengths, it took five lengths, along the tracks from the roundhouse, the needle on the stationary's gauge, luckily not yet quite dead from the day's work and whose fire-box Clarihue, the turner, now crammed with oil-soaked packing, began to climb, and they got an uncertain, weakly stream playing— uncertain, but a stream. After that, things went with a rush—both ways—the fire and the fight.

From the gambling hells and the saloons, from the streets and their homes came the population of Big Cloud, the Polacks, the Russians, the railroad men, the good and the bad whites, the half-breeds—and the local fire brigade. Two more streams they ran from the roundhouse and that was the limit—the rest of the hose was liquid rubber somewhere under the blaze.

Regan, with a bitter, hard look on his face for the shops were Regan's, was everywhere at once, and what man could do he did; but, inch by inch, the flames were getting the better of him. The yards were as bright as day now, and the heat was driving the circle of fighters back, stubbornly as they fought to hold their ground. It looked like a grand slam for the fire with the four aces in one hand. Twice Regan had been on the point of ordering the men to the roof, and twice he held back—once he had even ordered a ladder planted, only to order it away again. The building was only wood, and old, and the roof was none too strong at best; but now, under and supported by the roof of the fitting-shop, put in a month before in lieu of the old system of jacking and blocking by hand, making the risk a hundredfold greater, were the heavy steel girders and hydraulic traveling cranes that whipped the big moguls like jack-straws from their wheels preparatory to stripping them to their bare boiler-shells. Regan shook his head—it was asking a man to take his life in his hands. For the moment he stood a little apart in front of the crowd and just behind the nozzle end of one of the streams. Again he measured the chances, and again he shook his head.

"I can't ask a man to do it," he muttered; "but we ought to have a stream up there, it's——"

"Why don't you take it there yourself, then?"—the words came sharp and quick from his elbow, stinging hot like the cut of a whip-lash. It was "King" Gilleen, red-haired, blue-blooded, freckled-skinned Gilleen.

The master mechanic whirled like a shot, and for a minute the two men stared into each other's eyes, stared as the leaping flames sent flickering shadows across the grim, set features of them both, stared at each other face to face for the first time since that noon in the roundhouse days before.

"Why don't you take it there yourself, then?" said Gilleen again, and his laugh rang hard and cold. "*You* ain't a quitter, are you? There's nothin' wrong with *your* blood, is there? If you're not afraid—come on!"—as he spoke he stepped forward, pushed the men from the nozzle—and looked back at the master mechanic.

Regan's lips were like a thin, white line.

Gilleen laughed out again, and it carried over the roar and the crackle of the flames, the snapping timbers, the hiss and spit of the water, the voices of the crowd.

"Put up the ladder!"—it was Regan's voice, deadly cold. "Lash a short end around that nozzle, an' stand by to pass it up"—he was at the foot of the ladder almost before they got it in position, and the next instant began to climb.

Like a flash, Gilleen, surrendering the fire-hose temporarily, sprang after him—and up.

It wasn't far—the shops were low, just one story high—and both men were on the roof in a minute. Gilleen caught the coiled rope they slung him from below, and together he and the master mechanic hauled up the writhing, spluttering hose.

A shower of sparks and a swirling cloud of smoke enveloped them as they stood upright and began to advance. It cleared away leaving them silhouetted against the leaping wall of flame a few yards in front of them—and a cheer went up from the throats of the crowd below.

Not a word passed between the two men. Foot by foot they moved forward, laying the hose in a line behind them to lessen the weight and the side-pull, that at first had called forth all their strength to direct the play of the stream; foot by foot they went forward, closer and closer, perilously close, to the blistering, scorching, seething mass—for neither of them would be the first to hold back.

High into the heavens streamed the great yellow-red forks of angry flame, and over all, like a gigantic canopy, rolled dense volumes of gray-black smoke. Came at the two men spurting, fiery tongues, stabbing at them, robbing them of their breath, mocking at their puny might.

Another step forward and Regan reeled back, one hand went to his face — and the nozzle almost wrenched itself from the engineer's grasp.

"It's a grand race!" laughed Gilleen, but the laugh was more of a gasping cough, and the cough came from cracked and swollen lips. "It's a grand race, Regan; an' the blood———"

With a choking sob, Regan steadied himself and seized hold of the nozzle again.

They held where they were now — it was the fire, not they, that was creeping forward, pitilessly, inevitably, licking greedily at the tarred roof until it grew soft beneath their feet and the bubbles puffed up and formed and broke.

A cry of warning came from below, and with it came the ominous rending groan of yielding timbers. It came again, the cry, and rang in Gilleen's ears almost without sense. He could scarcely see, his eyes were scorched and blinded, his lungs were full of the stinging smoke, choking full. Beside him Regan hung, dropping weak. "Get back, for God's sake, get back!" it was Carleton's voice. "Do you hear!" shouted the super frantically. "Get back! The roof is sagging! Run for———"

Like the roar of a giant blast, as a park of artillery belches forth in deafening thunder, there came a terrific crash and, fearful in its echo, a cry of horror rose from those below. Where there had been roof a foot in front of the men was now — nothingness.

Gilleen, with a shout, as he felt the edge crumple under him, flung himself backward and as he leaped he snatched at Regan, His fingers brushed the master mechanic's sleeve, hooked, slipped—and he struck on his back a full yard away. He reeled to his feet like a drunken man, and dug at his eyes with his fists. Over the broken edge of the shattered roof, hanging into the black below, was the dangling hose—but Regan was gone. Weak, spent, exhausted, the master mechanic, unequal to the exertion of Gilleen's leap, had pitched downward, clutching desperately, feebly, vainly, as he went. Regan was gone, and twenty feet, somewhere, below— he lay.

Gilleen staggered forward. It was the far end of the beams that had given away and the six or seven yards of the roof that had fallen still separated him from the heart of the blaze. The advancing flames lighted up a scene of wreck and ruin below in the fitting-shop—girders and steel Ts and cranes and tackles, splotches of roofing, shattered timbers, lay over the black looming shapes of the monster engine-shells blocked on the pit.

"Regan!" he called; and again: "Regan! *Regan!*"

Above the roaring crackle of the fire, above the surging, pounding noises that beat mercilessly at his eardrums, faint, so faint it seemed like fancy, a low moan answered him. Once more it came and upon Gilleen surged new-born strength and life. He began to drag at the hose with all his might, dropping it foot by foot over the jagged edge of the roof until it reached well down to the snarled and tangled wreckage below. And then a mighty yell went up from a hundred throats—and again and again:

"Gilleen! King Gilleen! King! *King!*"

There was no gibe now—just a bursting cheer from the full hearts of men. "*King!*" they roared, and the shout swelled, but Gilleen never heard them as they crowned him. King he was at last in the eyes of all men, a king that knows no blood nor race nor throne nor retinue—Gilleen was lowering himself down the hose.

It was a question of minutes. The fire was sweeping in a mad wave across the intervening space. The engineer's feet touched something solid and he let go his hold of the hose—and stumbled, lost his balance, and pitched forward striking on his head with a blow that dazed and stunned him. Mechanically he understood that what he had taken for flooring was a work-bench. He got to his feet again, the blood streaming from his forehead, and shouted. This time there was no answer. Staggering, falling, tripping, stumbling, he began to search frantically amid the debris. The air was thick with the smothering smoke, hot, stifling, drying up his lungs. He began to moan, crying the name of the master mechanic over and over again, crying it as a man cries out in delirium. Bits of oil-soaked waste and wads of packing, catching from the glowing cinders, were blazing around his feet, the onrush of the flames swept a blighting wave upon him that sent him reeling back, scorching, blistering the naked skin of his face and hands. Again he fell. A great sheet of fire leapt high behind him, held for an instant, and then the dull red glow settled around him again—but in that instant, just a little to the right, pinned under a scanling, half hidden by a snarled knot of roof and girders, was the master mechanic's form.

On his knees, groping with his hands, Gilleen reached him, and began to tear furiously, savagely, madly, at the timber that lay across Regan's chest. He moved it little by little, every inch tasking his weakening muscles to the utmost. Blackness was before him, he could no longer see, he could no longer breathe, hot, nauseating fumes strangled him and sent the blood bursting from his nostrils. He tried to lift Regan's shoulders — and sank down beside the master mechanic instead. Feebly he raised his head — there came the splintering crash of glass, a rushing stream tore through a window, hissed against the boiler-shell above him, and, glancing off, lashed a cold spray of water into his face.

The window! Three yards to the window! He was up again, and pulling at the dead weight of the master mechanic. Just three yards! He cried like a child as he struggled, and the tears ran down his cheeks in streams. A foot, two feet, three — *two more yards to go*. Axes were swinging now in front of him, shouts reached him. Half the distance was covered — but he had gone to his knees. Everything around was hot, it was all fire and hell and madness. A yard and a half — only a yard and a half. Alone he could make it easily enough and maybe Regan was dead anyhow, alone and there was safety and life, alone — then he laughed. "It's a grand race, Regan, a grand race," he sobbed hysterically, and his grip tightened on the master mechanic, and he won another foot and another and another. A black form wavered before him, he felt an arm reach out and grasp him — then he tottered, swayed, and dropped inert, unconscious.

They got him out, and they got Regan out, and they got the fire out by the time there wasn't much left to burn; and, after a week or two, both men got out of the hospital. That's about all there is to it, except that Gilleen's red head now decorates the swellest cab on the division, and that he never fought for his title after that night—he never had to; though, if you feel like questioning it, you can still get plenty of fight, for all that—any of the boys will accommodate you any time.

Regan isn't an artist as a pugilist, but even so it is unwise to take risks—unscientific men by lucky flukes have handed knockouts to their betters.

"If Gilleen says so that's enough, whether it's so or not, what? "Regan will fling at you. "It's pretty *good* blood, ain't it, no matter what kind it is? Well then—h'm?"

IX
MARLEY

There are some men they remember on the Hill Division—Marley is one of them; and his story goes back to the days before the fire wiped out what the strike had left of the old rambling shops at the western end of the Big Cloud yards, back to the time when "Royal" Carleton was young in the superintendency of the division, when Tommy Regan, squat, fat and paunchy was master mechanic, and Harvey was division engineer, and Spence was chief dispatcher, when the Big Fellows, as they were called, wrestled with the rough of it, shaking the steel down into a permanent right of way, shackling the Rockies, welding the West and the East.

Marley was not a "Big Fellow" in either sense of the word.

Officially, when he started in, he wasn't anything—that is, anything in particular. Sort of general assistant, assistant section hand, assistant boiler washer, assistant anything you like to everybody—Marley's duties, if nothing else, were multifarious.

Physically, he was a queer card. He was built on plans that gave you the impression Dame Nature had been doing a little something herself along the lines of original research and experimentation—and wasn't well enough satisfied with the result to duplicate it! Anyway, as far as any one ever knew, there wasn't but one Marley produced. Maybe nature, even, isn't infallible; maybe she made a mistake, maybe she didn't. You couldn't call him deformed—and yet you could! That's Marley exactly—when you get to describing him you get contradictory. It must have been his neck. That lopped off two or three inches from his stature because he hadn't any! But if that shortened him down to, say, five feet five, which isn't so short after all—there's the contradiction again, you see—the length of his arms at least was something to marvel at, they made up for the neck. Regan used to say Marley could stand on the floor of the roundhouse and clean out an engine pit without leaning over. The master mechanic was more or less gifted with imagination, but he wasn't so far out, not more than a couple of feet or so, at that. Marley's hair, more than anything else that comes handy by way of comparison, was like the stuff, in color and texture, the fellows on the stage light and put in their mouths so as to blow out smoke like a belching stack under forced draft—tow, they call it. Eyes—no woman ever had any like them—big and round and wide, with a peculiar violet tinge to them, and lids that had a trick of closing down with a little hesitating flutter like a girl trying to flirt with you.

But what's the use! Marley, piecemeal, would never look like the short-stepping, springy-walked, foreshortened, arms-flopping Marley with the greasy black peaked cap pulled over his forehead, the greasy jumper tucked into greasier overalls who sold his hybrid services to the Transcontinental for the munificent sum of a dollar ten a day.

Marley's arrival and introduction to Big Cloud was, like Marley himself, decidedly out of the ordinary and by no manner of means commonplace. Marley arrived "'boing it" in a refrigerator car.

They ice the cars at Big Cloud and, luckily for Marley, the particular one he had, in some unexplained way, managed to appropriate required a little something more than icing. They pulled him out in about as flabby a condition as a sack of flour. He didn't say anything for himself mainly because he was pretty nearly past ever saying anything for himself or anybody else. The boys who found him cursed fluently because he wasn't a pleasant sight, and then carried him up Main Street on the door of a box-car with the hazy notion that MacGuire's Blazing Star Saloon was the most fitting Mecca available.

Marley continued to play in luck. Mrs. Coogan, the mother of Chick Coogan, that is, who went out in the Fall blizzard on the Devil's Slide some years before, spotted the procession as it passed her little shack, halted it, made a hasty, but none the less comprehensive, examination, amplified it by a few scathing remarks on discovering the proposed destination, peremptorily ordered them into her bit of a cottage and installed Marley therein.

He was pretty far gone, pretty far—and he hung on the ragged edge for weeks. Nobody knows what Mrs. Coogan did for him except Marley himself; but it was generally conceded that she did more than she could afford for anybody, let alone doing it for a stray hobo.

Marley got well in time, of course, for, than old, motherly Mrs. Coogan there was no better nurse, even if she had few comforts and dainties and less money to buy them with; and then Marley got a job—or rather Mrs. Coogan got one for him.

There wasn't anything Mrs. Coogan could have asked for and not got that was within their power to give her—she was Chick's mother, and with Carleton or Regan or any of the rest of them that was enough. But Mrs. Coogan never asked anything for herself—she had the Coogan pride.

"The good Lord be praised," she would say—Mrs. Coogan was sincerely devout. "I'm able to worrk, so I am, an' fwhy should I?"

Why should she? They smiled at her as men smile when something touches them under the vest, and they want to say the proper thing—and can't. They smiled—and gave her their washing.

Mrs. Coogan tackled Regan on Marley's behalf.

The master mechanic scratched his head in perplexity, but his reply was prompt and hearty enough.

"Sure. Sure thing, Mrs. Coogan," he said. "Send him down to me. I'll find him something to do."

To Marley he talked a little differently.

"I ain't quite sure I like the looks of you," he flung out bluntly enough, taking in the new man from head to toe. "There's no job for you, but I'll give you a chance."

Marley's eyes came down in a flutter.

"Thanks, sir," he mumbled nervously.

Tommy Regan wasn't used to being "sir" ed—the Hill Division did its business with few handles and it wasn't long on the amenities.

"Humph!" he ejaculated with a snort, and a stream of black-strap laid the dust on a good few inches of engine cinders. "You can hand any thanks you've got coming over to Mother Coogan. And say"—the master mechanic wriggled his fat forefinger under Marley's nose—"thanks are all right as far as they go, but I figure you owe her something over and above that, what?"

A faint flush came into Marley's cheeks and he darted a quick look at Regan. His eyes were on the ground and his hands had suddenly disappeared in his pockets before he answered.

"I'm going to board with her a spell," he said in a slow way, as though he was measuring every word before it was uttered.

"Are, eh?" grunted Regan, but the grunt carried a grudging note of approval. "Well, maybe that'll help some. You can report at noon, Marley, and make yourself generally handy around. I reckon you'll find enough to do."

"Thanks, sir," said Marley again, as he turned away.

Regan, leaning on the turntable push-bar in front of the roundhouse, followed with his eyes as the other crossed the tracks in the direction of the town, then he spat profoundly again.

"Queerest looking specimen that ever blew into the mountains, and we've had some before that were in a whole class by themselves at that," he remarked, screwing up his eyebrows. "Makes you think of a blasted gorilla the way he's laid out, what? Well, we'll give him a try anyway," and, with a final glance in the direction of the retreating figure, the master mechanic went into the roundhouse for his morning inspection of the big moguls on the pits.

It took the division and Big Cloud some time to size up the new man, and then just about when they thought they had they found they hadn't.

Marley, if he was nothing else, was a contradictory specimen.

Mrs. Coogan said it was like the good Lord was kind of paying her special attention, kind of giving her another son—"so quiet an' accommodatin' an' handy to have around. A good bhoy was Marley—a foine lad." One hand would rest on her hip, and the other would smooth the thin white hair over her ear with quick, nervous, little pats as she talked, and the gray Irish eyes, a little dim now, would light up happily. "Yes, ut's more than I deserve; but I always knew the Lord wud provide. 'Tain't so easy to move the tubs around as it uster be. I guess I knew it, but I wasn't willin' to admit it till I had somebody to do it for me. Sivinty-wan I was last birthday. 'Tain't old for a man, but a woman—indade he's a foine lad, an' 'tis myself that ses ut."

Down at headquarters Mrs. Coogan's praise went a long way, and after Carleton and Regan and the others in the office got accustomed to seeing him around they came to accept him in a passive, indifferent sort of a way. He was a curious case, if you like, but inoffensive—they let it go at that.

The men had their view-point. Marley didn't talk much, didn't draw out the way a new hand was expected to in order to establish his footing with the fraternity. Least of all did he make any overtures tending to anything like an intimate relationship with any of his new associates. Marley was never one of the group behind the storekeeper's office that had stolen out from the shops for a drag at their pipes and a breath of air; never on the platform to exchange a word of banter with the crews of the incoming trains; never amongst the wipers and hostlers in the roundhouse who lounged in idle moments in the lee of a ten-wheeler with an eye out across the yards against the possible intrusion of Regan or some other embodiment of authority. He was civil enough and quick enough to answer when he was spoken to, but his words were few—no more than a simple negative or affirmative if he could help it. And when he himself was in question there was not even that—Marley became dumb.

All this did not help him any — he wasn't what you'd call exactly popular! So, if he had little to say for himself, the men had plenty, and the general opinion was that he was a surly brute that by no possible chance was any credit to the Hill Division and by no manner of means an acquisition to Big Cloud.

A few, very few, took a more charitable view, basing it on the shy, slow flutter of Marley's eyelids — they charged it up to an acute sensitiveness of his grotesque and abnormal appearance. That isn't the way they put it, though.

"Looks like hell, an' he knows it," said they judicially. "Let the beggar alone."

It was good advice, whether their analysis was or wasn't — Pete Boileau, the baggage master, can vouch for that. As the time-worn saying has it, it came like a bolt from the blue, and — but just a minute, we're overrunning our targets and that means trouble.

Things had gone along, as far as Marley was concerned, without anything very startling or out of the way happening for quite a spell, and Regan, who had stood closer to Chick Coogan than any other man on the division before the young engineer died, had begun to look on Marley with a little more interest — as a sort of *deus ex machina* for Mrs. Coogan. It seemed to afford the big-hearted master mechanic a good deal of relief. He got to talking about it to Carleton one morning about a month after Marley's advent to the Hill Division.

"No, of course, I don't know anything about him," he said. "Nobody does, I guess they don't. But he minds his own business and does what he has to do well enough, h'm? The old lady's been getting a little feeble lately — kind of wearing out, I guess she is. I was thinking Marley was worth a little more than a dollar ten a day, what?"

They were sitting in the super's office, and Carleton's glance, straying out through the window from where he sat at his desk, fastened on Marley's clumsy, ungainly figure hopping across the yard tracks from the roundhouse toward the station platform. He smiled a little and looked back at Regan.

"I guess so, Tommy—if it will do her any good. I wouldn't bank on it, though. He's a queer card. Impresses you with the feeling that there's something you ought to know about him—and don't. I've a notion, somehow, I've seen him before."

"Have you?" said Regan. "That's funny. I've thought I had myself once or twice, but I guess it's imagination more than anything else. Anyway, he seems to remember what Mrs. Coogan did for him. I dunno what she'd do even now without the board money, little as it is, to help out. There's no use borrowing trouble I suppose, but later on I dunno what on earth she'll do. She's prouder than a sceptered queen—and she won't be able to wash much longer, nor take a boarder either, what?"

Carleton sucked at his briar for a moment in silence.

"We've all got to face the possibility of the scrap heap some day, Tommy," he said soberly. "But it's harder for a woman, I'll admit—bitter hard. Sometimes things don't seem just right. If you want to give Marley a small raise, go ahead."

The master mechanic nodded his head.

"I think I will," he announced. "He's queer if you like, but that's his own business. Never a word out of him nor a bit of trouble since——"

Regan's words stopped as though they had been chopped off with a knife. Both men, as though actuated by a single impulse, had leaped to their feet. Behind them their chairs toppled unheeded with a crash to the floor, and for an instant, as their eyes met each other's, the color faded in their cheeks. It had come and gone like a flash—a wild, hoarse scream of rage, a brute scream, horrid, blood curdling, like the jungle howl of some maddened beast plunged in a savage, blind, all-possessing paroxysm of fury.

Themselves again in a second, the master mechanic and superintendent sprang to the window.

On the platform, up at the far end, the great form of Pete Boileau rocked and swayed like a drunken man, and clinging to him, his legs twined around the other's knees, his arms locked around the baggage-master's body just above the elbows—was Marley!

Regan and Carleton gazed spellbound. There was something uncanny, inhuman about the scene—like a rabid dog that had leaped, snarling, for the throat hold.

Suddenly, Marley's legs with a quick, wriggling slide, released their hold, his whole form appeared to shrink, grow smaller, he seemed to crouch on his knees at the other's feet, then his body jerked itself erect to its full stature with a movement swift as a loosed bowstring, his arms flew up carrying a great burden, and over his shoulders, over his head, a sprawling form hurtled through the air.

"Merciful God! He's killed him!" gasped Carleton, dashing for the door. "Come on, Tommy. *Quick!*"

Both men were down the stairs in a space of time that Regan, at least, chunky and fat, has never duplicated before or since. Carleton, hard-faced and tight-lipped, led the way, with the picture beating into his brain of Boileau's senseless form on the ground and the other above tearing like a beast at its prey. He wrenched the door of the station open, sprang out on to the platform, stopped involuntarily, and then ran forward again.

The baggage-master's form was on the ground lying in a curled-up, huddled heap, and he was senseless all right—if he wasn't something more than that. But the rest of Carleton's mental picture was wrong, dead wrong. Right beside where the fight, if fight it could be called, had taken place was a baggage truck, and over this, his head down, his two great arms wound round his face, shoulders heaving in convulsive sobs, Marley was crying like a broken-hearted child.

Take him any way you like, look at him any way you like, Marley, whatever else he was, was a contradictory specimen.

Any other man with a skull a shade less tender than Boileau's—it must have been made of boiler plate—would never have drawn another pay check. And even granting the boiler plate part of it, it was something to wonder at. He had gone through the air like a rocket, and his head had caught the full of it when he landed. How far? Carleton never said. He measured it—twice. But he never gave out the figures of Boileau's aerial flight. Pete was a big man, six feet something, and heavy for his height. The strength of four ordinary men concentrated in one pair of arms might have done it perhaps; mathematically it wouldn't figure out any other way. Carleton never said. But what's the use! The division did some tall thinking over it—and Marley cried!

They picked up Pete Boileau and carried him into the station, and the contents of a fire bucket over his head opened his eyes. But it was a good fifteen minutes before he could talk, and by that time when they got over their scare and thought of Marley the baggage truck was deserted.

"What started it!" growled Boileau, repeating Carleton's inquiry. "I'm hanged if I know. I was jossing him a little—nothing to make anybody sore. I was only funning anyhow, and laughing when I said it."

"Said what?" demanded Regan, cutting in.

"Why, nothing much. He looked so queer hopping across the tracks like a monkey on a stick that I just asked him why he didn't cut out railroading and hit up a museum for a job, and then before I knew it he let out a screech and was on me like a blasted catamount."

"Serves you right," said the master mechanic gruffly. "I guess you won't nag him again, I guess you won't. And none of the other men won't neither if they've had any notion that way."

"He's a wicked little devil," snarled Boileau. "And the strength of him"—the baggage-master shivered—"he ain't human. He'll kill somebody yet, that's what he'll do!"

Pete's summing up was a popular one—the men promptly ticketed and carded Marley as per Boileau's bill of lading. There wasn't any more doubt about him, no discussions, no anything. They knew Marley at last, and they liked him less than ever; but, also, they imbibed a very wholesome respect for the welfare of their own skins. A man with arms whose strength is the strength of derrick booms is to be approached with some degree of caution.

Marley himself said nothing. Carleton and Regan got him on the carpet and tried to get his version of the story, but for all they got out of him they might as well have saved their time.

A pathetic enough looking figure, in a way, he was, as he stood in the super's office the afternoon of the fight. The shoulders were drooping giving the arms an even longer appearance than usual, no color in his face, the violet eyes almost black, with a dead, hunted look in them. Sorrow, remorse, dread—neither Regan nor Carleton knew. They couldn't understand him—then. Marley offered no explanation, volunteered nothing. Boileau's story was right—that was all.

"You might have killed the man," said Carleton sternly, at the end of an unsatisfactory twenty minutes. "You can thank your Maker you haven't his blood on your hands — it's a miracle you haven't. Don't you know your own strength? We can't have that sort of thing around here."

Marley's face seemed to grow even whiter than before and he shivered a little, though the afternoon was dripping wet with the heat and the thermometer was sizzling well up in the nineties — he shivered but his lips were hard shut and he didn't say a word.

Carleton, for once in his life when it came to handling men, didn't seem to be altogether sure of himself. An ordinary fight was one thing, and, generally speaking, strictly the men's own business; but everything about Marley, from his arrival at Big Cloud to the sudden beastlike ferocity he had displayed that morning, put a little different complexion on the matter. A puzzled look settled on the super's face as he glanced from Marley to the master mechanic, while his fingers drummed a tattoo on the edge of his desk.

"You had some provocation, Marley," he said slowly, "I don't want you to think I'm not taking that into consideration — but not enough to work up any such deviltry as you exhibited. You'll never get on with the men here after this. They'll make things pretty hard for you. I think you'd better go — for your own sake."

There was dead silence in the super's room for a half minute, then Regan, who had been sitting with his chair tilted back and his feet up on the window-sill, dropped the chair legs to the floor and swung around.

"I put Logan up firing yesterday," said he. "There's a night job wiping in the roundhouse. What do you say about it, Carleton?"

It was Marley who answered.

"*Yes!*" he said fiercely.

Carleton jabbed at the bowl of his pipe with his forefinger and his eyebrows went up at Marley's sudden animation. Marley's eyes met his with a single quick glance, and then the eyelids fluttered down covering them. There was something in the look that caught the super, something he couldn't define. There was a plea, but there was something more—like a pledge, almost, it seemed.

"All right," he said shortly; then, nodding at Marley in dismissal: "I hope you will remember what I've said. You may go."

Marley hesitated as though about to speak and changed his mind, evidently, for he turned, walked straight to the door and out, then his boots creaked down the stairs.

"He'll be away from the men there, all except a few," said the master mechanic, as though picking up the thread of a discussion. "And as for them, I'll see there's no trouble. There's Mrs. Coogan now that——"

"Yes, Tommy"—Carleton smiled a little—"I didn't put your interest all down to love for Marley."

"What gets me," muttered Regan screwing up his eyes, as his teeth met in the plug he had dragged with some labor from his hip pocket, "what gets me is the way he went to crying afterward. Like a kid, he was. It was the blamedest thing I ever saw, what?"

"I don't think he's responsible for himself when he gets like that," replied Carleton. "That's exactly what I am afraid of. It comes over him in a flash, making a very demon of him, and then the relaxation the other way is just as uncontrollable. I don't suppose he can help it, he's made that way. It wouldn't make so much difference in an ordinary man, but with strength like his"—Carleton blew a ring of smoke ceilingwards—"you saw what he did to Boileau."

"I ain't likely to forget it," said Regan. "But if he's left alone I guess he'll be all right. Any man that's fool enough to do anything else now will do it with his eyes open, and it's his own funeral."

Those of the night crew in the roundhouse were evidently of the same mind. They received him, it is true, with little evidence of cordiality, but their aloofness was decidedly pronounced, and they looked askance at the queer figure as it dodged in and out of the shadows cast by the big mountain racers, or, at times, stood silently by one of the engine doors under the dim light of an oil lamp staring out across the black of the turntable to the twinkling switch lights in the yard. They didn't like him, but they had learned their lesson well; and, as the weeks slipped away, they practised it—he was to be left alone.

One thing they grudgingly admitted—Marley could work, and did. Clarihue, the night turner, was man enough to give another his due any time, no matter what his own personal feelings might be, and there was some talk, after a bit, between him and the master mechanic about Marley getting the next spare run firing.

Clarihue even went so far as to hint at it as a possibility to Marley, and for his pains got a surprise—he wasn't used to seeing the chance of promotion turned down. Marley had shaken his head and would have none of it. He was satisfied where he was. That was all there was to that. Clarihue drew back into his shell after that. Marley could wipe till his hair was gray for all he cared.

So Marley wiped; but at Mrs. Coogan's cottage, as the summer waned, there wasn't as much washing done as there had been, and the company doctor got to dropping in too frequently to put his visits down to the old-time occasional friendly calls for an afternoon chat. And then, one day in the early fall, the washing stopped altogether, and the doctor's face was puckered and serious as he left the cottage and headed down Main Street to the station. He entered Carleton's office and, after a few words between them, the super sent for Regan.

That evening Carleton's private car was waiting on the siding when Number Two, the Eastbound Limited, Chick Coogan's old train, pulled in.

As the little yard switcher importantly coughed the super's car on to the rear Pullman, Regan, in his Sunday best, a store suit of black twill, with boiled shirt and stiff collar, came out of the station with Mrs. Coogan on his arm.

An incongruous pair they looked. The little old lady's walk was in painful contrast to the burly master mechanic's stride—her short steps had a painful, hesitating, uncertain waver to them. One hand gripped tenaciously at Regan's coat-sleeve, while the other held the faded, old-fashioned shawl close about her thin, bent shoulders. She carried her head drooped forward a little, hiding the face under the quaint poke bonnet.

A moment later Carleton, too, emerged from the station and joined them.

The station hands and the loungers eyed the trio with curiosity, and then stared in amazement as the two officials helped the old lady up the steps of the private car—Mrs. Coogan was getting the best of it, whatever it meant.

The three disappeared inside, but presently Regan and Carleton came out again, and the super dropped to the station platform. He held out his hand to the master mechanic as Frank Knowles, the conductor, lifted his finger to Burke in the cab.

"Good-by, Tommy; and good luck," he called, as the train began to move out. "Don't hurry, take all the time you need."

"All right," Regan shouted back. "Good-by."

Carleton stood for a moment watching the tail lights grow dimmer until, finally, they shot suddenly out of sight with the curve of the track, then he turned to walk back along the platform—and stopped.

Crouched back against the wall of the freight house, deep in the shadows, was Marley.

"Here you, Marley," Carleton called.

Marley, evidently believing himself to have been unobserved, started violently, and then came slowly forward.

"What are you hiding there for?" demanded the super.

"I wanted to see Mrs. Coogan off," Marley answered a little defiantly.

The tone of the other's voice did not please Carleton.

"You've a queer way of doing it then," he snapped shortly

Marley was twisting his hands, staring down the track.

"I said good-by before I came down to work,"—he spoke as though talking to himself.

"Oh!" said Carleton, and looked at Marley sharply, "I suppose you know what she went East for?"

"Yes," said Marley gruffly. That was all—just "yes." And with that he turned abruptly and started across the tracks for the roundhouse.

Carleton, taken aback, watched him in angry amazement, then the scowl that had settled on his face broke in a smile, and he shrugged his shoulders.

"Guess Tommy is right," he muttered, as he went on toward the office. "Marley's all in a class by himself. We've never had anything like him in the mountains before."

It was four days before Mrs. Coogan and the master mechanic came back. Days during which Marley slipped into Dutchy's lunch counter at deserted moments for his meals, and, if that were possible, drew into himself closer than ever.

The boys were curious about Mrs. Coogan, naturally; curious enough even to question Marley. He had one answer, only one. "She's sick, I guess," he said. They got nothing more out of him than that.

One thing Marley did, though, that Clarihue, while he thought nothing of it at the time, remembered well enough afterwards. He asked the turner to give him a sheet of railroad paper and a manila, and in his spare moments the night before Mrs. Coogan came back he labored, bent over the little desk where the engine crews signed on and off, scratching painstakingly with a pen. Clarihue caught a glimpse of the sheet in passing before Marley hastily covered it up—just a glimpse, not enough to read a single word, just enough to marvel a little at the wiper's hand. Marley was a pretty good penman.

Marley, of course, being on night duty slept daytimes, but the afternoon Regan brought Mrs. Coogan back to the cottage he must have heard them coming, for he was standing in the little sitting-room when they came in.

Mrs. Coogan kind of hesitated on the threshold, then she called out quickly in a faltering way:

"Marley, Marley, is that you?"

Marley was twisting his hands nervously. His eyes shot a rapid glance from the old lady to the master mechanic, and then the eyelids fluttered down.

"Sure," he said, "it's me."

She stumbled toward him and burst into tears, crying as though her heart would break.

"Marley, Marley," she sobbed, "don't lave them do ut. Don't lave them do ut, there's a good bhoy, Marley."

Marley never moved, just licked his lips with his tongue and his face grew whiter. Queer, the way he acted? Well, perhaps. Never a move to catch the frail, tottering figure, never a word to soothe the pitiful grief. He stood like a man listening as a judge pronounces his doom. Oh, yes, queer, if you like. Marley, whatever else he was, was a contradictory specimen.

It was Regan who caught the old lady in his arms, and led her gently into her bedroom off the parlor.

"You mustn't give way like that, Mrs. Coogan," he said kindly. "Just lie down for a. spell and you'll feel better. I'll ask Mrs. Dahleen, next door, to come in."

It took the master mechanic several minutes to quiet her and persuade her to do as he asked, but when he came out again Marley was still standing, exactly as before, in the centre of the room. With a black scowl on his face, Regan motioned the other outside, and, once on the street, he laid the wiper low. Hard tongued was Regan when his temper was aroused and he did not choose his words.

"What d'ye mean by treating her like that, you scrapings from the junk heap, you!" he exploded. "You know well enough what she went away for, and if you've any brains in that ugly head of yours you know well enough what she's come back to, without any printed instructions to help you out. What are you playing at, eh? What do you mean? You're not fit to associate with a dog! And she the woman that spent about her all to save your miserable carcass, you — you——"

"You'd better stop!" — the words came like the warning hiss of a serpent before it strikes. Marley's face was livid, and his great gnarled hands were creeping slowly upward above his waist line.

With a startled oath, Regan leaped quickly back: and then, separated by a yard, the men stood eying each other in silence.

It was gone in a flash as it had come, for Marley, with a shudder, dropped his hands limply to his sides, and the color crept slowly back into his cheeks.

"There is no chance for her?" — no trace of the passionate outburst of an instant before remained. The question came low, hesitating — more like an assertion combined with a wistful appeal for contradiction.

It took Regan longer to recover himself, and it was a minute before he answered. Then he shook his head.

"She'll be stone blind in a month," he said gruffly.

Marley's eyes came up to the master mechanic's—and dropped instantly with their habitual little flutter.

"Ain't no doubt, no chance of a mistake?" he ventured.

Again Regan shook his head.

"Not a chance. The best man we could find East made the examination. We're arranging to get her into an institute—a home for the blind somewhere."

"I thought you would"—Marley's voice was monotonous. "That's what she was talking about, wasn't it?"

"Yes," said Regan.

Marley wagged his head with a judicial air.

"That'll kill her," he remarked, as though stating a self-evident, but commonplace, fact. "That'll kill her."

"I'm afraid it will," the master mechanic admitted gravely. "But there's nothing else to do. It's impossible for her to stay here. She's got to have some one to look after her, and she has no money. God knows I wish we could, but we can't see any other way than put her in some place like that."

"I thought you would if it turned out bad," said Marley again, in dead tones. "I figured it out that way when you were gone." His hands were traveling in an aimless fashion in and out of his pockets. Suddenly he half pulled out an envelope, started, hastily shoved it back, and looked at Regan. "I—I got a letter to post," he muttered.

"Well, supposing you have," said Regan a little savagely—Regan wasn't interested in letters just then,—"supposing you have, you needn't——"

But Marley was well across the street.

The master mechanic gasped angrily, choked—and went into Mrs. Dahleen's cottage on his errand. It was wasted breath to talk to Marley anyhow.

It didn't take long for the news to spread around Big Cloud, and for three days they talked about Mrs. Coogan pretty constantly—after that they talked about Marley.

The Westbound Limited schedules Big Cloud for 2:05 in the afternoon, and on the third day after Mrs. Coogan's return Marley came down the street about half-past one, and crossed the tracks to the shops. Regan was in the fitting-shop when Marley walked in.

"I'd like to speak to you," said Marley, going straight up to the master mechanic.

"Well?" grunted Regan, none too cordially

"I'd like you to come over to Mr. Carleton's office with me."

There was something in Marley's voice, feverish, impelling, something in his face, that stopped the impatient question that sprang to Regan's lips. He looked at the ungainly, grotesque figure of the wiper for an instant curiously, then without a word led the way out of the shops.

They traversed the yard in silence, climbed the stairs in the station, and entered the super's room. Marley closed the door and stood with his back against it.

Carleton, at his desk, looked from one to the other in surprise.

"Hello," said he. "What's up?"

The master mechanic jerked his thumb at Marley, and appropriated a chair.

"He wanted me to come over. I don't know what for."

Carleton turned inquiringly to the wiper.

"What is it?" he demanded.

Marley walked slowly across the room until he reached the super's desk. His face was drawn, and he wet his lips with the tip of his tongue.

"It's about Mrs. Coogan," he said jerkily. "Five thousand would be enough, wouldn't it?"

Carleton stared at the man as though he were mad, and Regan hitched his chair suddenly forward.

"Will you swear to give it to her if I get it for you?"—Marley's hand, clenched, was on the desk, and he leaned his body far forward toward the super. There was no flutter of the eyelids now, and his eyes stared into Carleton's without a flicker. "*Swear it!*" he cried fiercely.

Carleton drew back involuntarily.

"Marley," he said soothingly, "you're not yourself, you——"

"No, I'm not mad." Marley broke in passionately. "I know what I'm talking about. I know she'd die in one of them charity places. It's up to me. She treated me white—the only soul on God's earth that ever did. And maybe, maybe too, it'll help square accounts. You'll play fair and swear she gets the money, won't you?"

"I don't understand," said Carleton slowly; "but I'll swear to give her anything you have to give."

Marley nodded quickly.

"That's all I want," he said. "There ain't much to understand." He fumbled in his pocket and brought out a newspaper clipping, a column long, which he laid on the desk. "I guess you'll get it all there."

The heavy "set" of the heading leaped up at Carleton. "$5,000 REWARD." Below, halfway down the column, was the reproduction of a photograph—Marley's.

Regan was up from his chair, bending over the super's shoulder.

"I thought I'd seen you somewhere before"—Carleton's voice sounded strained and hollow in his own ears. "It must have been the picture. I remember now. You—you killed a man in Denver a year ago."

"It's all there," said Marley, licking his lips again. "I never saw him before. I killed him like I almost killed Boileau this summer. I didn't know till afterward that he was rich, not until the family hung out that reward."

Carleton did not speak. Regan reached viciously for his plug. Marley stirred uneasily, and drew the back of his hand across his forehead. It came away soggy wet. In the silence the chime of the Limited's whistle floated in through the open window, then, presently, the roar of the train and the grinding shriek of the brake-shoes.

"My God," said Carleton in a whisper, "you want me to give you up and get the reward—for her!"

A queer smile flickered across Marley's face. Heavy steps came running up the stairs. There was a smart rap upon the door and a man stepped quickly inside. For a second his eyes swept the little group. Then he whirled like a flash, and the blue-black muzzle of a revolver held a bead on Marley's heart.

"Ah, Shorty," he cried grimly, "we've got you at last, eh? Put out your hands!"

Without protest, with the same queer smile on his face, Marley obeyed. There was a little click of steel, and he dropped his locked wrists before him.

"You're Mr. Carleton, aren't you?" the newcomer had swung to the desk.

"Yes," said Carleton numbly.

"I'm Hepburn of the Denver police," went on the officer. "We appreciate this, Mr. Carleton. Shorty here has been badly wanted for a long time. We got your letter yesterday."

Hepburn paused to reach into his pocket, and in the pause Carleton's eyes met Marley's—and he understood. Marley had written the letter himself and signed his, Carleton's, name. And, too, it was clear enough now, the telegram he had puzzled over the previous afternoon. It was lying before him on his desk. His eyes dropped to it. "Will be on hand on arrival of Limited, (signed) Denver."

"We can't give you any receipt for him as you requested," continued Hepburn, drawing a paper out of his pocket; "but here's an acknowledgment that his capture is due to information furnished by you. I guess that will answer the purpose. You won't have any trouble getting the reward." He handed the paper to Carleton.

The super took it mechanically, and started as it crackled in his fingers.

"Now," said Hepburn briskly, "I don't want to appear abrupt, but there's a local East at two-twenty. We'll move along, Shorty. Good-by, Mr. Carleton. Next time you're in Denver look us up." He took Marley's arm and moved toward the door.

"Don't—tell her, Mr. Carleton"—there was a catch in Marley's voice, and the words came low.

Carleton did not answer. He was staring at the paper in his hand—Marley's price.

Regan had turned his back, with a hasty movement of his fist to his eyes.

"Don't tell her"—the plea came again from the doorway.

Carleton tried to speak and his voice broke, then he cleared his throat.

"She will never know, Marley," he said huskily.

X
THE MAN WHO DIDN'T COUNT

He was a little gray-haired hostler, wiper, sweeper, assistant night man in the roundhouse at Big Cloud, anything you like, and this is the story he told me one night, leaning against the blackened jamb of one of the big doors, wiping his hands occasionally upon a hunk of greasy waste.

They were a rough lot out in the mountains in the days when the Hill Division was shaking her steel into something like a permanent right of way — a pretty rough lot. The railroaders because they had to be; the rest because they were just that way naturally. Miners and Indians made up the citizenship mostly, and there's no worse mixture. They've got the redskins corralled on reserves now; but they hadn't then, and it didn't take more than one bad word and one drop of bad whisky to set things in lively motion.

There's a few highfaluting poems, and some other things, about the noble red man that works you up so when you read them that you get to wishing the Almighty had seen fit to let you be a red man, too. Well, that's all right in its way because, after you've rubbed elbows with some of the real thing, you realize that the world owes the poets a living just as much as it does anybody else, and that what they say has to sound good; so you just come to keep the cautionary signals up by instinct, and let it go at that.

But, to give the poets their due, there's one thing they never trip up on, and that's the Indian's compound efficiency for smell. The Indian can smell. When he sticks out his chest, faces southeast, and begins to draw in the God-given mountain air, you're free to bet that the distilleries down Kentucky way are doing enough business to make regular dividend checks a sure thing. That's generally good whisky. Bad whisky, in smell and otherwise, carries farther—and it's only fifteen miles from here to Coyote Bend!

Coyote Bend wasn't even a pin prick on the engineers' blue prints when they mapped out the right of way, and there wasn't any such place w r hen the steel was all spiked down until the day some wandering prospector staked out a bunch of claims—and the news spread.

Gold in the Rockies? No; there's never been much of it *found*, but there's an all-fired big superstition that the mother lode of the whole country is tucked away here somewhere. That's why, in two days, the wilderness and a gurgling stream that trickled peacefully down through a high-walled canon became Coyote Bend; and that's why the local freight began to make regular stops to dump off supplies alongside the track. There was no station, of course, no agent, no nothing; the stuff was just dumped, that's all. The consignees picked out their goods if they could read, or guessed at it if they couldn't.

Maybe I ought to have told you this before; anyway, I'll stick it in now. There are three men that figure in this story, though one of them doesn't count for much. He was a young chap named Charlie Lee. A graduate of an Eastern college he was, and all he had to his name was his diploma and the clothes he stood in when he hit the West. He struck the super for a job, and he got it—braking on the local freight. Hell for a man like him, eh? Well, it was, in more ways than one! Anyway, from that day to this it was the best job he ever held down long enough to draw a second month's pay check.

The other two were Matt Perley and Faro Clancy—"Breed" Clancy, they called him behind his back.

Perley was a very good sort, pretty straight, pretty clean, measuring by the standards out here in those days; a little bit of a sawed-off, blond-haired, blue-eyed man, full of grit inside, and an out-and-out railroad man—only a freight conductor, conductor on the local, but he knew his business; he'd have gone up, 'way up, in time.

Clancy was a hellion, there's no other name for him, and even that doesn't express it—no one word could. Indian one way, Irish the other. He looked mostly Indian; the Irish came out in the brogue. Black, swarthy, small eyes like needle points, coarse dry hair that straggled down over his eyebrows, a hulking bony frame with the strength of a wrecking crane—that's Clancy, Breed Clancy.

Oh, yes, he was slick, slick as they're made—with his hands. Faro, stud poker, dice, anything—it was his business; that, and running booze joints. Mining camps and brand-new boom towns were Clancy's meat mostly—after Perley drove him out of Big Cloud.

Don't ask me. I don't know what there was between them. That was before my time. A woman probably—a woman's generally blamed anyhow. Anyway, one night Perley got the drop on Breed and marched him down the street in front of his pistol and out of the town. After that, Clancy kept away from Big Cloud. As I say, that part was before my time. I only know there was bad blood between them; wicked bad blood on one side, as you'll see. Clancy disappeared from Big Cloud, and the two didn't foul each other again until Coyote Bend started.

Breed Clancy hit the Bend with the first inrush of the miners, and before any of them had time to much more than get a pick into the ground he was busy knocking together a bit of a shack he called a hotel, and was ordering the furnishings—liquid furnishings, you understand—from Big Cloud.

There were three barrels of it, the hardest kind of fire water that ever went into the mountains waybilled to Clancy at Coyote Bend by the local, on the first trip that Charlie Lee ever made with Matt Perley. I'm getting back to Lee now, you see.

Well, it was about noon when they whistled for the Bend that day, and Lee, riding the brake wheels on the front end, could see about a dozen "blankets" squatting alongside the right of way about where the train would stop. Grouped behind these were a number of stragglers from the camp, among whom was a big fellow in a red shirt you could see farther than a semaphore arm.

Now, I don't say those Indians were attracted by the gold rush to Coyote Bend. Coyote Bend, or any other place, old or new, stale or prosperous, would get its share of the redskins. Where they came from or where they went nobody knew. They'd drop in from nowhere, and, if they liked the place, they'd grunt and settle down for a spell; if they didn't like it, they'd grunt, in benediction or otherwise, and leave.

I'm not saying they smelled the whisky in that train. I'm not saying they knew Clancy was importing fire water, and they were just there to feast their eyes on the barrels and meditate on what was inside. I'm not saying anything at all about that, or what followed. There's only one man that perhaps might have explained it—I say "perhaps" because he never did; and also, because he knew Indian nature as well as any white man in the West. That was Perley.

Whether Perley even knew that Clancy was at the Bend or not, I don't know. I only know that he could have known it if he'd bothered to read the waybills; and it was likewise on the cards that he might have learned the day before, down at Big Cloud, that the whisky was going up the following morning. I don't know, and that's straight. Sometimes I think he did; sometimes I think he didn't. I don't know.

Anyway, Lee slid to the ground as the train stopped, and went back to the car that held the consignment for the Bend. As he fumbled with the door, he got a whiff of raw spirit that nearly knocked him over. And then, right behind him, rose a chorus of appreciative "ughs!"

I told you an Indian could smell whisky, but I didn't tell you why. It's his ruling passion. That's straight. I'm not judging the Indian; the taste was born in him. There are some white men just as bad. I'm not judging them, either. Some drink for the same reason the Indian does, some for others, and some — some men drink because they have to.

What was I saying? Oh, yes, Lee getting that whiff. Well, before he got the door unfastened, the man in the red shirt had pushed through the Indians and come up beside him.

"Me name's Clancy," said he. "Did yez bring up any stuff for me?"

"There's three barrels for somebody," replied Lee, and slid open the door — and the next minute he had jumped back with a yell, colliding with Clancy.

"Ugh!" ejaculated the apparition that confronted him.

"He's drunk! Majestically drunk! An' on *my* stuff!" roared Clancy; and then, turning fiercely on Lee: "Fwhat did ye let him in there for, eh? Fwhat did ye let him in for, ye mealy-faced little——"

"Let him in nothing!" retorted Lee, getting back his grip on himself. "Here, you, get out — and *quick!*"

The Indian blinked gravely, but never moved. He sat cross-legged on the floor, exactly in the middle of the car between the doors, swaying slightly backward and forward. Beside him, up-ended and broached, was one of Clancy's kegs. The car reeked with the smell of it, for of the half kegful that had gushed out what hadn't gone into the Indian had gone on to the floor.

The half-breed was raving mad. I've a notion sometimes the man wasn't human at all. He had his hand on Lee's throat when Perley came running up from the rear end.

"What's the row?" he began, and then he stopped. He was a cool devil was Perley, and he never turned a hair as he stepped between the two men. "Ah, Clancy, it's you, is it, you copper-faced renegade?"—no loud talk, no bluster, he didn't raise his voice; but his insult, the worst he could have laid his tongue to, cut like the sting of a lash.

Clancy swung around like a flash—and stared into the muzzle of the conductor's ·45. His hands were clenching and unclenching as he recognized Perley, and the cords in his neck swelled into knotty lumps.

"Ut's your worrk, this job, is ut?" he snarled. "Some day, Perley, I'll show you."

Queer, you say, he'd act like that—nothing to warrant it. Well, maybe. I don't know. I don't know what was between them before; but I do know the awful deviltry of Breed Clancy, and I know that Lee, leaning back against the car, shivered at the look that passed between the two of them.

Perley cut the half-breed short off. "Once," said he contemptuously, still quiet, not a tone raised, and his voice the more deadly for it, "once, perhaps you'll remember, I warned you to keep out of my road. Lee, how'd that Indian get in the car?"

"I don't know," said Lee.

"Well, then, throw him out," said Perley shortly, snapping his watch with his free hand. "We can't stay here all day."

This little ruction between Perley and the half-breed has taken me longer to tell it, I guess, than it did to happen. Anyway, it didn't cause the excitement you might think it would. The "blankets" were too busy drinking in the smell of that whisky to let their hungry eyes wander very far from anywhere but the open door of that car. And as for the stragglers, by the time they'd caught on to the fact that there was something on the boards besides that drunken Indian, Perley, with the same cool contempt, had slipped his gun back in his pocket and was boosting Lee into the car.

The Indian offered no opposition as Lee tackled him. He couldn't—he was beyond all that—he was so full of dead-eye it was oozing out by the pores. He just sat there, and Lee slid him to the door just as he was, still sitting, and dropped him out. He struck the ground with a thud, rebounded a foot, rolled over, grunted, and lay like a log. There was a guffaw from the camp stragglers, and a deep and envious chorus of "Ughs!" from the "blankets."

No, I'm not joking—it's a long way from a joke, as you'll see. They *were* envious. It acted like a red rag on a bull—the possibility of attaining the condition, the state of heavenly bliss, that had been reached by their red brother, do you understand?

Clancy wasn't laughing. He stood where Perley had left him, sullen and with twitching face. I don't know, I think it was Parley's sheer nerve that kept the half-breed from drawing and shooting the conductor when his back was turned. I don't know—brute beast cowed by the human mind, perhaps. No one ever knew Breed Clancy. He had his yellow streak at times, and then again the blood that was in him made him worse than a frenzied madman. Yes, I guess it was a case of "brute" all right, for there was no cowing him when the frenzy was on him.

Perley wasn't laughing, either. He was opening and shutting his watch impatiently. "Come on! Come on!" he cried at Lee. "Get those barrels out. We've got to cross Number Two at the Creek. It'll be the carpet for ours if we hold her up."

Lee grabbed the broached cask and edged it toward the doorway. The contents slopped and sloshed inside as he moved it, and occasionally a little of the stuff would spill out through the bunghole. Then, somehow, just as he got it to the door, his hold slipped, out it went, bounded on the edge of the ties, and then went down the embankment right into the hands of those squatting "blankets." They didn't squat long; I don't need to tell you that. They were on it in a mob, and they got the taste—they'd had the smell—and the fill was to come presently.

Clancy was cursing in streams; and no fouler-mouthed man than Clancy ever lived. He tried once to get the Indians off the barrel, and the stragglers backed him up half-heartedly. You might as well have tried to move that mogul on the pit there behind you. He didn't try but once, then he fell back on cursing again, and Parley was the target for most of it.

Perley? He never answered him, but his face grew harder and harder—and his gun was in his hand again. "Throw out those other two barrels!" he snapped at Lee.

"The redskins will get every last drop if I do," objected Lee, hesitating.

"Owner's risk. We've no station here. Throw 'em out!" repeated Perley, grimmer than before, only this time loud enough for Clancy to hear him.

"Ye do," roared the half-breed, "ye do, an' I'll worse than murdher ye one of these——"

"Throw 'em out!" said Perley quietly, waving the go-ahead signal to the engine crew.

And out they went—down the embankment after the first.

Lee jumped to the ground and banged the door shut, just as the drawbars began to snap tight along the train and the local jolted into motion. He waited beside Perley to swing the caboose as it came up. And while he waited he watched and grinned.

Funny? I don't know; it depends on the way you look at it, depends on what you call fun. Lee thought it was funny — then. The air was full of curses, Indian yells, shouts, oaths; and there was one jumbled mess of arms, and legs, and barrels. The Indians were after their *fill*, and this time Clancy and the stragglers were in the game for keeps.

Up ahead the engine crew hung grinning out of the gangway. Behind, the other brakeman was occupying a reserved seat on the top of the caboose. A quarter of a mile away over by the camp, men, attracted by the shouting, were beginning to run toward the track. Inconsistent kind of a mix-up, eh? — Indians, miners, whisky barrels, and railroaders. I don't know; call it funny if you like, though perhaps you can size it up better when I'm through.

By this time the caboose was up to where Perley and Lee were standing. Perley motioned Lee aboard, and then swung on himself.

Just as he did so, Clancy's red shirt loomed up out of the mêlée, his arm lifted, and over the clack of the car trucks pounding the steel came the tinkle of breaking glass from the shattered pane in the door — the bullet had passed between the heads of the two men on the platform, missing them by a hair's breadth. Another shot followed the first, another and another, dangerously close; splintering the woodwork around them; and then Perley fired. The half-breed spun round like a top, clapped his hand to his face and pitched over.

Then the curve of the track shut out the scene, but for five minutes after they were out of sight they still got the whoops of the redskins, the shouts and curses of the miners, and the crackle of guns like the quick fire of a Catling. You see it came to that before it was through, and there was some blood spilled—a lot of it—and, not counting Clancy's, it wasn't all "blanket" blood, either.

Clancy? I'm coming to him. No, he wasn't killed—if he had been I'd never be telling you this story. It was two or three days before Lee and Perley got the details of what happened. The redskins fought like fiends after the miners began to fire on them and had killed one or two, and, though they were finally subdued, the casualties, as I've said, weren't all on their side by a hanged sight.

But I was talking about Clancy. Well, that bullet of Perley's caught him on the cheek bone, glanced in, plowed through his left eye, and landed up somewhere against the cartilage of his nose—a bullet will make queer tracks sometimes, worse than surveyors by a heap. They got him down to Big Cloud to a doctor's, and before he was half cured he disappeared. They had a sort of makeshift hospital here in those days, and when I say "disappeared" I mean they found his bed empty one morning, that was all.

I told you I didn't know whether Perley had any hand in putting that Indian in the car, or the other redskins at the Bend. I don't. I told you I didn't know what was between him and the half-breed before all this happened. I don't. Perley never said. But day after day as he and Lee pounded up and down on the local through the mountains, he began to grow silent and moody.

Lee, young Lee then, was the only one that could get anywhere near the inside of his vest. He took to Lee, and Lee liked him; but even Lee had his limits when it came to confidences. There was lots Perley never opened his lips about. No, I don't know as it makes much difference now.

Lee was the first of the two to hear that Faro Clancy was "loose." "It looks to me like a bad business," he said, after telling Perley the news.

Perley's eyes just narrowed a little. "It looks more like a bad shot, a rotten bad shot," he answered evenly.

"That, if you like," returned Lee; "but there'll be more to follow."

"One would think you *knew* Clancy," said Perley, cool as ever.

Lee was anxious. Call it presentiment or what you like, from that moment the thing was on his nerves. Perley had been pretty good to him; had made things a heap easier for the young fellow, green and raw as he was, in a hundred different ways. Things like that mean something.

"Look here, Perley," said he, "I've heard some talk, and I know there's something behind all this between you and that devil. I'm not asking for confidences——"

Perley cut him short, and caught him almost angrily by the shoulder. "Don't meddle!" he snapped. "Let it drop. *You* don't count in this, whatever happens. Your being at the Bend that day was an accident. What's between me and Clancy concerns ourselves. You don't count. Unless you're looking for another run besides the local, just remember that and don't meddle."

That was all. Lee never mentioned it to Perley again. Perley was right, wasn't he? I told you there were three men in this story, but that one of them didn't count. No, Lee didn't count. Why should he? What did he have to do with it? Perley was right, I leave it to you.

You've been over the division, and you know the Devil's Slide just west of the Gap from here. You know the grade—the worst in the mountains. The trains crawl up at the pace a man could walk, because they can't go any faster; and they crawl down just as slowly, because they don't dare do anything else.

I've seen the passengers get off the observation and walk—so have you. Done it yourself probably? I thought so. Extra engine on the rear end to push or hold back, and one in the middle if the train's heavy, to keep it from breaking apart—lessens the drawbar pull, you know. They're tunneling now to do away with that particular grade, but that's nothing to do with this story, nor, for that matter, with the night, some six weeks after that business at the Bend, when the local, eastbound, was climbing the Devil's Slide.

It was a dirty night outside the caboose. A storm had been racketing through the mountains all afternoon, and by the time it got dark it was a howling gale, raining hard enough to float the ties.

Lee's place was on the front end, going up that bit of track, but he wasn't well that night, and the other brakeman was doing his snatch. Touch of mountain fever, or something, nothing serious; just enough to make him shiver and boil alternately over the little stove in the caboose, sitting with his back to the door. Up above him in the cupola, holding down the swivel chair where he could watch the train—that is, see his engine fling up the sparks, for that's about all he could see, I guess—was Perley.

The car was swinging like a hammock with the heave and strain of the big pusher coupled right behind it—it acts queer, that does. Every time I've felt it I've always thought of a cat and a mouse. It's like the engine had the caboose by the scruff and was trying to shake the life out of it.

You've felt it a little if you've ever been in the rear Pullman going up—the difference is that a caboose hasn't any springs to speak of, you understand? Racket enough to raise the dead. You couldn't hear yourself think. Not so much from the noise of the train or the storm, but from the booming roar of the trailer's exhaust—like she was trying to cough her boiler tubes out every time the valves slid.

Now, there's just one more thing I want you to get. The engine crew of a pusher naturally can't see any track, roadbed, or anything of that kind, and it isn't their business to, either. All they watch is the leader and the intermediate, if there is one. Their headlight plays along over a few cars if it's high enough, or loses itself on the top of the door or the roof of the caboose if it isn't, understand?

Lee didn't hear anything. He was sitting bent over with his head between his hands, and it was the current of air from the opening door that made him twist around and look up, thinking it had blown open. I don't know as you'd call him a coward; maybe yes, maybe no; anyway, he was a white-faced, terrified man that next instant, as he started up from his chair. He never got to his feet. Instead, he shut up like a jackknife, and went down to the floor with a blow over the head from a revolver butt that knocked him senseless.

It all happened in a second, but in that second Lee got it with more vividness than a thousand hours would have given him—the great, hulking figure, the water trickling to the floor in little pools from the dripping clothes, the sickly pallor of the face, the thin new skin of the livid scar across the cheek, the sightless eye—Clancy.

Lee couldn't have lain unconscious more than twenty minutes, perhaps it was only fifteen, for it takes about forty minutes to climb the four miles of the Slide, you see. Call it twenty, that allows for what happened before and what happened after. When he came to his senses the light in the bracket lamp was out; blown out by the draft, for the door was open. A stray beam or two from the pusher's headlight filled the caboose with an uncertain, wavering light—from the jolt and swing, you know, though Lee thought at first it was his head.

He tried to get up, but he couldn't move. He was bound hand and foot, laid out on the flat of his back—helpless. For a minute he was too dazed to understand, then he remembered—Clancy. He stared up into the cupola above him. The swivel chair was empty—Perley had gone!

The car trucks were beating a steady *clack, clack-clack*, as they pounded the fishplates; from behind came the full, deep-chested thunder of the trailer's exhaust; around, the hundred noises of the creaking, groaning, swaying car; without, the patter of rain, the wail of the wind. But over it all, low though it was, came a sound that sent a chill to Lee's heart.

It was like a breathless moan, do you understand? That was the inhuman part of it; it was breathless—there was no break—a sort of sobbing monotone. It came from behind him. Lee shivered as he listened, and then his heart began to pound as though it would burst. He was afraid—*afraid*. Premonition, perhaps; I don't know. He rolled himself over on his side, and he saw——

How can I tell it! A figure was crouched against the side of the car in a half-sitting posture, the face was red—red with the blood that was flowing from the forehead. Lee shrieked aloud in terror. "Perley! Perley!" Then he grew sick with the horror that was on him. Worse than murder the half-breed had threatened—and he had kept his word. Perley had been scalped!

Lee's cry must have reached the poor wretch's consciousness, for he staggered to his feet, sweeping his eyes clear with both hands. Lee, sick to the depths of his soul, the sweat breaking out in great, cold drops upon his forehead, fought like a maniac with his bonds.

Perley never spoke, never paid any attention to Lee—he was past all that—but his brain, at least, was still capable of coherent impression. It must have been—to account for what he did. Right in front of him, as he hung there tottering and swaying, was a broken bit of mirror tacked up on the side of the car. He was staring into it.

His moaning stopped. The shock of his own awful horror must have revolted, shaken his very being. His hand groped weakly, subconsciously perhaps, for his pocket—his revolver—the end.

Again Lee shrieked as he struggled to free himself, and then, as Perley fired, he burst out into a peal of wild, discordant laughter. His mind was giving way. He began to gibber like a madman—that's the way they found him—with Perley's body pitched full across his chest.

Don't ask me. I told you Perley was a little, undersized, sawed-off man. I don't know, do I? The half-breed, physically, could have handled him like a baby, once he caught him unawares. That's all I know.

They buried Perley down at Big Cloud; and they buried Clancy where the posse dropped him, drilled full of holes. That's the story.

Lee? Charlie Lee? Why, he doesn't count, does he? He had nothing to do with it. Well, if you're interested in him I'll tell you. His college diploma never did him any good. Once he got ^better and out of the hospital, he took to drinking periodically—*hard*. Between times straight as a string, you understand, for six weeks say, then off again. That was fifteen years ago, and he's done it ever since. The doctors said that blow on the head unsettled him, skull splinter, or something like that; but medicine's not an exact science. The doctors were wrong. The trouble was deeper than the skull—it was in his soul. Lee drank to save himself from the madhouse—I told you, didn't I, that some men drink because they have to?

Carleton, the super, and the men before Carleton, understood what the doctors didn't, so Lee's working for the railroad yet. Not braking—he's not fit for that, but he keeps the job they gave him—and it's kept for him—when he gets back after his spells. I—there's the foreman shouting for me. Sorry, but I'll have to go.

If you're going out on Number One she's just coming down the gorge now. Good night, sir."

I lost him in the shadows of the big mogul on the pit behind me. Then I turned and walked slowly out of the roundhouse, over the turntable, and across the tracks to the station platform. Number One's mellow chime floated down from the gorge, then the flare of the electric headlight, and the rumble of the train. And in quick, fierce tempo, the beating, drumming trucks caught up the name I had heard the foreman shout, and rang it over and over again in my ears:

"Oh-you-Lee! Charlie-Lee! Lee! Charlie-Lee-Lee!"

XI
"WHERE'S HAGGERTY?"

The Hill Division was proud enough over it, of course, for Carleton was its old chief; but, none the less, it read General Order Number 38 with dismay and misgiving.

"T. J. Hale," the G. O. ran, "is hereby appointed Superintendent of the Hill Division, with headquarters at Big Cloud, vice H. B. Carleton promoted to General Manager of the System."

"Now who in the double-blanked, blankety-blanked blazes is Hale?" demanded the roundhouse and the engine crews.

"Carleton was all to the good, h'm? — what!" growled the dispatchers.

The train crews swung their lanterns with a defiant air, and the passenger conductors juggled their punches around their little fingers, smiling a superior smile to themselves. Hale might be a good man, perhaps he was, but Carleton was — "Royal" Carleton. "I guess he'll get along all right with us, *but* he don't want to get fresh, that's all. Where'd he come from, h'm?"

That question, at first, no one seemed able to answer. The general impression was that the Transcontinental had got him from some Eastern road. Certainly he was a new man, bran new, to the System.

And then the renown of one Haggerty, who was braking on a passenger local, became great, and, in consequence, the displeasure of the Division increased.

Said Haggerty: "When I was on the Penn five years back, this fellow Hale was assistant super. I knew him well. You wanter look out for him, you can take my little word for that. He's a holy terror, an' that's a fact. Got any chewin'?"

Haggerty got his chewing, being an egregious liar; and Hale got a damaged reputation for the same reason.

But Haggerty got more than his chewing—and he had not long to wait. On the day that the new super was expected, Haggerty, on passenger local Number Seven, got into Big Cloud about noon, and, taking advantage of the ten-minute wait for refreshments, straddled a stool at the lunch-counter. Between bites, he fired questions at Spence the dispatcher, who was bolting his mid-day meal.

"Hale come yet?" he demanded.

"Haven't seen him," replied Spence.

"When d'ye expect him?" persisted Haggerty.

"I don't know," Spence answered.

"Oh, don't be so blasted close!" snapped Haggerty. "You ain't givin' away any weighty secret if you let out what time his special'll be along, I suppose."

"I haven't heard of any special," said Spence. "Say, Haggerty, they tell me Hale's an old friend of yours, h'm? No wonder you're anxious. I forgot about that. As soon as I get word about him, I'll wire up the line to you so's you can jump your train, come back on a hand-car, and be here on the platform to meet him."

"You go to blazes!" retorted Haggerty, and scowled across the counter at an inoffensive looking little fellow who had taken the liberty of smiling at the dispatcher's words.

At Haggerty's look, the smile disappeared in a cup of coffee raised hastily to the lips. "Huh!" snorted Haggerty, by way of driving home to the other the audacity and temerity of his act, and likewise the inadvisability of repeating it. Haggerty was galled. Once before that morning he had been obliged to relegate this insignificant, squint, eye-glassed individual, who had persisted in riding on the platform, to a proper sense of submission. And the method employed had been no more delicate a one than that of jerking the man bodily into the car by the collar of his coat. "Huh!" he repeated, with rising inflexion.

"No, Haggerty," went on Spence pleasantly, "don't you worry. I won't fail you. When the super steps off the train, and the first words he says is, 'Where's Haggerty?' and you're not here to respond in kind I can plainly see there'll be doings. Oh, no, don't you fret, I'll not throw you down on anything like that—'twouldn't be wise for us, that's got to live with him, to rile him up at the outset! No, it certainly wouldn't, what?"

"You go bite on a brake-shoe, you're too sharp to be munchin' doughnuts," snarled Haggerty. And, swinging himself from his seat, he went back to his train.

An hour later when he reached Elk River, the end of his run, he found a telegram waiting for him from Spence. He sucked in his under lip as he read it.

"You sly joker," wired the dispatcher, "why didn't you tell us that your friend came up with you on Number Seven?"

Haggerty pushed his cap to the back of his head, and swore softly under his breath. He began to go over in his mind the passengers that had been aboard the train when they ran into Big Cloud. No one individual seemed to stand out carded and waybilled as the new super.

Then an idea struck Haggerty, and he climbed into the rear coach where Berkely, his conductor, was making up his report sheets.

"Say, Jim," said Haggerty, "was there any passes into Big Cloud this mornin'?"

Berkely looked up suspiciously. "You mind your own business, an' you'll get along better!" he snapped.

"Oh, punk!" returned Haggerty. "My *count's* the same as your'n, ain't it? What's the matter with you, then? Honest, Jim, I wanter know. Was there any passes?"

"No, there wasn't," grunted Berkely, cooling down a little.

"Well, then, you might have said so at first, instead of jumpin' a fellow for nothin'," said Haggerty, and went out of the car to hang meditatively over the handrail and spit reflectively at the ties.

"Now wouldn't that sting you?" he demanded of the universe in general. "Wouldn't that sting you? Who ever heard of a new super comin' on the job ridin' a local on a *ticket!* An' me askin' when he was goin' to turn up. Oh, yes, it sure would sting you! That funny boy Spence'll pass this along an'—oh, punk! I ain't sure it wouldn't have been better if I'd kept my mouth shut about knowin' Hale, but who'd ever thought he'd come up on *my* train! How was I to know, h'm?" And during all that afternoon's layup at Elk River, Haggerty pondered the matter. He continued to ponder it as they pulled out for the return trip in the evening, and he was still pondering it when they whistled for Big Cloud.

There was no moon up that night, and it was pretty dark as they ran in. Haggerty, with his lantern, was standing on the rear end. As the train slowed itself to a halt, a man came tearing down the station platform at a run.

"Where's Haggerty?" he called breathlessly. "Where's—
—"

"Here," said Haggerty promptly, leaning out over the steps and showing his light. "What d'ye want?"

"Oh, all right," said the man. "I'll be back—" and he disappeared in the shadow of the station.

"He acts like he was nutty," muttered Haggerty, and swung himself off the steps.

But, though Haggerty waited, the man did not come back, and he had not come back when the train began to roll out of the station, and Haggerty was again on the rear platform of the car. Then, just as his hand reached out to open the door, he stopped and started suddenly as though he had been stung.

A voice came out of the darkness from the other side of the track over by the roundhouse. "Where's Haggerty?" it demanded anxiously.

Then Haggerty tumbled, and his face went red with rage. He leaned far out over the rail, and, forgetful that the pantomime was lost in the darkness, shook his clinched fist in the direction from whence the voice had come.

"You go to he-ee-ll-lll!" he bawled, the exclamation shaken into syllables by reason of the car wheels jolting over the siding switches at that precise moment. And then, his senses being very acute, from where the light shone in the dispatcher's window he thought he heard, above the momentarily increasing rattle of the train, a laugh—a laugh that produced anything but a quieting effect on his already outraged sensibilities.

Now Haggerty was not the nature of those who can pass lightly over a joke at their own expense, especially if that joke be too prolonged and carries with it a hint of underlying venom. Therefore, as the "one on Haggerty" spread over the division, and scarcely an hour of the day passed that the cry "Where's Haggerty?" did not reach his ears, he began to sulk and treasure up his injury. The division was rubbing it in pretty hard. But the curious part of it all was that his bitterness was not directed against himself who was the direct cause of his discomfiture, nor against Spence who was the indirect cause, but against Hale, who was no cause at all.

Just once had Haggerty seen the superintendent. Hale was pointed out to him on the platform at Big Cloud, and Haggerty had ducked hastily back inside his train. Hale was the inoffensive little fellow he had treated with such scant courtesy at the lunch-counter, the insignificant, squint-eye-glassed individual he had hauled from the car platform by the coat collar! When Haggerty's mingled feelings of perturbation and amazement permitted him any speech at all, it was rather incoherent.

"*That*—the runt!" he gasped, and subsided into an empty seat.

And in this inelegant, but pithy, summing up of the capacity and dimensions of the new official the division was with him to the last section hand. Him — a railroad man! The Hill Division remembered "Royal" Carleton and was ashamed, and it rankled for the shame that it considered had been put upon it. Out of it all, Haggerty was the only thing of saving grace! So upon Haggerty they loosened, behind the humor, some of their bitterness. Haggerty became the safety valve of the division.

A month had gone by and Hale had lived well up to what his appearance had led them to expect. He might have been an automaton for all the signs of life that emanated from his office. Just routine, the routine business, routine, that was all. The disquiet and unrest that brooded over the division became contempt — the kind of contempt that made the car-tinks put on airs, and in their heart of hearts figure themselves better railroad men than he who sat over them in supreme authority.

Even Haggerty no longer ducked out of sight when circumstances required that he should breathe the same air as his superior. Haggerty had acquired a swagger; also, he now voiced his opinion, his cordially poor opinion, of Mr. Hale without restraint and with no check upon his tongue.

And then Haggerty got a shock. It was imparted by Spence.

"Got it from Hale's clerk last night," said the dispatcher. "He's going to run an inspection special over the division, and he's picked out the fag end of all things for the crew. He picked you first, Haggerty."

"Aw, forget it!" growled Haggerty, with a scowl.

"I think there's something behind it, though," Spence went on, his voice modulated confidentially. "Between you and me, Haggerty, the inspection trip is a bluff."

Haggerty pricked up his ears. "How's that?" he demanded.

"Well," said Spence serenely, backing to a safe distance, "I think he's hurt at the way you've cut him since he's been here. He's pining for your company, and——"

Haggerty sprang to his feet from the baggage truck on which he had been seated, and shook his fist frantically at the fast retreating figure. He was still gesticulating fiercely and muttering savagely to himself when the window in the dispatcher's room overhead opened softly, and Spence stuck out his head.

"Hey, there, Haggerty," he called, "quit practising that deaf and dumb alphabet. You haven't got any time to waste. You want to run along and get the missus to press out a pair of panties, and iron a boiled shirt for you. You'll get your orders in the morning."

"Come down for one minute," choked Haggerty, his rage fanned to a white heat by the knowledge of his own impotence, for Spence, as he well knew, was safely entrenched behind locked doors. "Just one minute, an' I'll make your face look like it had never been born. I will that!"

"Haggerty," said Spence in an injured tone, as the window closed, "you are disgruntled."

But Haggerty was to be still more disgruntled, for the next morning, true to Spence's words, he found himself assigned to Inspection Special Number Eighty-nine. Haggerty was not happy; but he boarded the forward car, as they pulled out for the mountains with the mental resolution that he would keep out of the super's way.

Resolutions, however, like many other things, are sometimes rudely upset in the face of conditions that are not taken into account in the reckoning. They had been running at a forty-mile clip, and were about into the yard at Coyote Bend, when Haggerty nearly went to the floor as the "air" came on with a sudden rush, and the train came jerking to a halt like a bucking bronco. The whistle was going like mad for the block ahead. Haggerty grabbed his red flag, dropped to the ground, and ran back past the super's car to take his distance.

Up ahead, he could see the tail end of a freight disappearing around the bend, crawling into safety on the siding. Nothing very interesting about that, somebody would get Tokio for laying out the Special, he supposed. Maybe the freight had had a breakdown, and was off schedule making the Bend. Personally, Haggerty did not care. It made very little difference to him. He picked up a handful of stones, and began to plug them at the nearest telegraph pole. Suddenly he changed the direction of his shots, and let fly with all his might at a gopher he had spotted squatting in front of his hole.

"Holy Mac!" he ejaculated in unbounded astonishment. "I believe I hit the cuss!"—and he went back to see.

Just as he got down the embankment, the Special began to whistle for her flag, one—two—three—four, and Haggerty, scrambling to the track again, began to run. But fast as he ran, he had only covered about half the distance when the train began to move. It was, therefore, a very breathless and panting Haggerty who just managed to grab the rail of the rear car—the super's car!

There was nothing for it but to pass through and Haggerty, with his acquired swagger, started. The super was alone in the rear compartment, seated at a table, a mass of papers before him. Haggerty was industriously rolling up his flag as he passed along.

"Haggerty!"

Haggerty stopped and swung around at the sound of his name.

Hale reached his hand into a box of cigars that lay open on the table, selected one carefully, lighted it, and leaned back in his chair. "I would like to offer you one, Haggerty," he said quietly, "but I am afraid you would misunderstand."

Haggerty shifted a little before the super's look. Somehow, there wasn't any squint at all; instead, behind the glasses, the gray eyes were remarkably bright and clear, and their steadiness was discomposing—to Haggerty.

"It seems," said Hale, a little smile playing around the corners of his mouth, "that they don't measure men by the same standard out West here that they did when we were back on the Penn together, eh?"

Haggerty reddened. His only belief would have been in bluster; but, curiously enough, there was something about this little man, he couldn't tell just what, that made bluster impossible. Therefore, Haggerty held his peace, and his fingers played nervously with the flag, twirling it around and around awkwardly.

"Don't make any mistake, Haggerty," the super continued pleasantly. "I'm not trying to rub it in. I want you to know that I've heard the story. I want you to know that I didn't nose it out. I heard it at the lunch-counter that day after you went out, and before the men there knew who I was. I want to start straight with you, Haggerty."

Haggerty was puzzled and flustered at this opening. "Well, sir," he blurted out, "of course you know it was all a lie. I only did it for a josh."

"Yes, I understand," Hale answered. "In itself it didn't amount to anything, but the consequences are a little more than you reckoned on, aren't they? It's acted like a boomerang, and you're pretty sore, Haggerty, aren't you?"

The openness and friendly tones of the super took hold of Haggerty, and he warmed toward the other.

"Well, yes, sir, I suppose I am," he admitted.

Hale nodded. "Now, I want you to see the other side of it, Haggerty—my side. No division of any railroad, or anything else for that matter, can do itself justice unless everyone connected with it is pulling together *for* it. I want *every* man out here with me, and first of all I want you. There is nothing destroys respect so much as ridicule. The division, much after the fashion that an epidemic of measles springs up amongst children, took it into their heads to dislike the successor of Mr. Carleton, no matter who he might be. Now, unfortunately, instead of having checked the spread, the germs are being fostered because, back of their fun with you, a description of contempt for me is constantly kept alive. So I want you to coöperate with me, Haggerty, and show them that, after all, whether I'm a holy terror or not, whether I'm a runt of a giant, no matter what, I'm entitled to a fair deal out here in the West. There, Haggerty, that's a pretty long sermon for me. I'm not much at preaching. Just turn what I've said over in your mind, that's all. I think I can safely offer you a cigar now. Will you have one?"

Haggerty accepted the cigar with a flustered mumble of thanks, and as he went forward to the other coach he chewed the end pensively.

"Well, how's the little fellow? Hope the ride ain't makin' him car-sick," sneered Slakely, the conductor.

Haggerty strode up to the other, and shoved his fist savagely within an inch of Slakely's nose.

"I'll have you know, the super's all right, you wall-eyed coyote, you! I'm tellin' you he's a *man*. Do I hear any *re*-marks to the contrary?"

"Say," gasped Slakely blankly, retreating down the aisle, "what's the matter with you, anyway?"

"That's what's the matter!" — Haggerty's explanation was more forcible than explicit, though the meaning of his clenched fist which he shook at the other was pointed enough in its inference. "That's what's the matter, my bucko," he repeated fiercely, "an' don't you forget it! I'm givin' it to you straight, an' I'll take none of your lip about it neither! See?"

Haggerty had raised the standard. Not, perhaps, as the super had expected; but according to his own ideas, or rather to his fiery temper which led him to act blindly on the spur of the moment as his impulse directed.

But it was not this method of Haggerty's, if such a term could by any stretch of the imagination be applied to Haggerty, that was to bring about the desired result, and at the same time rid him of his tormentors — tormentors who continued to sound the cry, "Where's Haggerty?" with undiminished frequency — tormentors who were much too wary to allow themselves to be caught anywhere within striking distance, for Haggerty's forearm was a thing to wonder at. Instead, the end came from another source as totally different as it was unexpected. It came on the third day of the inspection trip, up in the Rockies at the new bridge across the Stony River — and it was the new bridge that did it.

They were to lay out there for the morning, and Haggerty started in to employ the two or three hours of leisure this gave him by looking over the work. It wasn't much of a bridge as bridges go, for the Stony wasn't much of a river; but the approaches were enough to pull the heart out of the stoutest bridge crew that ever toiled and sweated and slaved. Just rock, solid, gray, massive; and so it was blast, blast, blast, hour after hour all through the day, day after day. One span, resting on the shore abutments, was to bridge the cañon that yawned six hundred feet below, where the Stony swirled and eddied, a foaming, angry, chattering, little stream.

On the eastern side, where Haggerty stood, the anchorage was pretty well under way, but over across on the western shore they were still pitting their blasting powder against the stubborn rock of the mountainside. Haggerty crossed over on the old bridge to take a look at this. Just as he reached the other side a stationary engine blew shrilly for a blast, and the men began to run for cover. Haggerty pulled his watch and marked the time—one minute and fifteen seconds. Then the blast thundered, echoed, reechoed, and died away through the mountains. He joined the men as they went back to their work.

"Holy Mac!" he exclaimed to the foreman, as he peered over the edge of the excavation and looked down some fifteen or twenty feet to the ledge where the men were already busy again. "Holy Mac! You've got to look sharp, eh?"

"Oh, I dunno," replied the foreman. "We give 'em plenty of time. When the whistle blows the men hump it. We don't touch the button till the last one is crawlin' over the top of the bank. Then, with the time fuse, there's a minute, lots of time."

Haggerty looked on for awhile, then he turned away, sat down by one of the shanties, and loaded his pipe. The pipe once alight, he settled himself in a more comfortable position by sprawling on his back, his hands under his head. From where he lay, he commanded a view of the other side of the river as well as the work before him. He could see Hale across there talking to one of the bridge engineers. He watched the two men lazily, in drowsy contentment, until he lost sight of them as they started to come over to his side, then his attention became riveted again on his immediate surroundings.

They were getting ready for another blast. Haggerty sat up. It was rather exciting to see the men come scrambling out of the hole. The whistle had just gone three toots. They were coming now, one head after another popping up over the edge, then the shoulders, and finally the men on their feet running like deers for shelter—not far, only a few yards, for the excavation itself afforded protection, once clear of it. Haggerty himself was not fifteen yards away.

He counted the men as they came out. It was the eighteenth who, just as his head and shoulders appeared, waved an arm and shouted: "All out. Let 'er go!" He saw the foreman bend over the battery and make the connection that would spark the time-fuse at the other end, and then a groan of horror went up around him. Number Eighteen, with a cry and a desperate effort to pull himself over the top, had slipped back and disappeared from sight!

Haggerty's pipe dropped to the ground from between his teeth, his heart seemed to stop its beats, a cold sweat broke out upon his face. He was on his feet now, and the foreman's words were ringing in his ears: "Then there's a minute, lots of time! *Then there's a minute, lots of time!*"

He began to run, and the seconds, as he ran, lengthened into years and cycles. "My God!" he muttered in a catchy way.

But fast as he ran, someone was faster than he. Five yards from the edge of the excavation, a figure, small, short, speeding like the wind, passed him. It was Hale—the super!

Behind, the foreman's voice bellowed hoarsely: "Come back! Come back! Ye can't get to the fuse! D'ye hear!"

"Mabbe," mumbled Haggerty between his teeth, "mabbe we can get the *man*. Mary, Mother, help us!"

Hale, flat on the ground, was making to swing himself over as Haggerty, for the second time, caught him by the collar of his coat. "You ain't strong enough," he grunted, yanking the super back. "You help me from the top"—and over the edge he went himself.

"Then there's a minute, lots of time!"—the words came again unbidden. How much, in God's name how much, of that minute had gone, how much was left? His teeth were set, his heart pounds so fierce and rapid that his breath came hard and choked, as he lowered himself to a little ledge, projecting out some seven or eight feet below the surface that had caught and held the body of Number Eighteen. The man lay there groaning. It was easy to see what had happened. A misplaced step in the climb, then a loosened rock, his balance gone, and the stone had crashed down upon his legs and ankles.

There was a look of helpless terror in the eyes of the wounded man as Haggerty reached and bent over him. "Get out," the white lips quivered. "You ain't got time. I give the signal. The blast'll be goin' now."

"There's a minute, lots of time," said Haggerty in a sing-song, crazy way. He was trying to fit the words to an air he had heard somewhere. Queer he couldn't remember it, the words were straight enough! Then he laughed—foolishly—as he worked like a madman!

He had raised the man in his arms and now, heaving with all his strength, was gradually pushing him up, up. The strain became terrific. Haggerty's muscles cracked. One of his arms was almost useless to him owing to the narrowness of the ledge that, to maintain even a precarious footing as, little by little, he rose to an upright position, forced him tight against the wall of rock and earth. Haggerty panted with cruel, gasping sobs. "Then there's a minute, lots of time!" The repetition of the words came surging upon him with a shock of horror, lending him a frenzied strength. A desperate twist, and he had made the half-turn that brought his back to the cutting. His other arm was free now. A heave, and he had swung Number Eighteen above his shoulders within reach of the super's outstretched hands. A second more, and, with Hale pulling above and Haggerty lifting below, the man, with a cry of agony as his wounded leg banged limply against the ground, was forced up over the bank.

"Quick, Haggerty! For God's sake, be quick yourself," cried Hale. "Hurry, man, *hurry!*"

"There's a minute"—Haggerty sprang for the top of the bank, clutched it—"lots of—" The last word was blotted out as he dragged himself over the edge, and heard Hale's sharp command: "Lie flat!" From behind and below him came the roar of the detonation, he felt the ground shake and quiver beneath him, the echoes were rolling and reverberating like a park of artillery—then Hale's low, fervent: "Thank God!"

It was Hale who got it first as the mob of men rushed forward, cheering, laughing, gabbling hysterically. And it was at Hale's uplifted hand that the clamor died suddenly away, and in its stead came the super's voice in quiet tones: "Where's Haggerty?"

"Aw, gwan!" sputtered Haggerty sheepishly, trying to fight his way out of the crowd that pressed upon him to haul and maul him, to thump his back, to shake his hand. "Aw, gwan! I wanter get me pipe that I left over by the shanty."

XII
McQUEEN'S HOBBY

There isn't much use in talking about the logical or the illogical when you come to couple up with a man's hobby, because a hobby is a hobby and that's all there is to it with nothing left to be said on the subject. Most men have a hobby. McQueen's was coal—just coal.

McQueen talked coal with a persistence that was amazing. On all occasions and under any pretext it was coal. Was he off schedule with a regularity that entailed his presence on the carpet before the division superintendent, it was coal. Did he break down between meeting-points with the attendant result that the dispatchers fretted and fumed and swore as they readjusted their schedules and rearranged their train sheets, it was coal. Everlastingly and eternally coal.

"What's coal?" McQueen would demand oracularly. "It's carbon and oxygen and hydrogen with a dash of nitrogen, ain't it? Well, then, what are you talking about? Coal *ain't* just coal, some of it's mostly slate. Two hundred and ten pounds all the way, all the time, with the grate bars cluttered with that, huh! What?"

No purchasing agent that had ever hit the division had been quite able to satisfy McQueen with the brand of the commodity that was supplied in accordance with the requisition orders that he drew. And so, day in and day out, big 802 puffed her way through the mountains, and McQueen, in the cab, absorbed coal statistics, coal data, coal everything, with an avidity, a thoroughness, and a masterliness of detail, that would have put some noted geologists to shame and given the rest a run to hold their rights on the marked-up schedule.

Up at headquarters—when things were running smoothly and McQueen was behaving himself with no scores chalked up against him on the time-card—they treated his hobby as a joke. So that when his whistle boomed out of the gorge to the westward, or shrilled across the cut to the eastward, followed a moment afterward by the sight of the big, flying mogul with her string of slewing dark-green coaches, the staff on duty at Big Cloud would lean from the upper windows and watch the Limited as she shattered the yard switches with a roar—watch as, with a hiss of the air and the grinding of the brake shoes as they sparked the tires, she would draw up, panting, at the platform, and the big engineer would swing himself from the cab for an oil around. Then the badinage flew thick and fast while McQueen swabbed his hands on a hunk of waste and punctuated the remarks with squirts from his long-spouted can as he filled the thirsty oil cups.

So the big fellows laughed and joked, and the Brotherhood chaffed him unmercifully.

If anyone had asked McQueen what had started, let alone caused him to exhaust the subject of coal with such painstaking and conscientious insistence, he couldn't for the life of him have answered. It had started—just started, that's all—and, fascinating him, had pursued its insidious advance unchecked and unquestioned—that is, unquestioned until one morning when Clarihue, the turner at the Big Cloud roundhouse, kind of jerked him up a little on the proposition.

"You're against the red, you and your coal, Mac, all right, all right," Clarihue chuckled, as the engineer came in to sign on for the day's run.

McQueen was patting 802's slide bars affectionately. "How's that?" he asked.

"Oil!"

"Oil?" repeated McQueen, puzzled.

"Sure thing! No more coal—no more slate—no more cinders—you touch her off, and there you are! You'll have to cut out the coal and plug up on oil, Mac."

"Oh!" said McQueen, enlightened. "Oil-burners, eh? I saw one of 'em down East. They're evil-smelling, inhuman, stinking brutes, that's what they are! Don't you let 'em side track you like that, son. They may do down there, but not in the hills. Not while you and me are pulling throttles, and don't you think so."

Clarihue grinned.

"Well, mabbe," said he. "But say, honest, Mac, what's the sense of gassing about coal the way you do? What's to come out of it? What's the good of it? You just get the laugh from the boys, what?"

McQueen's answer was to scratch his head. To put the matter into the concrete class of practicability was a phase of the subject that he had not considered. He scratched his head when the turner had gone; and, also, he scratched his head for several days thereafter. Then he caught at a happy inspiration whereby to solve the riddle, and therein he fell—but of that in a moment.

Things were booming on the Hill Division. Traffic was doubled, trebled. Everything on the train sheets was in sections. Promotions flew thick and fast. Wipers were set to firing, and the firemen moved over to the right-hand side of the cabs. Every wheel the division could beg, borrow or steal was doing fancy time stunts smashing records. Everyone from car-tink to superintendent, was on the jump. Even the directors, not to be outdone in the general order of things, worked overtime rubbing fat hands in gleeful anticipation of juicy, luscious dividends to be; only *they* neglected to figure in Noonan as an item on the balance sheets.

Noonan? Where is the Brotherhood that does not number among its members men with grievances, fancied or real? Noonan had a grievance, — no particular grievance, just a grievance — and Noonan was a power in that branch of the Brotherhood that held sway over the Hill Division. Noonan always had a grievance; due, primarily, to the fact that he had a deep and long-seated grudge against himself. It dated way back — he'd been born that way.

"Grievances!" he spluttered to a group of his admirers. "Grievances? Why, we're against the worst of it all the time. We're not track-walkers, are we? Well then, who runs the road? It's us on the throttles, what? Who's to blame for our measly schedule of hours and pay? We are, 'cause we haven't the sand to stand up for our rights. That's what, and don't you forget it!"

There was a chorus of assent. "Noonan's right," said one Devins, "only it don't look to me like now was what you might rightly call the time to growl. Times are good, everything's double-headed, and the paycar's running carload lots."

Noonan glared. "You've got the brains of a piston head, that's what you have," he exploded. "It's times like these we'd win hands down. Perhaps you'd like to wait till there's nothing doing, and they're laying the boys off and everybody, mostly, is running spare! What chance d'ye think any demands would stand then?"

Of a truth it was the accepted time and a most glorious opportunity. In that, Noonan was right. Only one obstacle lay between him and the accomplishment of his cherished ambition to make something of his trouble-hunting proclivities and become a leader of men — in a strike. That obstacle was McQueen.

McQueen was a company man. Out and out a company man; though nothing would have surprised McQueen more than to learn that he was looked up to as a leader by the conservative element of the Brotherhood. True, he and his coal was the joke of the division; but that was only a joke, and in no wise to be held up against him. His influence, of whose existence he was oblivious, was based on things apart from that. Big, kindly, honest, incapable of deceit, simple, straightforward, staunch in his friendships, somewhat inclined to stubborness in his beliefs perhaps, easily ruffled but as easily pacified, such was McQueen. Such was the McQueen the officials honored, and such was the McQueen with whom the boys would gladly and loyally have shared their pay checks to the last cent.

All this Noonan knew. Knew, too, that to gain his end he must first win over McQueen. And to that object he began to devote himself. He and McQueen shared the honors of the fast mail, and under ordinary conditions communication between the two men was limited to a flirt of the hand from the cab as one or other of them tore by the siding designated as their meeting-point by the lords of the road, the dispatchers. But now things were a bit different, everything was more or less off schedule. And while the Limited, East and West, was nursed along as near her running time as possible, and generally got the best of it over everything else, there were, nevertheless, occasions when both men were stalled together on time orders at the same point.

Noonan tackled McQueen at the first opportunity. He picked his way cautiously as though not quite sure of his rights and ready for a quick reverse.

"Say, Mac," he began, "what do you think of all this talk that's going 'round?"

"Talk?" said McQueen. "What talk?"

"You don't mean to say," gasped Noonan, in well-simulated surprise, "that you haven't heard it? And the boys are slinging it pretty hot, at that!"

"I haven't heard anything," McQueen answered, slightly suspicious that Noonan was about to spring one at his expense. "What you giving us?"

"Straight," confided Noonan earnestly. "It's strike, Mac, that's what."

"Strike!" ejaculated McQueen, bewildered. "What for?"

"What for!" cried Noonan. "What for? That's a sweet question to ask. Well, pretty dashed near everything,"—he waved his hand expansively—"hours, scale, and—and—"

McQueen shook his head. "I'm not kicking," he said. "I don't see anything to strike about. Looks to me as though you fellows were hunting trouble. You'll probably get it, what?"

"You never see anything," Noonan blurted out, irritation getting the better of diplomacy. "Nothing but the blamed coal you're forever yapping about."

"What I know about coal," returned McQueen with dignity, "you'll never know. It's a subject that requires brains."

"Is that so!" Noonan jeered. "You tell it!"

"It requires brains," McQueen repeated stolidly.

"It's a shame that the only man on the division that has 'em, don't know how to use 'em, then," Noonan prodded. "Who cares about your blazing old coal and what it's made of? Talk's cheap. There's no sense to it, anyhow."

"Maybe there isn't, and then again maybe there is. At any rate, there's a dollar a day for every man pulling a throttle," McQueen announced triumphantly. "I don't know yet just how much for the firemen, I haven't figured it on their schedule."

Noonan pricked up his ears. "What's that you say, Mac," he demanded.

Here was McQueen's vindication. They'd laugh at his absurd, pointless theories on coal, would they? Well then, he'd show them! And it wasn't any of their business, either, how many days he'd racked his brains, puzzling out an adequate solution to the question Clarihue had flung at him! He shook two impressive fat fingers at Noonan.

"One dollar a day, every day, and the spare men proportionately, that's what! Do you get that, Noonan?"

"Rats!" said Noonan. "You'd better go into the shops for repairs. You need new stay-bolts on your dome cover!"

"Never you mind my dome cover," McQueen flung back, beginning to get exasperated. "It may need a little tinkering, but it's not ready for the scrap-heap yet, the way some are I could mention—but won't. It all goes back to what I said. It's a subject that requires brains—which you haven't got. There's no use explaining anything to you because——"

"You can't," Noonan interrupted craftily. "You're only long on wind, Mac."

"You listen to me, you rust-jointed disgrace to the throttle!" cried McQueen, stung into retort. "You listen to me! What are you paid for? Mileage, ain't it? How do you get your mileage? Steam! What makes steam? Coal! D'ye hear? Coal! Coal, and don't you forget it. Well then, poor coal means poor steam, and poor steam means poor mileage, don't, it, what?"

Noonan burst into a loud and derisive guffaw.

McQueen glared. "You're a wild, uneducated, hee-hawing ass!" he choked. "What do you know, anyway? Nothing! But *I* know! A dollar a day I said, and I say so now. I figured it out. It's the difference between high grade coal and the muck we burn. It's the difference between the mileage we make and the mileage we *could* make in the same time. That totes up one dollar a day. Supposing they wouldn't let us have any more mileage than they do now, well, we'd do it in better time, and the difference would be ours, wouldn't it? And time's money. And *that* totes up one dollar a day just the same. It's the same either way—time or mileage. Take your choice!"

"There, Johnny, that's a good boy, run along and fetch me a bucket of steam," Noonan scoffed.

With a snort of unutterable contempt, McQueen turned to swing himself into his cab.

"Hold on a minute, Mac," Noonan cried, afraid that he had overstepped himself. "Don't get whiffy. I swear, I believe you're right. Let's see how you figure it."

And McQueen, mollified, figured it. Figured it with the stub of a pencil in greasy, scrawling characters on the back of a time order. As to the process by which the conclusion was arrived at, that was something of which Noonan was in profound and utter ignorance. Whether it was right or wrong, he did not know. He never knew—and cared less! Certainly the result was there.

McQueen completed the last figure of his calculation with a flourish. "There!" he cried exultingly. "How about it now, eh?"

Noonan took the paper, wrinkled his brows, pursed his lips, and stared at it with the air of a connoisseur of calculus. "H'm," said he slowly, "are you dead sure it's right, Mac?"

"Right!" McQueen fairly yelled, touched in another tender spot. "Right! Confound you, it's there in black and white, ain't it? Figures don't lie, do they? Well, what in thunder's wrong with you, then?"

"I wanted to be sure, Mac, that's all. Holy fishplates, I knew it was bad, rotten bad, but I didn't think they were handing it to us like this."

"You bet it's bad. It's the worst ever. There's more kinds of coal than there are spikes in the right of way from here to Big Cloud and back again, but the coal we get is the last on the list. Bad! It's what I've always said, ain't it?"

"It's fierce!" continued Noonan with rising emphasis. "And when the boys hear this, it'll be the last straw. They'll fix 'em!"

"Fix who?" inquired McQueen, blankly.

"Why, ain't I telling you! The company."

"I—I was talking about the coal," said McQueen a little uneasily.

"Sure you were," Noonan agreed heartily. "Sure you were, and how the company is robbing every engineer on the division of a dollar a day, to say nothing of the firemen and the train crews. It's enough to make a man mad. Well, I should say yes!"

"I—I didn't say the company was robbing us," protested McQueen.

"What's that!" cried Noonan sharply; then in apparent disgust: "So your crazy old figures are just gas-bag filling like the rest of your coal talk, eh? They *did* look pretty scaly, and that's a fact. I had my suspicions. That's why I asked you if you were sure they were right. But I might have known they weren't without asking."

"Oh, you might, might you?" exploded McQueen, goaded once more into angry outburst. "You and your suspicions! Who are you! I tell you they *are* right, and that's the end of it!"

"Well, if they're right, why don't you stand by them, then? We're being robbed every day we work, ain't we?"

"Ye-e-es, I suppose we are," McQueen admitted reluctantly; "but I didn't figure it out for the purpose of——"

"Mac," Noonan interrupted unctuously, "'tain't for you nor me to say the purpose it's to be put to. There's others besides us. But I do say, Mac, you're almighty smart."

McQueen shook his head. "I'm a company man," he said dubiously.

"Company man! Of course you are. We're all company men. But right's right and wrong's wrong before anything else. Well, ta ta, Mac, see you again. I'm off. There's Hake with the tissue. I'll tell the boys where you stand."

It was a somewhat dazed McQueen that in turn pulled himself up into his own cab. He stood in the gangway and squinted meditatively at the coal heaped high on the tender. To his conscientious self-communion, his triumphant vindication had somewhat the appearance of a boomerang. "I don't know," he reflected. "It *is* damn poor coal, and—and figures *don't* lie. We—we've been getting the worst of it, and—and a man *should* stand up for his rights."

And while McQueen, busy with new and momentous problems, was steaming west into the Rockies, Noonan, with his tongue in his cheek, was cutting along for Big Cloud with a wide-flung throttle.

That night, at Big Cloud, Noonan's cronies got the story. That is, they got what Noonan saw fit to tell them. And the burden of his tale was that McQueen was with the Brotherhood and against the company. That was sufficient. They looked with appreciative admiration at the man who had done the trick, and then they flew to obey his orders.

By morning, every engineer on the division had the news. On way freights, on stray freights, on regulars, specials, and sections, they got it—every last one of them. And McQueen coming east again on Number Two got it, and marvelled a little at his new importance, never seeing Noonan's hand in the marked deference paid to him.

First and last it was a bad business. Bad for the company, bad for the hot heads led by Noonan, bad for the others, and bad for McQueen. It caught the company none too well prepared, and Carleton, for this happened in the days of his superintendency, was hard put to it to move anything. There was pretty bitter feeling; and before it was over there was blood spilled. But the roughs at Big Cloud, who didn't know the pilot from a horn-block, were responsible for the most of that, though, in their own way, too, they ended it.

It came to a show-down the night they carried young Carl Davis home from the yard on a door they had wrenched from a box-car. Davis was braking in the yard then, and he was a nephew of McQueen's. He had lived with the engineer ever since, as a little chap of ten, he had come out to the West. Childless themselves, McQueen and his wife thought as much of the lad as though he had been their own.

McQueen in his grief didn't get the rights of it. Only in a confused sort of a way he understood the roughs had winged the boy with a cowardly shot, meaning perhaps to do no more than shoot out his lamp as he swung by on the top of a car. And while his wife with tender hands busied herself in rendering such assistance to the surgeon as she could, McQueen sat in a chair and stared, dry-eyed and bitter of heart, at the white face on the bed.

Also McQueen was getting sense. Certainly, he had never intended to strike. Now, the shock of Carl's hurt had sobered his judgment and he saw things as he should have seen them, saw them as he cursed himself for not having seen them before he had allowed his senseless egotism to carry him off his feet. As the thoughts came crowding through his brain, his cheeks burned dull red at his own shame. But through it all he blamed only himself, with never an inkling that he had been used as a cat's-paw by the crafty Noonan—that was to come afterward.

McQueen waited only to wring a half-grudging assurance from the doctor that the boy would pull through, then he took his hat and left the house. It was getting on toward eleven o'clock when he walked into the hall across from the station where the boys had their headquarters, and had been in the habit of congregating each night ever since the strike began. Usually noisy in a good-natured, devil-may-care way, there was a subdued and serious quiet pervading the room as McQueen stepped in. The shooting in the yard was something they had not counted on and, like McQueen, it was acting on them as a tonic. All except Noonan who, evidently bolstered up with a few drinks, was more noisy, hilarious and quarrelsome than ever.

McQueen answered the questions they crowded at him as to the boy's condition soberly, and going over to Noonan took him by the arm and led him into a corner.

"The game ain't worth it," he said shortly. "I've had my lesson to-night and I'm through!"

"What for?" demanded Noonan aggressively. "We didn't have anything to do with it. We're not responsible, are we?"

"We are," said McQueen sturdily. "Morally responsible."

"Morally responsible!" Noonan mocked with a sneer. "Oh, mamma, listen to him! Streak of yellow, that's you, McQueen." Then fiercely: "You play the scab and I'll bash your head to jelly."

"You're drunk," retorted McQueen contemptuously.

"Drunk, eh? I'm not so drunk but that I know who's running this strike. It's me, and don't you foget it! And what I says goes, d'ye hear?"

"I'm asking you to call it off. Blood on our heads I won't stand for. Our grievances don't warrant what's likely to happen here if things go on. You owe it to the men who followed you into the strike, Noonan."

"Oh, I do, do I? Followed *me* into the strike, eh? How about the men that followed *you*?"

"That followed me?" repeated McQueen in amazement.

"Sure, that followed you! You didn't think I took any stock in your batty coal talk, did you? You must think I'm green! All I wanted was *you* — you bit fast and easy enough — the rest of the softies came along then like a pack of sheep. What d'ye think now about *me* owing it all to the men, Mr. Morally Responsible, eh?"

It took McQueen a minute to get the whole of it — the bitter whole of it. Then the blood rushed to his face in a crimson flood. He reached out and grasping Noonan by neck and shoulders shook him as a terrier shakes a rat. "You cur!" he cried hoarsely, and flung the other suddenly away against the wall.

The men at the sound of the scuffle came running over.

"He's a scab! Kill him!" shrieked Noonan.

McQueen turned to face the men. "If beating this strike's a scab, I'm a scab," he said quietly. "I'm out to beat it right now! I've been a fool and I'm ready to admit it. But I didn't know until to-night that I'd been bait for a whining thing like that!" pointing at Noonan. "He says some of you men came in on the strike because I did. If that's so, then get out of it because I do. Get out of it before there's more on our hands than we'll be able to answer for when we go into Division for the last time. That's all I've got to say. I'm going over now to ask Carleton to put me on again, if it's nothing better than pulling a way freight. And — and I hope you'll come with me."

As the flood follows the fracture in the dam, so the breaking of the tension filled the room with pandemonium. Cheers, yells, hisses, curses, shouts — the Brotherhood was divided against itself. But ten minutes later, the majority of them were clustered behind McQueen in the super's office.

Carleton and his staff were sleeping at headquarters those days, and they gathered in a group around the green-shaded lamp on the dispatcher's table to face the delegation.

"Mr. Carleton," McQueen began, "we——"

That was all. He never got any further. From the platform outside came hoots and cat-calls, and above the chorus Noonan's voice:

"Soak the scab! Kill him! If he's so fond of it, let him have it! *Now!*"

The window pane was shivered with a crash, and McQueen, struck full in the head by a huge hunk of coal, sank without so much as a moan to the floor.

They cured him of brain fever in the course of time all right, but they never cured him of coal. Up and down from one end of the division to the other, when he got around again, he talked coal harder than ever—it was his business. McQueen was doing the buying for the road.

"There wasn't anything wrong with what I said about coal," he asserts with a smile, when the boys put it up to him. "Not for a minute! Good coal makes better steam, better everything, and pays the company. They saw that all right. That's why I'm buying it, see? As for figuring it into the schedule, the sum was too hard and they couldn't do it. Me? Oh, I can't, either, I lost the paper I did it for Noonan on. I ain't so good on figures as I was, what?"

XIII
THE REBATE

He was known as Dutchy, but his name was Damrosch. This is Dutchy's story when Dutchy and the Transcontinental were in the making; and before, as has been recorded elsewhere, he came to Big Cloud. He started railroading as cook's helper on a construction gang that was laying track across the prairie. As the mileage grew, so Dutchy grew. At first lank and lean, he took on, little by little, the appearance of being comfortably nourished, until, by the time they hit the Rockies, Dutchy's gait had become a waddle and his innocent blue eyes were almost hidden by the great rolls of fat that puffed out his face like a toy balloon. Then Dutchy, slow of body and likewise of brain, and yearning for a quiet and peaceful existence, secured the lunch-counter rights for Dry Notch.

Now, Dry Notch, half-way across the prairie, consisted of a water-tank, a small roundhouse, a smaller station and a diminutive general store. But because of its geographical position, it was headquarters for the Mid-Plains Division.

Here, T. V. Brett was superintendent; Thornley was his chief clerk; and MacDonald was dispatcher. And these, with the railroad hands and train-crews comprised the population of Dry Notch, unless there might be added a few ranchers somewhere in the neighborhood.

The staff bunked in a room over the station, and the men had their quarters in the roundhouse, but one and all they ate at Dutchy's counter. Sinkers and coffee, apple pie and sandwiches they stood as a steady diet for a month after he had appeared upon the scene, and then a delegation waited upon him and demanded dishes more substantial.

"You can make meat pies and chicken stew and all that sort of thing, can't you?" they demanded.

"Sure!" said Dutchy. "But dot iss expensive."

Money was no object, they assured him, and thereupon proceeded to fix a schedule of prices—fifteen cents for a meat pie; twenty cents for a chicken stew—with two slices of bread and butter thrown in for good measure.

"Vell" said Dutchy, "so iss it."

And a few nights later, true to his promise, they got their chicken stew—canned chicken stew.

The huge pot, full to the brim, had been emptied, and Dutchy, his face beaming with smiles, had bustled into the back room for a further supply, when MacDonald's voice rose plaintively:

"It's—it's *chicken*, isn't it?"

The crowd looked inquiringly at the dispatcher.

"Because," went on MacDonald softly, "I—never heard of any chickens in Dry Notch."

And then, amid the laughter that ensued, Thornley rose dramatically from his seat, and, picking up a bone from his plate, waved it aloft.

"Gentlemen, this is no time for mirth!" he cried. "We are the victims of a swindle. We are in the clutch of an octopus—that is to say, a food trust, composed of Dutchy and the dining-car conductors of Numbers One and Two. It is my painful duty to assert that I recognize this bone as the identical bone on which I fed two nights ago coming up the line on Number One."

Dutchy entered, staggering under the load of the replenished pot, when Thornley solemnly demanded a rebate on the spot.

"Vat iss it?" said Dutchy, halting and peering anxiously into the pot; then, evidently reassured that no essential ingredient had been forgotten, he looked up at the ring of faces that were regarding him with grave inquiry. "Vat iss a repate?" he demanded. "It something iss mit der bread und butter for twenty cents to go, yess?"

The crowd roared, and up and down the division train-crews, engine-crews, and section-gangs got the joke and passed it on until the lunch-counter became known to every man on the system as "The Rebate."

They did not explain the joke to Dutchy, and for days he endured the chaff stolidly, though with much bewilderment, until, one afternoon, MacDonald patiently and ploddingly acquainted him with the unhallowed baseness of one Thornley—helping himself, by way of compensation, to the heap of doughnuts under the glass cover.

Dutchy listened, his cheeks getting redder and redder as MacDonald, exaggerating some hundred-fold, suavely rubbed it in.

"Dot Thornley iss—iss a pig!" shouted Dutchy suddenly, as the light burst in upon him.

MacDonald nodded assent, his mouth too full of doughnut to speak.

"Und I a fool iss, yess?" continued the proprietor, pounding a fat fist on the counter.

Again MacDonald nodded, smiling sweetly—and reached for another doughnut.

But this time Dutchy's fingers were firmly clasped around the cover, and he peered suspiciously through the glass at the number of doughnuts remaining, then glared at the dispatcher.

"You—you git out from here!" he said slowly, but with rising emphasis.

And MacDonald, chuckling, went.

It was not until after supper that same evening, when Number One pulled in, that Dutchy made any move toward retribution—then Dutchy cut loose. It was Taggart who got it—little Shorty Taggart, the driver of Number One, who was red-haired and an inveterate joker, and likewise a great crony of Thornley's.

The first intimation MacDonald had that anything was up was an enraged howl that, rising above the tumult of the station, reached him where he sat in the dispatcher's office. There was no mistaking the voice — it was Dutchy's. MacDonald stuck his head hastily out of the window, while Thornley, who was in the room, leaned over his shoulder.

Dutchy was bellowing like a mad bull. "Say it! Shusht say it. Oh! py golly! "

Here followed a volcanic eruption of guttural German with one or two words common to all languages intermingled.

Then, flying through the doorway of the lunch-room, dashing down the platform, scattering loungers, passengers, and car-tinks in all directions, in a mad rush for the engine end of the train, tore a short figure in tight-fitting, bandy-legged overalls, whose flaming red hair presented a shining mark for the plate that whizzed past his ear and smashed into a hundred pieces against a baggage-truck.

And Dutchy, blowing hard, his sleeves rolled up over the fat of his arms, waddled to the center of the platform and shook a frantic fist after the retreating engineer.

"I a fool iss no longer yet, don'd it?" he screamed, and, puffing his cheeks in and out like a whezzy injector, he turned, reentered the restaurant, and the door closed behind him with a resounding bang.

MacDonald drew in his head, and the tears were running down his cheeks as he held his sides.

Thornley groped for a chair.

"Guess Taggart was asking for a rebate," he gasped. "It was worth pay to see him run."

"You bet!" said MacDoneld eloquently, when he could get his breath.

The door opened, and Brett, the super, came in.

"D'ye see Taggart and Dutchy, Brett?" cried Thornley.

"Yes," said Brett, laughing. Then, more seriously: "Look here, you'd better patch it up with Dutchy. There's no use rubbing it in too hard. MacDonald, tell Blaney to put my car on Number Two when she comes in. I'm going east to-night."

The patching, however, was quite a different matter than talking about it.

The next morning the lunch-room door was ominously closed—and the staff went breakfastless. By listening at the keyhole, and from an occasional glimpse through the window, they knew that Dutchy was inside.

But to pleadings, threats, and door-kickings the occupant was, to all intents and purposes, oblivious. Things began to look serious for the staff and station hands who were wont to depend on Dutchy for their grub-stakes.

Thornley whistled softly and pulled at his pipe, his feet on the dispatcher's desk.

"He'll *have* to open up when Number Ninety-Seven pulls in," Thornley was saying, more by way of reassuring himself than of presenting any new view of the case to MacDonald. "The company won't stand for any inconvenience to the passengers—that is" he hastened to amend, "not of this kind. What? They've got a sort of lien on that joint, and if he waits for them to get after him he'll get into trouble. Wish Brett were back—he'd make him open up quick, I guess. What's the matter with Number Ninety-Seven, anyhow? Thought you said she was on time?"

"So she is," said MacDonald, grinning. "Hear her?"

From the eastward came the hoarse shriek from the whistle of a five-hundred class.

"Guess I'll go down," said Thornley. "Coming?"

MacDonald nodded and got up from his chair.

The two men reached the platform in time to acknowledge a flirt of the hand from Sanders in the cab as the big machine, wheel-tires sparking from the tight-set brakes, rolled slowly past them, coming to a halt farther on.

Simultaneously the door of the lunch-room swung wide open, and on the threshold, completely filling the opening with his bulk, stood Dutchy. In his left hand he held his bell, which he began to ring clamorously; in his right hand, almost but not quite concealed behind his apron, was no less a weapon than a substantial-looking rolling-pin. A crowd of passengers began to surge toward the restaurant, and among them mingled the hungry railroad men of Dry Notch.

"Come on!" shouted Thornley exultantly. "I knew he'd have to open up. Here's where we feed—h'm?"

"Vait!" cried Dutchy imperiously, as the head of the column reached him. "You, yess; you, no. Vat iss it?" He was sorting the sheep from the goats, allowing the passengers to enter, pushing the railroaders ruthlessly to one side.

"You, yess; you, no. You, yess; you—oh! py golly

He had caught sight of Thornley, and, swinging suddenly, struck out viciously in that direction with the rolling-pin. Being obliged, however, to maintain his position in the doorway, the strategic key to the situation, the jab fell short by two or three inches, barely missing Thornley's nose.

Thornley fell back instinctively.

"Look here, you old ass!" he yelled angrily, "we've had about enough of this. It's past a joke. The company's got a lien on that joint of yours, and we'll close it up so tight you'll never open it again—d'ye hear?"

Dutchy stopped short in the monotonous, "You, yess; you, no," on which he had recommenced, and his paunch began to shake.

"Yah!" he cried. "Dot iss a joke. Oh, py golly, *lean!* Dot iss ven you ge-starving get, yah? Ho, ho! Ha, ha!"

In Dutch's burst of merriment first one and then another joined, until even Thornley, his good nature getting the better of him, roared with the rest at his own expense.

But if this apparent return to good humor on Dutchy's part inspired any hope in the minds of the railroad men that he had relented and that former friendly relations were to be resumed, they were doomed to disappointment, for Dutchy stolidly continued to allow the passengers to go in and as stolidly barred the entrance to the others.

Then they gave it up, and bought out the slender stock of canned goods and biscuits from the shelves of the general store.

They messed in the baggage-room and they swallowed their scanty portions to the tune of "Die Wacht am Rhein," bellowed out by a strong and sonorous voice, through the partition, on the other side of which, laid out in tempting confusion, as they were painfully aware, was plenty.

What they had, however, did little more than whet their appetites, and by three o'clock some of the men were talking of carrying the position by storm, helping themselves, and doing a few fancy stunts with Dutchy.

"We can't have any row," said Thornley, pulling at his mustache and staring at MacDonald. "What had we better do? The boys'll be pulling the old shack down around his ears. He'll fight like blazes, and some one'll get hurt. And then the company 'll want to know what's what. Say, the old geeser has got us where he wants us, sure—eh, what?"

MacDonald nodded.

"I'll tell you what it is," Thornley went on impressively, "there's some one besides Dutchy in this. They've been giving him a steer, and *I'd* give a few to know who it is. It's mighty queer Dutchy would wake up so suddenly to the fact that he was a joke. Then, there isn't enough to that rebate josh to make him so sore. Some one's been stringing him good and plenty. What had we better do?"

"I don't know," MacDonald answered. "Let's go and see if we can't talk him over."

At the sight of Thornley and the dispatcher heading for the lunch-room, the trainmen and station-hands fell in behind them.

MacDonald halted a few paces from the door.

"You boys, stay here," he directed. "Let me see what I can do."

Thornley and the men halted obediently, while MacDonald went on and knocked at the door. There was no response.

"But—Mr. Damrosch!" he called. "It's MacDonald. I want to talk to you."

This time his knock was answered, and so suddenly as to cause him to jump back in surprise.

"Vell, vat iss it?" demanded Dutchy, scowling belligerently.

"We're—we're—" stammered MacDonald, his confidence a little shaken at the proprietor's attitude. Then, desperately: "Oh, I say, confound it all, Dutchy, we're hungry."

"So!" Dutchy's exclamation was a world of innocent astonishment and kindly interest.

"Yes," went on MacDonald, diplomatically. "You bet we are. It's been a good joke, but you've had the best end of it. Let's call it quits, there's a good fellow, and—and give us all a handout."

Dutchy listened attentively to the appeal.

"I, a fool iss no longer yet, don'd it?" he queried softly.

"You most decidedly are not," MacDonald assured him.

"You vill for repates no longer ask, yet?" persisted Mr. Damrosch.

"Not on your life!" replied the dispatcher earnestly, beginning to see daylight. "That's all off. We'll apologize, too, if you like. I promise you, we are quite willing to apologize."

"Vell, den," announced Mr. Damrosch, "ve vill aggravate"—and he slammed the door in MacDonald's face.

"Oh, hold on, Dutchy!" cried MacDonald piteously, for he was very hungry. "What did you say?"

"Vat I said iss dot ve vill aggravate!" shouted Dutchy from the other side of the door. "Dot iss English, don'd it? Aggravate!"

"He means arbitrate," prompted Thornley from the platform.

"Oh, all right!" said MacDonald. "We'll agree to that, Dutchy. Come on——open up!"

"I vill not mit you aggra—arra—*do it*—hang dot vord!" Dutchy asserted decisively, but again opening the door. "But mit Mister Brett I vill do it."

"But Mr. Brett isn't here, you know that," retorted MacDonald, beginning to get exasperated. "And, what's more, he won't be back until the day after to-morrow. I guess you know that, too, don't you?"

Dutchy smiled a patient, chiding smile. "Dot iss too bad," he remarked regretfully. "But dot Thornley a pig iss, und you—oh, py golly! you—I could not you pelief. Ve vill vait for Mister Brett."

He was closing the door again, when MacDonald put his foot against the jamb and, leaning toward Dutchy, said quickly, in an undertone:

"Look here, Dutchy, you're going too far. If I couldn't see any farther than you, I'd wear glasses. Now's the time to make your deal. I'll help you see? You can get anything out of the boys now, but you push them too far and they'll pull the whole outfit down over your ears. You say what you want, and I'll get it for you."

Dutchy looked meditatively into MacDonald's face, and shook his head with a sad smile of wisdom.

"I could not you pelief," he repeated.

"You don't have to. You don't have to believe anybody. Whatever you want us to do we'll do before you let us in to eat. You can't lose. What do you say?"

Mr. Damrosch scratched his head pensively, without taking his eyes off the dispatcher. After a minute he tapped MacDonald on the shoulder.

"Vell," he announced, "I vill tell you. Listen."

MacDonald listened—incredulously. Then he whistled a low, long-drawn-out note of consternation.

"Well, you've got a nerve!" he gasped. "What do you think, eh? The boys'll never—" He stopped suddenly, a smile came over his face, and he chuckled softly to himself. "Dutchy, you're great! It'll be meat for the boys to make Thornley stand for it. That's what you want to do—make Thornley stand for it. Will the boys make him? Oh, will they! Give them the chance. That's the way to handle it. I told you I'd help you. Now, make your *spiel*."

MacDonald turned to the group on the platform. "Dutchy'll arbitrate!" he cried.

At this the men began to push forward, but Dutchy stopped them. "Vait as you iss! Ven der—der—hang dot word—iss, den iss it. Vait!"

They waited, and Dutchy began to count on his fingers. "Dere iss sixteen dot breakfasted didn'd," he began. "Dot—iss—iss——"

"Average 'em up at a quarter apiece," prompted MacDonald in a whisper. "That makes four dollars."

"Iss four dollars—yess," went on Dutchy. "Vell, I vant dot. Dere iss der crews dot in-came und out-vent und didn'd eat ven der door vas closed. Dot iss two dollars—yess? Vell, I vant dot."

The men came to, and a roar of derision rent the air, in the face of which even Dutchy was a little shaken.

"Stand pat," encouraged MacDonald. "You've got them coming and going."

Dutchy held up his hand for silence. "Dere iss der sixteen over again yet dot dinnered didn'd. Dot iss four dollars—yess? Vell, I vant dot. Dot iss four und two and four. Dot iss ten dollars—don'd it? Veil, I vant dot, und den you come in—yess, one py one—for a quarter py each."

Then, amid the storm of abuse and jeers that greeted Dutchy's ultimatum, MacDonald, with a final injunction to the proprietor to stand by his guns, turned and joined Thornley and the men.

"Vell, py golly!" screamed Dutchy above the din. "Vat iss it? Who was der commencer of dot joke dot iss ten dollars to pay? It iss dot Thornley!"

"Why, you wretched old thief," yelled Thornley, "do you think we're going to pay you for grub we didn't get, because you wouldn't let us have it, and then pay you for it again when you do dole it out? We'll see you further, first."

"It vas agreed in front of der—hang dot word!—py der—"

"Agreed nothing!" snorted Thornley.

"Dot you vill for repates no longer ask, yet, don'd it? Vell, der price ten dollars iss. Dere iss no repate. Oh, py golly, Mister Thornley, dot vas an expensive joke—yess? Dot vas your joke, und I shusht thought me dot I hope you will pay dot yourself."

Thornley paid. With no good grace, but because, as MacDonald had said they would, the men made him. Disgruntled and angry, he led the file into the restaurant, placing ten dollars and twenty-five cents in Dutchy's hand before he crossed the threshold.

Behind him followed MacDonald and the grinning line of men, each contributing their quarters—in advance—for the first square meal they had had that day.

"Eat vat you like," said Dutchy magnanimously.

Thornley glared. "Eat vat you like! Eat vat you like!" he mimicked savagely. "I like your colossal generosity at my expense!"

For a long time there was no other noise save the rattle of dishes and the busy clatter of knives, forks, and spoons. Then Thornley beckoned to Dutchy.

"Vell, vat iss it?" inquired the proprietor from behind the counter.

"Who put you on to this?" demanded Thornley. "I've had to stand for it, and I'd like to know. I would that!"

MacDonald, sitting beside Thornley, noticed, with some misgivings, a peculiar expression sweep over Dutchy's face, but to his relief the proprietor's only reply was a grunt, as he answered a call for more coffee.

"By the hokey, I'll bet it was that red-haired Taggart!" exclaimed Thornley suddenly, turning to the dispatcher.

MacDonald buried his face in his cup, ostensibly to drain the last drop, then he set it down quickly and jerked his watch from his pocket.

"Holy Moses!" he ejaculated, and fled from the room.

An hour later, as Thornley was again sitting with his feet on MacDonald's desk, Dutchy stuck his head into the room and beckoned to the dispatcher. MacDonald walked across the floor and joined him. Dutchy pulled him out of the room and closed the door.

"Dere iss one thing dot I forgotted did," announced Mr. Damrosch.

"What's that?" inquired MacDonald.

"Dere iss five doughnuts dot iss paid for not."

"Oh!" said MacDonald.

"Dot vas der time you told dot it vas Thornley—yess? Dot vas von dollar py each. Vell, I vant dot—yess?"

"Really!" laughed MacDonald. "Well, I guess *not!*"

"Dot—vas—der—time"—Dutchy was raising his voice, each word growing louder and more distinct than the preceding one. Thornley's chair inside creaked ominously. MacDonald glanced furtively toward the door, and his face grew red—"you—told—dot———"

With a hasty movement, MacDonald clapped one hand over Dutchy's mouth, and with the other thrust a five-dollar bill into his fingers.

"Get out!" he choked, and shoved Dutchy violently toward the stairs.

At the bottom, Dutchy halted, turned and looked up with a grin.

"Py golly," said he, "I shusht thought me dot I like jokes pretty good, and I hope dot——"

"Oh, shut up!" said MacDonald.

XIV
SPECKLES

This happened at a period in the history of the Hill Division when trade was very bad, and the directors, scowling over the company's annual report, threw up their hands in holy horror; while from the sacred precincts of the board-room there emanated the agonized cry:

"Economy!"

The general manager took up the slogan and dinned it into the ears of the division superintendents.

"Operating expenses are too high," he wrote. "They must be cut down." And the superintendents of divisions, painfully alive to the fact that the G. M. was not dictating for the mere pleasure of it, intimated in unmistakable language to the heads of departments under them that the next quarterly reports were expected to show a marked improvement.

John Healy had charge of the roundhouse at Big Cloud, in those days, and the morning after the lightning struck the system he came fuming back across the yards from his interview with the superintendent, stuttering angrily to himself. As he stamped into the running-shed his humor a shade worse than usual the first object that caught his eye was Speckles, squatted on the lee side of 483, dangling his legs in the pit. That is, it would have been the lee side if Healy had come in the other door.

"Cut down operatin' expinses, is ut?" Healy muttered. "Begorra, I'll begin right now!"

And he fired Speckles on the spot.

Now, Speckles—whose name, by the way, was Dolivar Washington Babson—had been fired on several occasions before, and if he swallowed a little more tobacco-juice than was good for his physical comfort it was rather as a gulp of startled surprise at Healy's appearance than because of any poignant regret at the misfortune that had overtaken him. Nevertheless, he felt it incumbent on himself to expostulate.

"Git out an' stay out!" said Healy, refusing to argue.

And Speckles got out.

For a day he kept away from the roundhouse, the length of time past experience had taught him was required to cool the turner's anger; then he sauntered down again and came face to face with Healy on the turntable.

"I came down to ask you to put me on again, Mr. Healy," he began, broaching the subject timidly.

"Phwat?" demanded Healy.

"I came down to ask you to put me on again, Mr. Healy," Speckles repeated monotonously.

"Oh, I heard you—I heard you," said Healy, a little inconsistently. "On ag'in, is ut? Ut'll be a long toime, me son, mark that!"

This being quite different from Healy's accustomed, "Well, git back to yer job," it began to filter vaguely through Speckles' brain that his name was no longer to adorn the company's pay-sheets.

"Am I fired for good, Mr. Healy?" he faltered.

"You are!" said Healy. "Just that!" Then, relenting a little as Speckles' face fell: "If 'twere not fer the big-bugs down yonder"—he jerked his thumb in the general direction of the East—"I might—moind, I don't say I would, but I might—put you on ag'in. As ut is, we've instructions to cut down the operatin' expinses, an' there's an ind on ut!"

Speckles stood for a moment in dismay as Healy went back into the roundhouse; then he turned disconsolately away, crossed the tracks to the platform of the station, and, seeking out a secluded corner of the freight-house, sat down upon a packing-case to think it out.

To Speckles it was no mere matter of cutting down expenses. It was a blasted career!

Whatever Speckles' faults, and he was only a lad, he had one redeeming quality, before which, in the eyes of the business he had elected to follow, his strayings from the straight and narrow path dwindled into insignificance—railroading was born in him.

At ten he had started in as caller for the night-crews, and, during the five years the company had had the benefit of his valuable services in that capacity, there was not a man on the division but sooner or later came to know long-armed, bony, freckled-faced, red-haired Speckles—came to know the little rascal, and like him, too.

Then Speckles had been promoted to the post of sweeper in the roundhouse, and occasionally, under Healy's critical inspection, to washing out boiler-tubes. Fresh fuel thereby added to the fire of his ambition, he began to figure how long it would be before he got to wiping, then to firing, and after that—even Speckles' boundless optimism did not have the temerity to specify any particular date—the time when he would attain his goal and get his engine.

Now, instead, at the age of sixteen, he found himself seated on a cracker-box, his dreams for the future rudely shattered—thanks to Healy, old Sour Face Healy!

So Speckles sighed, and as he sighed the shop whistle blew. It was noon, and the men began to pour out of the big gates. Then Speckles, remembering that the schools were also "letting out," hurried down the platform and up the main street. He would confide in Madge. Madge would understand.

Madge Bolton was the daughter of the ticket agent at the station, and between Mr. Bolton and Speckles there existed a standing feud, the *casus belli* being fifteen-year-old, blue-eyed Madge. Speckles kicked his heels on the corner until she appeared; then he turned and fell into step beside her, reaching a little awkwardly for her strap of books.

"Hallo, Dol!" was Madge's greeting. She was the only person in Big Cloud who did not call him Speckles.

"Hallo, Madge!" he returned.

Madge glanced at his face and hands. "Haven't you been to work?" she asked.

"Nope."

"Why, Dol?"

"Fired," said Speckles laconically.

"Oh, Dol, again!" she cried reproachfully. "What for?"

"'Tain't only the third time, and 'twasn't for nothin',' said Speckles, a bit sullenly. "I was only restin'."

"Dolivar Babson," she accused, "you were loafing. Oh, Dol, you'll never get to firing, and — and — " She hesitated and stopped, her cheeks a little red with the hint of boy-and-girl castle-building that would have increased her father's ire against the luckless Speckles had he seen it.

Speckles, somewhat shamefaced, and having no excuse to offer, trudged on in silence.

"Did you ask Mr. Healy to take you back?" she inquired, after a moment.

"He won't," said Speckles.

"What are you going to do, Dol?"

"I dunno."

"Well," said Madge, hopefully, "perhaps you could get a job in one of the stores. I'll ask Mr. Timmons, the grocer, if you like. I know him pretty well."

Speckles came to an abrupt and sudden halt, cast in Madge's face one look that carried with it a world of unutterable reproach, handed over her books in silence — and fled.

He, a railroad man, go into a *store!* And this from Madge! Madge, who, of all others — it was too much! Speckles ate his dinner, dispirited and crushed. Everything and everybody was against him.

His mother's curt inquiry as to when he was going back to work did not in any way tend to mitigate his troubles — rather, on the contrary, to accentuate them.

"Old Sour Face won't put me back," he jerked out, in response to his mother's repeated question.

"No wonder he won't," said his mother sharply, "if you're as disrespectful as that. I'm ashamed of you, and you ought to be ashamed of yourself."

Speckles was too much depressed to offer any defense. He finished his meal in silence, gulped down his cup of tea in two swallows, took his hat, and started out.

Unconsciously he directed his steps toward the yards, and, some five minutes later, arrived at the station. Here, about half-way down the platform, he spotted Mat Bolton in the open doorway of the ticket office.

As he approached, the nonchalant air with which the other leaned with folded arms against the jamb of the door aroused Speckles' suspicions. To reach the seat of his meditations — the cracker-box in the freight shed which had now become his objective point — he would be obliged to pass Mr. Bolton. He therefore began to incline his course toward the edge of the platform nearest the rails, so that, when he came opposite the office door, some fifteen feet were between him and his arch enemy.

Mr. Bolton awoke from his lethargy with surprising suddenness.

"You young rascal," he shouted, "what you been doing to my girl? I'll teach you to make girls cry, you little speckled-face runt, you!"

He made a dash for Speckles, but by the time he had recovered his balance and saved himself from toppling over the edge of the platform to the tracks, Speckles had reached the safe retreat of the freight-shed door. And as the irate parent, after shaking his fist impotently, walked back and disappeared within his domain, Speckles indulged in a series of pantomimes in which his fingers and his nose played an intimate and comprehensive part.

Perched once more on the cracker-box, Speckles again resolved himself into a committee on ways and means. His little skirmish with Madge's father had exhilarated him to such an extent that his heavy and oppressing sense of despondency had vanished, and in its place came a renewed determination to resume, somehow or other, the railroad career that Healy had so emphatically interrupted.

He turned over in his mind the feasibility of applying to Regan, the master mechanic, for a job in the shops, but dismissed the idea almost immediately on the ground that shop men were not, strictly speaking, railroaders.

He might start in switching and braking, and work up to conductor. That, at least, was railroading — not to be compared with engine-driving, not by long odds, but still it was railroading. His face brightened. He would interview Farley, the train-master.

Farley was in his office. Speckles had not very far to go, only a few steps down the platform. All the offices and Big Cloud was division headquarters — were under the same roof.

At Speckles' request, Farley swung around in his swivel-chair with a quizzical expression on his face. Then he grinned.

"Want to go on with the train-crews, eh? What do you think, kid, that I'm running a kindergarten outfit, even if some of 'em do act like it? How old are you?"

"Sixteen," said Speckles, with a sinking heart.

"Sixteen, eh? Well, come back in a couple of years, and——"

But, for the second time that day, Speckles fled. He was in no mood to stand much chaffing, and Farley, as he well knew, had a leaning that way. Speckles halted outside the door, undecided what move to make next, when the clicking of the instruments in the dispatcher's room overhead came to his ears like an inspiration.

Why hadn't he thought of that before? Spence, who had been on the night trick most of the years that Speckles was caller, was now chief dispatcher. If he had any friend anywhere, it was Spence, the man at whose elbow he had sat through those long, dark hours of the night that beget confidences, and into whose ears he had so often poured the tales of his cherished aims and ambitions.

Speckles covered the stairs three steps at a time, in his new-found exuberance. Spence looked up from his key and listened as Speckles told his story.

"So you're Healy's contribution to economy, eh?" he said when Speckles had finished. "And he won't take you back?"

"No," said Speckles.

"Well, that's pretty rough. But I don't see how I can help you any, Speckles. I haven't any rights over Healy, you know."

Speckles hesitated a moment and fidgeted nervously from one foot to the other. "I know you ain't," he began, "but I thought maybe you'd put me on here."

"W-what!" ejaculated Spence. Then, smothering a laugh at the sight of Speckles' woebegone countenance, he demanded gravely "You mean dispatching?"

Speckles nodded.

"No, no, Speckles, that would never do. You go back and see Healy. I'll do what I can for you with him."

"'Twon't do no good," said Speckles hopelessly. "I've asked him twice already."

"Well, ask him again. Look here, Speckles, it's up to you to square yourself with Healy, somehow or other. If you want your job very badly, you ought to be sharp enough to find a way of getting it. Go on, now."

So Speckles descended the stairs to the platform and irresolutely began to cross the tracks in the direction of the running-shed. He reached the roundhouse and skirmished cautiously along its front. No Healy was in sight, so he dived in between two engines and made his way to the rear of the shed. Here, by peering around the end of a tender, he could see Healy's cubby-hole — Healy called it an office — a bit of space about four by six partitioned off from the back wall in the corner, with a greasy book the engine-crews signed, and two or three others, equally greasy, in which Healy kept tabs on things in general.

In spite of his trepidation, Speckles grinned. Healy was there, bending over a very flimsy, spindle-legged table that he had wheedled out of the claim-agent some months before. His brows were puckered into a ferocious scowl, and he growled and muttered to himself, now laboring furiously with a stubby pencil on the sheets of paper in front of him, now pausing to bite that unoffending article almost in two in his desperation.

Healy was working on his invention. All the division knew about Healy's ideas on Westinghouse and "air," and that these ideas, when perfected, were to be patented. As to what the consensus of opinion of their value was is neither here nor there, except that in Healy's presence, when referred to at all, the subject was treated with dignity and respect, for Healy's physical powers were beyond the ordinary, and dearest to Healy's heart and most sacred in his eyes was this creation of his brain, or, to be more accurate, fancy.

Speckles sidled up to the cubby-hole, and, without any peroration, took the plunge.

"I came to ask you to put me on again, Mr. Healy," — he spoke rapidly, as though he feared his courage might ooze out before he could finish.

Healy wheeled round with a grunt.

"Oh, ut's you, is ut?" he demanded grimly.

Speckles, ready to run at the first sign of violence, acknowledged the impeachment by nodding his head affirmatively, and smiled sheepishly while Healy scrutinized him with a long stare from head to foot.

"Well," said Healy, "you wait a minute an' I'll give you me answer."

Speckles' heart bounded in joyous hope. Healy very deliberately gathered up his papers, folded them carefully, and opening the cupboard where his coat hung — it was a hot day, and Healy was in his shirt-sleeves — tucked them into the inside pocket. Then, like a flash, he turned and reached for the first thing in sight. It was a broom.

But, quick as he was, Speckles was quicker, and he led Healy by the length of the pit as he dodged around the tail end of a tender and darted out of the running-shed across the tracks to the freight-house.

Healy followed no farther than the turntable. There he halted, and Speckles, from his retreat, saw him shake his fist and listened to the threat that thundered across the yards:

"Show yer face around here ag'in, you young rascal, an' I'll bate the loife out av you, so I will!"

Speckles betook himself to the cracker-box; and from his lips there flowed a fluent and unrestrained expression of his opinion on things in general, but more particularly of Healy, and more particularly still of Healy's invention. Then, his indignation subsiding, it was followed by a fit of the blues; so that when, at the expiration of half an hour, Healy, still in his shirt-sleeves, came out of the roundhouse and walked up the tracks in the direction of the shops, Speckles, through the freight-house door, remarked the incident in complete apathy and as one in which he had no interest whatever.

Ten minutes later, however, his apathy vanished and he sprang to his feet at the sound of the excited shouts of the men in the running-shed. Some were hastily swinging the big engine doors wide open, others were setting the table in position, while one started on a run in the direction Healy had taken.

Another minute and the shop whistle had boomed out its warning, and as Healy, with the man who had gone after him, came tearing down the track like mad, Speckles saw the smoke beginning to curl up over the roof at the back. The running-shed was afire.

With a whoop, Speckles traversed the platform, leaped to the rails, and was hard on Healy's heels by the time the turntable was crossed. Healy paused but an instant. The thing to do was to get the engines out, and Healy was the man to do it.

"Get tackle rigged on 463," he ordered. "She's cold, an' we'll have to haul her out. Set the table fer 518; I'll take her."

Then he started on the jump for the cubby-hole and his precious papers.

Now, the tackle that Healy had referred to was stored in the rear of the roundhouse in the same general direction as the cubby-hole, and as the order had been given to no one in particular, Speckles, shouting "I'll get it," started after Healy.

Some grease and waste had caught and was rolling up a nasty smoke. Through it, even while he tugged manfully at the heavy tackle, Speckles saw Healy run into his office, snatch his coat, rush out again, and dash for the cab of 518, throwing the coat up on the tender. As he did so, something fell from the pocket.

Speckles dropped the tackle and pounced upon it. It was the bundle of papers he had seen Healy put in his coat-pocket a little while before.

It was Healy's invention!

Speckles' first impulse was to shout to Healy, but just then 518 glided out of the shed, and the men in front of 463 were yelling in chorus for the tackle, so Speckles put his tongue in his cheek and the papers in his pocket.

It wasn't much of a blaze, but it looked bad while it lasted. Even after the shop-hands had got their hose-lengths connected and a stream playing on the fire, and the engines were all in safety in the yard, the smoke continued to roll out in clouds, with here and there a vicious tongue of flame.

Then Healy, his duty done, bethought him of his coat on the tender of 518. And Speckles, as he heard Healy's gasp of dismay on discovering that his papers were gone, had an inspiration.

"Me papers! Me papers!" wailed Healy. "Fer the love av Mike, I must av dropped thim on the flure!"

"I'll get them for you, Mr. Healy," said Speckles, quick as a shot.

"You'll not!" said Healy. "I'll have no wan risk his life fer thim, bad as I want thim. Hey, come back, you runt!"

But Speckles was gone. Headed straight for the big, yawning doors that vomited their smoke and flames? Oh, no, not Speckles! Hardly! Speckles would make his attempt from the rear! And around the end of the shed and in behind he raced.

Some of the men were fighting the fire from that side, but they were too busy to pay any attention to Speckles. A dab of soot and dirt on his face which he obtained by rubbing his fingers along the blackened wall, an artistic smudge of generous proportions on the outside of the papers, which he took from his pocket, and Speckles' make-up was complete and convincing.

Now, Speckles had an eye for the dramatic and an appreciation of its value. He peered in through one of the windows. It was not nearly as bad inside as it had been, and he decided there would be no risk and very little discomfort in carrying out the plan that had popped into his head.

So he climbed in through a window and dropped down to the floor on the other side. The next minute he had dashed through the running-shed, and emerged from a whirl of black smoke into the open in front of the turntable, the papers waved aloft in his fist.

It was effective — decidedly effective! A cheer went up, and the men crowded around, while Healy rushed forward and began to pump Speckles' arm up and down like an engine-piston.

"Ut's a hero you are, me bright jool av a lad!" he cried in his delight. "'Tis mesilf, John Healy, that ses ut, an* the bhoys are me witness. Come back to yer job in the mornin' an', by my sowl, Speckles, I'll niver fire you ag'in, niver! An' ut's more I'll do — I'll promote you. Ut's a wiper you are from now on, me son, an' to blazes wid cuttin' down operatin' expinses! Where did you foind the papers?"

"On the floor," said Speckles — and he told the truth.

XV
MUNFORD

Munford came to the work before the gangs were deep enough into the hills to lose daily, or rather nightly, touch with Big Cloud. And the way of his coming was this: The town, springing up in a night, had its beginning in the wooden shanty the engineers built as headquarters for the Hill Division that was to be. Then, with mushroom growth, came shacks innumerable; and these shacks, for the most part, were gambling hells and dives and saloons, and the population was Indian, Chinese and bad American. To these places of lurid entertainment flocked the toilers at night, loading down the construction empties as they backed their way to the spurs and sidings that soon spread out like a cobweb around headquarters.

Naturally, rows were of pretty frequent occurrence between the company's men and the leeches who bleed them with crooked games and stacked decks over the roulette, faro and stud-poker tables. But of them all in the delectable pursuit of separating the men and their pay-checks, Pete McGonigle's "Golden Luck" saloon was in the van, both as to size and crookedness. And that high station of eminence it maintained until the night a stranger wrecked it by no more delicate a method than that of kicking over the roulette table, sending it and the attendant, who was presiding over the little whirling ball in Pete's interest, crashing to the floor. That stranger was Munford. And that was how Munford came to join the army of the Rockies.

A number of the company men were present and they sided in with Munford. Before this amalgamation, Pete and his hangers-on went down to ignominious defeat, and the "Golden Luck," to utter demolishment and ruin. News of the fracas spread rapidly to the other "joints." The dive-keepers joined forces, the company men did likewise, and that night became the wildest in the history of Big Cloud.

Munford took command of his new-found friends from the start. In the street fight that followed he did wondrous things—and did them with zest, delight and effectiveness. With his great bulk he towered above his companions, and the sweep of his long arms as they rose and fell, the play of his massive shoulders as he lunged forward to give impetus to his blows, was a marvelous sight to see. But the details of that fight have no place here. Its result, however, was that Munford, previously unknown and unheard of, became thereafter, a marked man in Big Cloud.

When the fight was over the company men, elated with victory though somewhat the worse for wear, retired to the yard to wait for the construction trains to take them up to their work. And while they waited they spent the time gazing in admiration at Munford who sat on the edge of a flat-car, his legs dangling over, blowing softly on his knuckles, a smile of divine contentment on his face.

What was Munford going to do? demanded McGuire and the cronies of his particular gang who had had the honor of being present at Pete's when the evening's proceedings were instituted, and who therefore felt they had a prior claim to the hero's consideration over and above that of the men from other sections of the work who had taken part in the fight. Munford did not know. Would he go up the line with them and take a job with their gang if they promised to get him one? Munford would. So he kept his seat when the construction train pulled out just as the dawn was breaking, and twenty miles up the road at Twin Bear Creek they tumbled him off and introduced him to Alan Burton, foreman of Bridge Gang No. 3.

At the sight of his battered and jaded crew, who in no wise appeared fit for the day's work before them, Burton swore savagely and with great bitterness of tongue bade them get to their work. Then he turned in his ill-humor to Munford, who was still standing beside him.

"Who the devil are you? What you doin' here? Where d'ye come from?"

The questions came quick and sharp like a volley of small arms.

Munford eyed the wiry little chunk of a man, scarcely up to his own shoulders, in silence, taking him in from head to foot.

"Well," snapped Burton, "speak up!"

"Munford's my name," said Munford, coolly. "I'm here for a job. Where I come from ain't none of your blamed business, is it?"

"Ain't it?" said Burton. "Well, then, you can walk back there, my bucko!" and he turned on his heel and followed the men to their work.

Munford sat down on the doorsill of the camp shanty and with a laugh pulled out his pipe and began to smoke. He was still sitting there a half-hour later when the foreman came back.

"If you've got far to go," grinned Burton, you'd better get started."

"No hurry," replied Munford, imperturbably.

"You're a queer card," said Burton, after a moment. "What's this about the trouble down at Big Cloud last night the boys are so full of they can't do anything besides talk?"

Munford chuckled quietly. "Nothin' much," said he.

"Nothing much, eh? They say you put the "Golden Luck and Pete McGonigle to the bad, and then cleaned out every dive in town. You're quite a reformer, ain't you? I'll tell you this, though, it won't be healthy for you around these parts from now on."

"Oh, I don't know," said Munford. "Say, how about that job?"

Burton laughed. "You've got a sweet nerve to ask for a job, and you responsible for a gang that won't be able to do a day's work among the lot of them between now and night. Did up McGonigle's, eh? Well, I don't know, I reckon in the long run that'll be worth more to the company than the day's work. All right, sport, you can go to work—until Pete and his crowd scare you out, which I predict won't be long. And while you're here, if you get itchy for trouble don't look for it among the men, come to *me*."

"Well, I'll—" gasped Munford. "Why, I could twist you like—" Then he laughed in pure delight at Burton's spunk. "Oh, sure! *Sure*, I will."

It took Munford no longer than a day to get the hang of the work. He was already more than a demigod in the eyes of Bridge Gang No. 3, and that counted for much. They were eager and ready to show him what they knew themselves, whereas the ignorance and rawness of any other newcomer would have been turned to good account in the shape of gibes and jests at his expense. In two days, from a natural adaptability coupled with his great strength, that was the strength of two men, Munford had fitted into place with the same nicety that one part of a well designed machine fits into another.

To the crews of the construction trains bringing up the bridge material he was pointed out with pride by his mates — though, indeed, that action was superfluous — as "the boy who did the trick at Pete's." And from these in turn Munford learned that down at Big Cloud, Pete and others of his ilk had sworn that, sooner or later, they would fix him for it. At this he only laughed and, doubling his great arm bared to the shoulders, intimated that there could be no greater pleasure in life for him than to have them try it. And that night sitting outside the camp after supper, McGuire, as spokesman, alluding to the threat, proposed that under Munford's leadership they should make another raid on Big Cloud.

Burton, passing by, caught the gist of the conversation. "I want to see you a minute, Munford," he called, shortly.

Munford got up and followed to the foreman's little shanty that stood a few yards away from the main camp. Once inside, Burton shoved him into a chair and shook his fist under Munford's nose.

"Didn't I tell you yesterday morning," he spluttered angrily, "that if you were looking for trouble to come to me and leave the gang alone? And here you're at it again, what? Go down to Big Cloud and raise hell, eh? You great, big overgrown calf!"

Munford blinked at the foreman, speechless. It was a long time since he had taken words like these from any man, much less a little spitfire like Burton.

"Trouble!" continued the irate Burton, hardly pausing for breath. "You live on it, don't you? Eat it, eh? Well, you'll get a fill of it before long that'll give you the damnest indigestion you ever heard of. I promise you that! But you keep your hands off my crew! Now you listen to what I'm saying!"

"Aw, go hang!" said Munford, contemptuously. "I can't help it, can I, if they want to go down to Big Cloud? If you're so blamed anxious about them, it's a wonder you don't go around every night and tuck 'em into their bunks!"

For a moment Burton looked as though he were going to jump into Munford and mix it then and there; but instead, with a short laugh, he turned and walked to the other side of the room, sat down on the edge of his bunk and pulled out his pipe. He cut some tobacco from his plug, rolled it between his palms, packed his pipe slowly and lighted it. It was five minutes before he broke the silence; Munford was beginning to feel uncomfortable.

"I don't suppose throwing a few timbers across Twin Bear Creek means much of anything to you, Munford, eh?" he asked quietly.

"Not so much," replied Munford carelessly, a little puzzled at the question.

"No? Well, it means a lot to me, a whole lot! Until that trestle is up, we can't shove material over to the other side, ties and rails and heavy stuff. Progress on the Hill Division depends just at this minute on Bridge Gang No. 3, and concretely on me. I don't propose to have it interfered with by the men going down to Big Cloud and getting their heads broke, understand?"

"Oh, I guess we can take care of *our* heads, if that's all that bothers you," drawled Munford. "And I furthermore guess your bloomin' little bridge you seem so stuck on won't take any hurt by lettin' the boys have their fling. Anyway, whether it will or not, what's the use of you shootin' off all your talk? You can't stop 'em! If they want to go, they'll go. And say, Burton"—an inspiration coming to Munford—"come on down with us. I'll promise you the time of your life."

"I ought to have put it up to you differently, I guess, and saved my breath," said Burton in disgust. "You're just a hulk of bone and muscle and your head's wood. You can lift a timber and swing a pick or axe because you've got the strength. But that's all you know, or all you're good for!"

The cool contempt in Burton's voice stung Munford more than the words themselves.

"Is that so!" he snarled, resorting to his favorite habit of blowing on his knuckles. "I'd show you fast enough what I'm good for, you runt, if you was a little bigger!"

"Maybe you'll find I'm big enough one of these days," said Burton, sharply. "Now I'll put it to you straight so that you'll understand. I'll show you whether I can stop the gang going to Big Cloud or not. No man rides on the construction trains after to-day without a pass signed by me. That's orders! If the men don't like it, you can tell them it's your fault. The next row in Big Cloud wouldn't stop at fists. And as for you, you wouldn't come out of it alive."

"You needn't worry about me," sneered Munford. "I'm——"

"You're a fool! The thickest-headed, trouble-hunting fool it's ever been my cursed luck to run against!" exclaimed Burton angrily.

Munford brushed his great shock of hair out of his eyes with a nervous sweep of his hand. "I ain't ever before taken the back talk from any man that I've taken from you—without hurtin' him," he said thickly, rising from his chair. "And I'm goin' to get out of here before I hurt *you!*" He walked quickly across the shanty and swung around in the doorway. "By God, I wish you was bigger!" he flung out.

Munford walked back to the men's camp and listened to their conversation awhile in sullen silence. They were still on the same topic and were waxing more enthusiastic each minute.

"Aw, dry up!" said Munford, cutting in at last. "It'll be a long time before any of you see Big Cloud again."

"Who says so?" demanded McGuire, aggressively.

Munford jerked his thumb in the direction of the foreman's shanty. "Him," he said laconically.

"How's he goin' to stop it? What for? What's the matter with him, anyway? It's none of his business!" the men were talking in chorus.

"He's fussy about gettin' his dinky little bridge through," sneered Munford. "He says he ain't goin' to have broken heads interferin' with it, either. From now on you've got to get a pass to ride on the construction train. Likewise, he said if you didn't like it I was to tell you"—here Munford paused to glance around the circle—"that it's my fault and I'm the cause of all the trouble."

"What did you tell him?" demanded the crew.

"I told him to go hang. What else would I tell him?"

"Bully for you!" shouted McGuire, slapping his leg in delight. "Did he fire you?"

This was something Munford had not thought of. "Fire me?" he repeated. Then slowly, pondering the idea: "No, he didn't. It's funny he didn't, though; I gave him back talk enough."

"Aw," said McGuire, with a sneer, "that's easy. He'd have fired you quick enough if he dared."

"Why," said Munford innocently. "I wouldn't have touched him if he had. He's too small to touch—I told him that, too."

"'Tain't that," McGuire returned. "He ain't afraid of any man, big or little. I'll give him credit for that. It's his bridge, and that means his job, that he's afraid of."

"What's my gettin' fired got to do with the bridge?" demanded Munford, in amazement.

"Aw, go on; you know what I mean. If Burton has trouble with us the bridge work stops, don't it? And the company'll be askin' Burton the reason why, won't they? Well, Burton knows there's some things we won't stand for, and firin' you after we brought you up here is one of them. And that's right, too, eh, mates?"

There was emphatic assent from the men.

Munford, a little flustered at this wholesale exhibition of homage, fidgeted nervously. "Much obliged," said he, clumsily. "Don't put yourselves out on my account. I——"

"That's all right," broke in McGuire. "Burton won't try it; he knows better. As for gettin' a pass to get out of camp, I dunno about *that*." He got up, stretched himself and yawned. "The way I look at it, it's more up to Munford here than it is to Burton. I'm goin' to turn in, but I'll say first that the night Munford says Big Cloud, then Big Cloud it is for Bridge Gang No. 3. That's the way we talked it before we knew about Burton mixin' in, and I reckon it stands just the same now."

And the camp retired to their bunks and to sleep, voicing McGuire's sentiments and swearing a unanimous and enthusiastic allegiance to Munford; all but Munford himself who did not sleep but lay awake tossing restlessly though, withal, in a very self-satisfied frame of mind.

This outburst of popularity pleased Munford exceedingly. The more so that it was directly traceable to his great strength and physical courage of which he was inordinately vain. He began to regard Burton with contempt. Burton was a man whose backbone wobbled when it came to a showdown! As Munford turned the situation over in his mind his contempt grew stronger until he came to decide that he despised the little foreman heartily. Would he, he demanded of himself with a snort, have fired a man that had talked to him as he had talked to Burton, had he been in Burton's place? He would! And the gang, bridge, job and everything else could go to blazes! Munford sat up to emphasize his feelings on this point with a crash of his fist on the side of the bunk. He thrilled with the fierce joy of enacting just such a role as his imagination depicted, despising Burton accordingly for lacking in what were, to him, the essentials of a man. He decided, as he fell asleep, to make the foreman's life a burden to him — and he did.

No flagrant violation or disobedience of orders was there, instead the inauguration of a petty little system of nagging that embraced every indignity Munford could think of. And the range of his attack was from profound and exaggerated attention and politeness to the utter and complete ignoring of the very existence of such a person as Alan Burton, foreman of Bridge Gang No. 3. While the gang, taking their cue from Munford, would shift from one extreme to the other with a precision and significance that cut deeper into a man of Burton's high-strung, nervous temperament than any other form of torture they could have devised.

Three times during three days Burton, who was afraid of no man or aggregation of men, took the bull by the horns and struck Munford a violent blow in an effort to bring matters to a head. On the first occasion the gang watched the action with a gasp of mixed pity and admiration—looking for Burton's instant annihilation. But Munford, with a bit of a laugh, only reached out and grasping Burton's neck held him wriggling, helplessly, impotently, at arm's length. "You got to grow, boy; just keep quiet now, I ain't going to hurt you," he taunted. And the gang promptly lost their faint appreciation of Burton's nerve in their relish of the ridiculous figure cut by the white-faced, raging foreman.

It was dirty work, and deep down in his heart Munford knew it. But his better nature no sooner manifested itself by sundry pricks of conscience than it was smothered beneath the new sense of authority and command that was now his for the first time in his experience; and which, catering as it did to his peacock vanity, was paramount to all things else. The work lagged sadly and fell behind. The daily reports Burton signed and sent down to headquarters became worse and worse.

Each day, too, the feud between the dives at Big Cloud and Bridge Gang No. 3, fanned by the crews of the construction trains, who taunted McGuire and the men with cowardice, grew stronger. For the train-men, having no idea of disregarding Burton's orders and allowing the bridge men to ride down on the empties, rubbed it in until the gang writhed under their gibes.

Munford did not come in for much of this personally. The trainmen, none of them, seemed to display any particular hankering for discussing the question in his presence; but he got it second-hand from McGuire and the gang. The outcome of it all was a decision one night after supper to board the construction train the following evening, Burton, the train crew and the company to the contrary, and go down to Big Cloud if they had to run the train themselves. Munford concurred in the decision by blowing very gently on his knuckles. It looked bad for the peace and quiet of Big Cloud; and it looked bad for Burton's standing with the company.

Munford, as commander-in-chief, and McGuire, as chief of staff, withdrew from the circle and strolled off by themselves to perfect their plans for the next day's campaign, taking the trail in the direction of Big Cloud — a trail still called, but now a passable road due to the traffic incident to the building of the Hill Division, whose right of way it paralleled from Big Cloud to the ford at Twin Bear Creek. At the end of a quarter of a mile the two men sat down on a felled tree by the side of the trail to talk. Some ten minutes had passed when McGuire, in the midst of a graphic description of what they would do to Pete McGonigle and the rest, suddenly stopped and gripped Munford tightly by the shoulder.

"Keep mum," he cautioned. "There's someone comin'!"

In the bright moonlight they could make out the figure of a man about a hundred yards down the road coming toward them from the camp.

"He walks like Burton," whispered McGuire.

"What the devil is he followin' us for? Get back into the trees and let him pass."

They moved noiselessly a little deeper into the wood that fringed the road, and lying flat, watched the man who was approaching.

"It's Burton," McGuire announced at last.

Munford grunted assent.

"He's been followin' us all right, and now he's goin' to wait for us to come back," continued McGuire, as Burton halted within a few yards of them and sat down to smoke. "Well, we'll give him a run for his money. He can wait a while, I'm thinkin'."

Five, ten, fifteen minutes passed. McGuire began to tire of his self-selected game of hide and seek. "Come on," said he, "let's go out and see what he wants."

"Wait," Munford answered. "There's someone comin' from Big Cloud way. It's not us Burton's after. Listen!"

There was the faint beat of horse's hoofs gradually drawing nearer. Then presently rider and horse loomed out of the shadows and Burton, getting up, stepped out into the middle of the road.

The horseman drew up beside him. "That you, Burton?" he called softly.

"Yes," said Burton, shortly.

"You got Pete's letter, then," the man went on, dismounting from his horse. "I suppose it's all right to talk here. No one around, eh?"

"As well here as anywhere. Only cut it short."

"Oh, there ain't any hurry," returned the man, with a laugh. "Wait till I tie my horse, then we can sit down and chew it over comfortable."

"Now," he went on, that task performed, "what I came to see you about was this fellow Munford."

"Well," demanded Burton, "what about him?"

"It looks to us down to Big Cloud, from the way the fellows on the construction trains are talkin', you ain't got any cause to love him, eh? So Pete figured you and him could deal. You want to get rid of him, don't you?"

"I wish to God I'd never seen his face!" exclaimed Burton, with great bitterness.

"Sure! That's the idea. You don't want him; we do want him—bad! There's nothin' against the rest of the men; we'll forget all about that. It's just Munford we're after."

"Why don't you get him, then?" said Burton curtly.

"We're going to," the man replied, with a nasty laugh. "We're goin' to, all right. It's a fair deal. You're on, eh? Pete said you'd jump at the chance to sit in. We want you to fire him."

"That all I'm to do?" asked Burton, quietly.

"Sure, that's all there is to it—except this."

Munford's hand closed on his companion's arm in a tight, spasmodic grip as Pete's emissary produced a wad of bills and began to peel off the outer ones.

"Three hundred plunks," said the man, extending the money he had abstracted from the roll to Burton. "Pretty good for just firin' a man we've been lookin' for you to fire for the last week, anyway. Besides, there's been some talk down at headquarters about you not bein' able to handle your men, and about them gettin' someone that can. Pete says not to bother about that, he'll fix it for you. Here, take the money."

"Suppose I fired him," said Burton, slowly, "where'd he go?"

"What do you care where he goes, so long as you get rid of him?"

"He couldn't go West," went on Burton, paying no attention to the other's remark; "so he'd have to go East—that's Big Cloud—and *murder!*" He turned fiercely, savagely on the man. "You dirty, low-lived hound!" he flashed. "You offer me three hundred dollars to murder a man, do you? You wonder why I've stood for what I did, do you, you scrimp! Fire him, eh, to get a cowardly knife or shot in his back! You think I didn't know what would happen if I let him out, eh? Get out of here, you cur! And get out now—while you *can!*" Burton's voice rasped, hoarse with passion. He turned abruptly away and strode quickly in the direction of the camp.

"Hold on, wait a minute, Burton," cried the other, following him. "Don't get batty."

Unconsciously Munford had tightened his grip on McGuire's arm until the latter whimpered with the pain, and now Munford lifted him bodily to his feet making cautiously for the spot where the horse was standing. The two figures were still discernible, and Burton's angry voice continued to reach the listeners, though the words were now indistinguishable.

Munford's face in the moonlight was colorless, the muscles around his mouth twitched convulsively. "D'ye hear what they said? D'ye hear what they said? *My God!* d'ye hear it all?" he was mumbling incoherently in McGuire's ear, his eyes strained up the road.

"Yes, I heard it. Let go of my arm, you're breakin' it!"

"He's comin' back," said Munford, hoarsely.

Burton had disappeared around a turn in the road and the man, after hesitating a moment, began to retrace his steps to his horse, muttering fiercely to himself as he came along. As he reached for the bridle, Munford leaped out and grasped him by the throat, choking back the man's cry of terror.

"You make a noise," snarled Munford, "and I'll finish you! Oh, it's you, eh? Look here, Mac, it's the cuss that ran the roulette wheel that night at Pete's. So my price is three hundred, eh? Well, hand it out. *Quick!*"

Slowly the fellow put his hand in his pocket and for the second time that night pulled out his roll.

Munford's anger seemed to have vanished. He laughed softly as he took the money.

"What are you going to do with me?" whined the gambler.

Munford made no answer. In the imperfect light, he was laboriously counting the bills. McGuire watched the operation, at the same time keeping an eye on their prisoner.

"Two sixty—eighty—three hundred," said Munford at last, cramming that amount into his pocket and handing back by far the larger part of the roll to the man. "What am I goin' to do with you? Nothin'! You get on that horse and ride back to Pete. I want him to know this. Tell him all about it. Tell him Munford told you to tell him. That's worth more than breakin' your neck—and that's all that saves you from gettin' it broke, savvy? You tell him *I've* got the three hundred, and I'll give him his chance at me for it one of these days. And when I do— My God, *you ride* before I begin with you!"

The fellow glanced fearfully from Munford to McGuire and back again to Munford to assure himself that he was free to go. Then he clambered frantically into the saddle and lashing his beast in a frenzy of terror disappeared down the trail.

Munford, with swift revulsion of mood, threw himself down on the grass, burying his face in his hands. Not a word from McGuire; he walked awkwardly up and down, whistling under his breath. After a minute Munford looked up.

"I got to square this with Burton," he said brokenly.

McGuire nodded.

"He's a better man than you and me and the whole gang put together"—Munford's tones were fiercely assertive.

"He is that," assented McGuire, with conviction.

There was silence for a moment between them; then McGuire spoke: "Why didn't you take it all?" he asked.

"Take it all!" flared Munford. "I'm no thief, am I? Well, then, what's the matter with you? That's my price, ain't it? Three hundred. That's what Pete offered for a chance to get his paws on me. Well, *I'll* give him his chance, you heard me promise, didn't you? That's right, eh? That's Pete's proposition, and the money's mine, ain't it?"

"It is," said McGuire.

"It is, and it ain't," said Munford. "Burton *could* have had it if he'd sold me out, couldn't he? Well, then, I'm goin' to see he gets it anyway."

"He wouldn't take it, not by any means, he wouldn't," objected McGuire.

"Not outright, he wouldn't," agreed Munford. "I know that well enough. We got to fix it so he won't know where it come from, and so it will square me with him, and you fellows, too."

"How you goin' to do that?" demanded McGuire.

"I dunno," said Munford. "We'll talk it over with the boys. Come on back to camp."

The next day and the day after, the gang worked like Trojans, and the lack of any sneer or incivility on their part, coupled with a subdued, expectant excitement that the men tried fruitlessly to hide, made Burton more anxious and ill at ease than during the days that had gone before. It looked like the lull before the storm; and he wondered bitterly what culminating piece of deviltry they were hatching.

To the taunts of the train crews the gang grinned and said nothing.

On the second day a package, addressed to Munford, came up from the East, and at noon hour the men handed it around from one to another in awe-struck wonder at the magnificence of the solid gold repeater that chimed the quarters, halves and hours, and split the seconds into fractions. It was indeed a beauty. Maybe the chain was a little massive, but the men opined that it was therefore strong. They pried open the case to read the inscription over whose wording they had wrestled most of a night.

"Nifty, ain't it?" cried McGuire, admiringly; and he read it aloud: "'This is to certify that Alan Burton is as square as they make them, and Munford and the gang are sorry. So help us!' They delivered it solemnly to Munford, who was to make the presentation, and started in a body for Burton's shanty. Burton met them at the door, his face hard and set.

"So it's a showdown at last, eh, boys?" he laughed grimly. "Well, what is it?"

The men shoved Munford bodily forward and he stood balancing himself sheepishly, first on one foot and then on the other, as he faced Burton. He cleared his throat painfully once or twice, then he found his voice. From a point of oratory or rhetoric it was perhaps the lamest presentation speech on record, for Munford suddenly thrust the watch and chain into the astounded Burton's hands.

"Here, take it," he sputtered. "It's all written out on the inside." And breaking through the men, he turned and fled incontinently.

THE END

CPSIA information can be obtained
at www.ICGtesting.com
Printed in the USA
LVOW05s1014240217
525354LV00012B/133/P

9 781541 009714